Praise for
New York Times bestselling author
Lindsay McKenna

"McKenna steadily ratchets up the tension...
a good blend of romance and action
makes this an amazing read."
—*RT Book Reviews* on *High Country Rebel*

"Another masterpiece."
—*Affaire de Coeur* on *Enemy Mine*

"Talented Lindsay McKenna delivers excitement
and romance in equal measure."
—*RT Book Reviews* on *High Country Rebel*

Praise for *USA TODAY* bestselling author
Delores Fossen

"Suspense, charm and a complicated plot
keep the action revved up."
—*RT Book Reviews* on *The Baby's Guardian*

"Fossen delivers a flawless roller-coaster adventure
that careens through the countryside with the velocity
of a speeding bullet. It will take your breath away."
—*RT Book Reviews* on *Outlaw Lawman*

Praise for favorite author Geri Krotow

"A poignant and sweet military romance
that reminds us of the many sacrifices made by those
who serve in the military and those who love them.
A heartwarming story."
—*Night Owl Reviews* on *Navy Rules*

"Krotow's deep, rich characters are perfect for this
story fraught with tension and emotional growth."
—*RT Book Reviews* on *Navy Orders*

LINDSAY McKENNA

is proud to have served her country in the U.S. Navy as an aerographer's mate third class—also known as a weather forecaster. A *New York Times* bestselling author, she pioneered the military romance subgenre and loves to combine heart-pounding action with poignant romance. True to her military roots, Lindsay is the originator of the reader-favorite Morgan's Mercenaries series. She does extensive hands-on research, including flying in aircraft such as a P3-B Orion sub-hunter and a B-52 bomber. She was the first romance writer to sign her books in the Pentagon bookstore. Visit her online at: www.lindsaymckenna.com, www.twitter.com/lindsaymckenna and www.facebook.com/eileen.nauman.

DELORES FOSSEN

Former Air Force Captain Delores Fossen is a *USA TODAY* bestselling author, and she has received a Booksellers' Best Award for Best Romantic Suspense, as well as an RT Reviewers' Choice Award. In addition, she's had nearly a hundred short stories and articles published in national magazines. Delores is currently at work on her next Harlequin Intrigue novel. Visit her website at www.dfossen.net for news on upcoming releases and more.

GERI KROTOW

A U.S. Naval Academy graduate and former Naval Intelligence Officer, Geri left her military career to write full-time. She has traveled the world, living in such far-flung places as Whidbey Island, Washington state and Moscow, Russia. Geri enjoys creating love stories for Harlequin Superromance that stand the test of time and have settings that she has personally experienced. She's lived it, now she writes it! Visit her website at www.gerikrotow.com to join her Loyal Reader Program, and connect with her on Facebook, Twitter, Pinterest and Goodreads.

New York Times Bestselling Author

LINDSAY McKENNA

Coming
Home

FOR

Christmas

USA TODAY Bestselling Author

DELORES FOSSEN

GERI KROTOW

ISBN-13: 978-0-373-83804-2

Coming Home for Christmas

Copyright © 2014 by Harlequin Books S.A.

The publisher acknowledges the copyright holders of the individual works as follows:

Christmas Angel
Copyright © 2014 by Nauman Living Trust

Unexpected Gift
Copyright © 2014 by Delores Fossen

Navy Joy
Copyright © 2014 by Geri Krotow

Recycling programs
for this product may
not exist in your area.

This edition published by arrangement with Harlequin Books S.A.

For questions and comments about the quality of this book, please contact us at CustomerService@Harlequin.com.

® and TM are trademarks of Harlequin Enterprises Limited or its corporate affiliates. Trademarks indicated with ® are registered in the United States Patent and Trademark Office, the Canadian Intellectual Property Office and in other countries.

HARLEQUIN®
™ www.Harlequin.com

Printed in U.S.A.

CONTENTS

To my Italian chef friend, Giovanni Scorzo-Andreoli.
I've been to Italy and I know the food,
which is to die for. It was such a delight to
find real Italian food in Scottsdale, Arizona!
My thanks to Pamela Kimbrough and Vesna Ajic,
my lunch buddies, for finding this Italian jewel and
the many wonderful meals we share there together.
www.andreoli-grocer.com.

CHRISTMAS ANGEL

Lindsay McKenna

Dear Reader,

It was a delight and honor to be part of this very special Christmas anthology for several reasons. I want to thank Birgit Davis-Todd, Senior Executive Editor, for allowing this project to become a reality, and especially for asking Harlequin writers who are military vets to write the military romance novellas you will read in this book.

I was in the U.S. Navy as an AG3 (weather forecaster) and pioneered the military genre in 1983 with *Captive of Fate* (Silhouette Special Edition). My other two sister writers, Delores Fossen, U.S. Air Force, and Geri Krotow, U.S. Navy, are also military vets, so the readers are getting the real deal. The novellas will have a uniqueness that no one else can produce because we were in the military and understand how it works from the inside out. We're able to lend an insider's knowledge to the novellas as a result.

With the drawdown and our heroic military men and women finally coming home from Afghanistan, it makes our stories all the more heartrending and poignant. Delores, Geri and I know what it's like to be stationed somewhere else in the world when the holidays hit. And it's a very lonely time for everyone because of the separation involved. Christmas is the single most important holiday a military person yearns to be home for and celebrate. And so often it doesn't happen. The sacrifices our military people make are many.

To our military personnel, thank you for your service, your hours alone overseas, so far away from your home and family. And equally, let's praise those wives/husbands and children who also make those sacrifices in different ways when their loved one is so far away from them. It's hard on everyone. Just know that you are not forgotten by any of these military women vets and authors here at Harlequin.

Hooyah!

Lindsay McKenna

CHAPTER ONE

SNOW TWISTED, TURNED and sparkled around Kyle Anderson as he eased out of the rental car. He closed the door and thrust his hands deep into the pockets of his leather bomber jacket. The cold snowflakes landed in his hair, slid across his jacket and melted upon touching his face as he slowly walked toward the White Sulphur Springs Ranch house. The wind was inconstant and he hunched his shoulders, hearing his combat boots crunching in the foot of snow across the graveled parking area.

His heart squeezed with anticipation and worry. Anna Campbell, the woman he loved and had walked away from, had been in a serious auto accident two weeks ago. She'd been in a coma, though now was recovering at home.

Kyle had been notified only three days ago because his SEAL team had been out on a two-week mission. He didn't think twice before leaving to see her.

His mouth tightened and he opened the creaking white picket-fence gate. Snow had covered the bright red tiles he had helped place there as a ten-year-old. Kyle had grown up with Anna on her parents' ten-thousand-acre cattle ranch. There were so many good memories here. He halted for a moment on the covered sidewalk, looking around.

The sun was setting, the sky a light gray. He could

see the sharp pointed tips of the evergreens behind the massive two-story log house. To his left were three large red barns. To his right were pipe-rail fences where the cattle were kept. Most of the animals were probably in nearby pastures, huddled in herds, their butts to the wind, keeping warm. The barns would house the wrangler's horses in box stalls, the grain and hay to feed these herds.

No one was out in the coming blizzard. The car-rental place at the Great Falls, Montana, airport had warned him that a major storm was on its way. It was expected to dump three to four feet of snow in the next one or two days. He'd arrived home just in time.

Turning, he wiped his wet face and spotted something in the window nearest the bright red wooden door. It was an electric candle sitting in the window.

Old memories flowed through Kyle as he stared at the light, filling him with remorse and yearning. When she was eighteen, Anna had bought the electric candle in a scroll-like saucer of green copper at a hardware store in Great Falls. She told Kyle she would keep the candle on during the holidays, as a light, so he could find his way home to her. Pain squeezed his heart.

The window was partly frosted over in the corners, the ice crystals making the soft yellow light look like some kind of halo an angel might wear. Anna was his angel. She always had been. His mouth pulled in at the corners as he stood there on the walk, his gaze on that candle, the memories filling him like warm, spiced red wine tainted with bitterness.

Kyle couldn't remember a time when he hadn't loved Anna. They had grown up together on this ranch, attended the same small school, played together, laughed together and had so much fun. He'd joined the Navy at eighteen and later became a SEAL. He'd left Anna crying in this very driveway that cold December day. Rubbing his chest, grief, loss and concern warred within Kyle.

Of all the people in the world he loved, Anna had always owned his heart. And he'd broken hers. Dragging in a ragged breath, Kyle tried to steady his emotions, but it was impossible. He knew from several phone calls with the head wrangler at the ranch, Jepson Turner, that Anna had a grade-three concussion, a serious one, but was steadily improving. For that, Kyle had breathed in a sigh of relief so deep that he was overwhelmed with gratefulness in that moment.

He had always expected to die in combat, not be called home because Anna teetered between life and death for two weeks in a hospital.

What could he say to her? Kyle stood with the snow falling silently around him, his gaze never leaving that candle, or the hope Anna had clung to that he'd someday come home and stay here forever. With her. The starry-eyed idealism of an eighteen-year-old girl helplessly in love with him. He'd loved her and she'd blindly loved him. At first, as children, it was puppy love. In junior high, the love turned serious. But then, she'd turned down his marriage proposal when he'd come home at twenty-two.

No one in his platoon saw him weeping. Kyle had gone off by himself. He'd cried for what he'd selfishly thrown away: Anna. He'd never talked or emailed her again, not wanting to cause her more pain. And then, five years later, he got an email from his mother, telling him that she'd divorced her wrangler husband, Tom

Carter. Kyle hadn't even known she'd married. It came as a shock. But he couldn't leave the SEALs and come home and marry her. His heart wanted that, but his loyalty to his team had been a stronger calling.

Until now.

News of her accident—that she'd almost died—changed everything. It changed him. But Kyle wasn't sure about anything right now. And it was the uncertainty that made him tense and edgy as he forced himself to move the last twenty feet toward that red-painted door and press the buzzer. He tried to ignore the circular wreath composed of sprigs of pine with a bright red ribbon and silver-glittered pinecones fastened to it. That was Anna's work. She loved Christmas and made beautiful arrangements to celebrate the season. When he was younger, he had helped her.

What would Anna look like now? She knew he was coming home to see her. So many years ago, at her parents' urging to protect the family property, Anna had made out a will and had given him power of attorney, if she ever got seriously injured. Kyle had completely forgotten about it because she'd made this decision so far in the past. Part of her eighteen-year-old idealism, he supposed. Even though she had gotten married, she'd never changed that in her will. Throughout the years, had Anna hoped he would return someday to her?

Now he was twenty-nine. Never had he thought he'd be pulling emergency medical leave to see Anna. Kyle had always expected to be the one to die, not her. She was too beautiful, too filled with life, to ever die. And she almost had.

The door opened. Kyle stared at Anna. She was tall and lean like a willow, dressed in a bright red cable-knit

sweater, jeans and sensible leather boots. Her ginger-
colored hair lay in thick red-gold tresses around her
shoulders. As Kyle gazed into her forest green eyes,
his breath hitched. Anna had always reminded him of
a gossamer fairy found between the pages of a book.
Her face was oval, eyes wide set with a full mouth that
had always curved into an infectious smile.

Now Kyle saw her once-perfectly aligned nose had
been broken. When had it happened? The break didn't
ruin the soft beauty of her face, but it bothered him
that she had suffered. As he hungrily sponged her into
himself, he saw more unsettling signs of her injuries.

Usually, her cheeks were tinged pink, flushed with
life, but not now. There was gauntness to her face, telling him she wasn't eating well. And the dancing gold
highlights that had always dappled the green depths of
her eyes were missing. Anna was pale, her eyes life-
less, her full mouth compressed, as if she were still in
pain. Her hand came to rest on the wooden jamb, and
Kyle saw her waver just a bit. Was she dizzy? Was the
head injury causing all of this?

"I'm sorry I couldn't get home sooner," he said simply, hands at his side. "How are you doing, Anna?"

She stared up at him, gripping the jamb with her
long, slender fingers. Her voice broke and she stepped
to the side, gesturing for him to enter the warmth of the
foyer. "You didn't have to come, Kyle."

He moved past her and took the door and closed it
behind him. As he stomped his feet on the thick rug, the
snow fell off his boots. His heart beat hard in his chest.
He ached to open his arms and sweep Anna into them.
He saw the wariness in her eyes and sensed how fragile
she really was. When Anna turned her head to his left,

he saw a two-inch scar above her ear, the area still red. Kyle assumed it was the blow that had caused her coma.

"I wanted to come, Anna. I didn't get the emergency message about your condition for two weeks because my team was out on a long-range patrol." Wearily, he added, "I would have come sooner, but I couldn't." He watched her wrap her arms around her waist, as if chilled. Or defensive. He hated helplessness and felt it crawling through him.

"I—I didn't really expect you to come home at all," she offered quietly, giving him an understanding look. "I know your SEAL family comes first."

Frustration thrummed through him. "I was out on an op, Anna. I returned three days ago from it and found out about your medical condition." Emotion colored his deep tone. "I wanted to come home. To be here for you." And he saw a bit of life come to her eyes over his sincere words. "You put me down as POA. Remember that? When we were eighteen? It was a long time ago."

"Jepson reminded me of it. I'd completely forgotten about it."

God, how badly he wanted to haul Anna into his arms. She appeared not only fragile, but more wraith than human, as if she might disappear at any moment, gone forever. His heart raged with need for her and Kyle flexed his fingers, forcing himself not to reach out and touch Anna. He'd made it clear seven years ago that the SEALs were his family, not her. He never regretted his words more than he did right now. He'd spoken them out of anger and hurt after she refused to marry him.

"I *wanted* to be here for you, Anna." His throat tightened. Aching in ways he couldn't even name or control, Kyle added a slight smile, "Hey, you were always there for me. Remember? When I fell off that horse and landed in barbed wire?" He held up his left hand, pulling back the sleeve on his jacket, revealing the thin crisscross of white scars from that day. "You took care of me? Tore up part of your T-shirt to make a bandage out of it to wrap my bleeding arm?"

She looked down at her feet, her mouth softening. "Yes, of course, I remember."

To hell with it. Kyle stepped forward, placing his finger beneath her chin, making eye contact with Anna. There was such longing in her eyes that it momentarily shocked him. Longing for him? Could it be? Dropping his finger, he rasped, "Well, you've just fallen into another kind of barbed wire, Anna. And I want to be here for you if you want me."

Above all, Kyle didn't want to stay if she didn't want him around. The years between them had been long and desolate, but dammit, he felt that same warm, powerful connection with her right now. His feelings had never dimmed through the years. Not once. Now he felt an amplified intensity to them.

She lifted her head a little more confidently, held his gray gaze. "It's...just that it's a shock to see you, is all, Kyle. I never really expected you to come home even though you were my POA."

That hurt worse than a bullet going through his leg, which it had. Trying not to wince at her barely spoken words, Kyle saw how changed Anna was from before. It had to be due to the concussion. "I'm here," he told her firmly. "I've got thirty days of medical leave, Anna. There's no other place I'd rather be."

"That sounds good," she whispered unsteadily,

searching his eyes. "I know it's hard for you to leave your SEAL family."

Kyle wanted to deny all of that right now. Instead, he rasped, "Right now, you're the center of my universe, Anna. Just you. Okay?" He forced himself not to lift his hand and caress her pale cheek. For a moment, he saw hope flare in her dark eyes. And then, it vanished. He swore he could feel Anna's yearning for him as much as he felt for her right now. But it was all water under the bridge.

"Are you hungry? You've been traveling. I made a pot of vegetable beef soup earlier today. Why don't you come into the kitchen and eat? We can talk there."

Kyle watched her walk. Anna wasn't steady and he slipped his hand beneath her left elbow, cutting his long stride for her sake.

"It smells great," he offered. "Are you okay?" He searched her profile. Anna was a cattleman's daughter. She was the only child of Paul and Nancy Campbell. The family had a hundred-year ranching history in this part of Montana. Anna had always been strong and confident, but now she seemed just the opposite to Kyle. And it scared him.

She grimaced. "My head." She pointed to the scar above her left ear. "The neurologists are telling me with a grade-three concussion I'll have some dizziness and maybe other symptoms for a while. Eventually, they said, they'd go away." She opened her hand. "Right now, since being released, I deal with dizziness. It just comes and goes. I don't have any control over it, and I wish I did." She looked up, no doubt seeing his concern. "I'll be okay, Kyle."

"You've been out of the hospital how long?"

"Three days. Every day is better," she assured him, stopping at the entrance to the kitchen. "I'm going to let you get the bowl down from the cupboard and take as much soup as you want." She gestured toward the gas stove, where a five-quart pot sat. "I don't trust my equilibrium that much tonight."

Kyle guided Anna to one of the heavy oak chairs and pulled it out for her. His fingers tingled where they met her elbow. "Do you remember where everything is?" she asked.

He smiled and shrugged out of his coat, placing it over the chair next to Anna. "I think I do. Are you hungry? Can you eat a little something, too?"

Anna had become thin, and it pained him. He knew her parents had died in an auto wreck a year ago. Running a huge ranch like this took more than one person. All the weight of responsibility had fallen on Anna's slender shoulders. Automatically, Kyle found himself wanting to protect her, lift her burden, give her the time she needed to heal herself.

"Maybe I'll try just a little."

Kyle moved to the drain board and opened up a cupboard where the blue-and-white Delft-patterned bowls were kept. It was so easy to fall back into the routine of how they'd grown up together. He and his parents had eaten with Anna's parents every night. His father had been the foreman for the ranch. They were like extended family, and damned if anything had ever felt so fitting as this right now. "You're thin, Anna."

Walking to the stove, Kyle unhooked a metal ladle from the wall, opened the lid and inhaled the flavorful scents of the soup. He piled his bowl high with beef chunks, potatoes, carrots, onions and peas and put about a third as much in a bowl for Anna.

"It's the work," she admitted, resting her hands on the long, rectangular oak table.

"Don't you have a foreman?" he asked, handing her the bowl and giving her a soup spoon. And then Kyle remembered that Jepson had told him Trevor Bates, the foreman, had been driving the truck to Great Falls with Anna when the accident had occurred. It had killed Bates outright and damned near killed Anna. As he sat down at her left elbow, he noticed how her eyes darkened with grief.

"I did…but Trevor died in the accident." She dragged in a ragged breath and slowly moved her spoon through the thick, hearty soup. "I still don't remember the accident. Nothing…. I couldn't even be there for his funeral."

"I'm sorry," Kyle murmured, reaching out and briefly touching her arm.

"There's a lot to do around here," Anna uttered tiredly before sipping the soup.

Kyle hungrily dug into the beef and veggies. He watched her eat, and she seemed tentative about the food. Between bites he asked, "Are you not hungry?"

"I am." Then Anna shrugged. "I get nauseated off and on. Sometimes, food triggers it. The doctors said in time that will go away, too."

Which was why she was so pathetically thin, Kyle thought. He smiled into her eyes. "Can I give you my appetite? I can guarantee you, I'm going back for another bowl here in a few minutes." He was starved for good home cooking. Anna had cut up the vegetables and added the spices, and this soup had been made with love as far as Kyle was concerned. She seemed to rally beneath his teasing and picked at her clothes. "I lost twelve pounds in two weeks. Can you believe that?"

"Yeah," he said bluntly. "You look like a toothpick, Anna. And that worries me." He motioned to her bowl. "Come on, get some of the meat into you. I'll even spoon-feed you if you want."

Her cheeks suddenly flushed pink. Anna was blushing. She used to do that all the time when they were growing up. The first time Kyle had leaned over on his horse and given Anna a peck on the cheek when they were thirteen, her cheeks turned as red as an apple.

Giving him a wry look, Anna said, "No, I can feed myself. You're wolfing down your food."

Kyle felt heat steal into his cheeks as he looked down at his nearly emptied bowl. "That's what we do. When I first joined the Navy, I learned to eat fast."

There was that sadness in her eyes again. Anna had once dreamed of them being married, having a family, sharing their love here on this sprawling ranch. His heart clenched and he felt guilty. He could remember when Anna was eight and she had her dolly in her arms, telling him that someday they would be married and they'd have more dollies. *God, the innocence of childhood.* And he'd gone off to the Navy and left her.

He'd tried to convince her to marry him at twenty-two and follow him out to the West Coast, out to SEAL Team 3 headquarters at Coronado Island. Anna had refused. Kyle never forgot that tearful, gutting day. He'd bought a set of wedding rings and come home on leave to propose to Anna. And she had burst into tears, sobbing, making him feel like a selfish bastard.

Kyle couldn't handle a woman's tears very well at all.
He didn't know any man who could.

How many times had he replayed that conversation
in the living room of this ranch house? That Anna was
afraid he'd be killed in combat. And where would that
leave her? What if she was pregnant? Or they had children? Where would he be? Never home. Never there as
a father to his children, or a husband to her. Anna was
right on all accounts.

In the end, he took the rings, pocketed them and
understood why she refused to marry him. He could
give her nothing except worry, loneliness and maybe a
funeral because SEALs led dangerous lives. And they
were rarely home to help the wife or be a parent to their
children even when stateside. It all fell on the shoulders
of the wife. He never blamed Anna for her decision. He
blamed himself.

Sliding the chair back, Kyle walked over to the stove
and put another heaping amount of food into his bowl
and then sat down. "How can I help you while I'm
here?" he asked her.

"You can help Jepson. We have wranglers, but many
of them are going home for Christmas and it's leaving
us shorthanded. He needs another wrangler."

"Okay. What else? What about you, Anna?" He
looked around the bright white kitchen with red and
green curtains across the heavily frosted windows.
There was a huge fireplace in the living room that
moved heat everywhere within the two-story ranch
house. Already the blizzard outside was coating the
double-paned windows, the temperature dropping dras-
tically.

"I'll be okay, Kyle. If you could just help Jepson, that would take a huge load off my shoulders."

"Do you need to be driven into Great Falls to see your doctors? Any other medical appointments?"

She wrinkled her nose. "No one is going anywhere with this blizzard. I have my medications and I'll be fine. Just lots of sleeping and rest are what they prescribed. I have an appointment in Great Falls in two weeks."

Nodding, Kyle watched her sipping her soup. She was trying to eat, he realized. For him. He felt euphoric. And then reality crashed down on him. Was Anna going to count the days until he left? Again? Always? That tormented him. It had to hurt her, seeing him again. Did she still want a life with him that she couldn't have?

Anna was a good person who always did right by others. She was a hard worker, honest as the day was long, and was always there when Kyle had needed her in the past. He would be here for her.

"I noticed a tree holder in the corner," he said, hitching a thumb toward the flagstone living room. "For your Christmas tree?"

"Trevor had just put it down before the accident. He and I were planning to go up to Christmas Tree Hill the day after we got back from Great Falls, and cut two trees down. One for here and one for the wranglers' bunkhouse."

Kyle nodded, holding her gaze. "Would you like to do it with me? Remember every year as kids we'd go up there with our parents? They'd let us find just the right trees for our homes." His heart squeezed with all those fond memories, the laughter and fun they'd had choosing the Christmas trees. He saw Anna considering his idea and wasn't sure if she was well enough to drive up there and tromp around in the snow, looking for a tree.

"Yes, I'd love to do that, Kyle."

Hope and emotion were combined in her suddenly husky tone. For a split second, Kyle swore he saw moisture in Anna's green eyes, but just as suddenly, it was gone. Had he imagined it? The look of longing in her expression was there to read. The joy in her eyes was there, too. Kyle felt his heart expand. God, he wanted nothing more than to lift her depressed spirits. He'd give his right arm to see her smile instead of that sad curve to her lips that always haunted her mouth instead.

She had a lot to be grieving about. The loss of Trevor was a huge blow to a ranch of this size. Anna had the innate ability to make everyone feel nurtured by her maternal warmth, to be inclusive of everyone, as if those who worked at the ranch were like family to her, too. And that was just the way Anna was built.

Right now, Kyle was feeling that warmth exuding from her toward him. That invisible sensation of being special, of being loved and cosseted by her.

"This blizzard isn't a good time to do much of anything," he said, eating the hearty soup with enthusiasm. Kyle saw she'd finished just about everything in her bowl, a good sign. He was grateful Anna had an appetite. Kyle knew from too many experiences that on patrol, if a team member got wounded or killed, no one had an appetite. They forced themselves to eat because there was no choice. The only way to get back to the FOB was to continually eat food and keep hydrated.

"Maybe in three or four days?" Anna asked.

"Yeah," he murmured, cleaning up the last of the food in his bowl.

"Let's see what Jepson says about the road up to the hill," she counseled, pushing the emptied bowl away.

"Sounds like a plan." Giving her a fond look, he said, "You ate everything."

Touching her stomach, Anna made a slight shrug. "It must be you, Kyle. I haven't eaten this much since returning home from the hospital."

Preening inwardly, Kyle wanted to believe her. He knew he had influence over Anna. Despite her hesitancy, her reluctance to share any feelings with him, he sensed it. If the SEALs didn't give him anything else, they had given him a powerful, unquestioned intuition. And if Kyle was accurately reading Anna, she was more than glad to see him.

It almost felt like old times when they were young, naive and innocent to the ways of the world. And Kyle was aware that his decisions had made Anna sadder than anyone else's actions had in her life.

"Where would you like me to bunk?" he asked her, holding her gaze. Once again, her cheeks flamed pink. Why? Kyle knew there was a bunkhouse for wranglers near the main ranch house. He found himself resisting going there because he wanted to remain close to Anna in case she needed help. If nothing else, he could at least support and assist her if necessary. It ate at his sensitized conscience that he would be here for only a month.

"You can have the guest bedroom down the hall." She gestured gracefully toward that direction. "If that's okay with you?"

Okay? Hell, it was perfect. And already, Kyle was plotting and planning when he could kiss Anna, feel her lush lips blossom beneath his onslaught, feel her heat combine with his. Because when they kissed, the real world went away and only the two of them existed in that exquisite, heated moment. And damn, he wanted to take her to bed, love her gently, love her until he would hear those beautiful sounds caught in her throat, feel her convulse around him.

Was it all a dream? Kyle was a realist. He knew from past experience Anna would refuse to go to bed with him ever again. Because if she did, Kyle knew she would agree to whatever he wanted from her. And the Montana woman, the pragmatist, knew better. She would not sell her heart for one night in his arms. Or even thirty nights. It had to be forever or not at all.

CHAPTER TWO

FOUR DAYS... ANNA closed her eyes, standing near her bedroom door, hand upon the brass knob. She had changed into an old pair of jeans that had seen better days, two layers of sweaters beneath her dark blue nylon parka and good boots to traverse the knee-deep snow. As she opened her eyes, the slats of sun filtered through the burgundy drapes in her bedroom. Kyle waited for her out in the living room. They were going to go find the perfect Christmas tree for the ranch house and the wranglers' bunkhouse. Her house was now painfully empty, no longer filled with the booming laughter of her father or the teasing from her mother. It seemed longer than a year that they'd been gone. And on days like this, particularly around the holidays, it felt as if someone was carving up her heart with a dull knife.

She felt weak and needy. Four days with Kyle under her roof triggered the powerful emotions of loving him once more. He was charismatic. His eyes were a deep gray with a black ring around the iris, making him look like the focused hunter he really was. He hunted men, just as raptors hunted their kind of food.

And his smile was devastating to her, dismantling all logic as to why she shouldn't get involved with him. Did he know how his smile undid her? Did Kyle read the desire in her expression?

At twenty-two, seven long years ago, he had come home and they'd made love, giving their hearts to one another. Even after their breakup, she wore her heart on her sleeve. She couldn't hide how she felt about Kyle. She never could. And right now, her heart pined so powerfully for any little touch, any smile or gaze from Kyle.

There was no mistaking what lay in his gray gaze, that intense craving for her alone. Kyle seemed cautious about touching her during the past four days. He'd been circumspect, as if respecting her space, her needs. But at night in bed? She hurt so much, the ache in her body for this man with the careless smile and dancing gray eyes haunted her. Kyle exuded life times ten. To Anna, he was like the force of sunlight come to earth in the shape of a human. Just being around him had increased her appetite, chased away so much of her dizziness and infused her with his energy, his love. Within days she felt ten times stronger than before.

Kyle cajoled her into eating a little more each day. He made them breakfast, and his buttermilk pancakes were mouth-waveringly good. She was surprised he knew how to cook, but in the end, she left no crumbs on her plate, either. Anna would swear she'd gained five pounds. It was Kyle's love for her, she realized, that was feeding her soul, infusing her heart and body. He had always had that kind of magical effect upon her in every way.

Her fingers tightened around the doorknob. What was she going to do? She felt the intense longing to be in his arms, resting against his stalwart body, knowing he would hold her safe. Kyle would love her if she allowed him. Every cell in her body trembled with need. The last time he had loved her, kissed her, was seven years ago. And she could still remember the strength of his mouth upon hers.

What did that make her? A fool forever? Hadn't she tried to erase Kyle from her heart? They were children who grew up together. Running through fields of purple clover, rolling in lush, green grass and lying together, hands behind their heads, watching the white clouds change shape above them.

A small sound, part desperation, part desire, slipped from between her lips. Anna wanted to blame her neediness for Kyle on her concussion, but she knew that wasn't true. Her heart wanted this man who was so tall, so confident and such a warrior among men. And she knew she was chasing a dream that would never come true. Kyle had said it himself: his family was the SEALs. Not her. She was second in his life. She had been first before he'd turned eighteen. The sweet, stolen kisses they'd shared still danced in her heart's memory. They had been so young, innocent and so much in love with one another.

Opening her eyes, Anna stared down at her hand, felt the dampness and coolness of her fingers around the brass knob. Kyle had loved the SEALs more. And that was what she had to remember. No matter what happened today, out at Christmas Tree Hill, Anna had to keep that knowledge that she was second in his life. Her heart didn't want to remember it, but her head did.

Slowly, she twisted the knob and the door quietly opened before her. Anna heard the soft snap and crackle of wood in the massive fireplace down the hall. Those natural sounds always soothed her. This afternoon, she knew Kyle was there, warming himself by the fire, waiting for her.

Her heart cried out in anguish to go to him, wrap her arms around his narrow waist, rest her head against his well-sprung chest, feel his arms slide around her, enclose her, hold her close. In four days, the desperation had built within her so much that Anna felt like a crazed animal, wanting to throw caution to the wind. Take Kyle to her bed, love him with all the passion she possessed and allow him to return it to her. She saw the look in his eyes. Saw the hunger for her in them. Anna knew he didn't possess the ability to hide how he felt toward her. With her, Kyle wore his heart on his sleeve, too.

Numbly, she walked down the flagstone hall, the hollow sound of the tread of her boots against the caramel, white and sienna–colored sedimentary rock. As she emerged, Kyle lifted his chin, his gaze narrowing on her. Heat began to build in her breasts, tightening them, and then that arc of blazing heat dived below, nestling and restless deep within her. All Kyle had to do was look at her. *Just a look.*

"Ready?" he asked, studying her closely as she drew up to him.

"Yes," she said, a little breathless.

"Blue sky and sunshine out there," he said, slipping his hand beneath her elbow. "A beautiful day. Jepson said it was going to get above freezing."

Anna barely heard his low, dark voice that always made her shiver with anticipation. She felt the monitored strength of his long, strong fingers cupping her elbow as he opened the door and guided her into the crisp afternoon air.

Kyle led her outside the gated fence to a black Chevy truck. He opened the passenger door for Anna and she stepped inside the cab. The sky was blindingly blue, and she put on her red baseball cap and dark glasses. Watching Kyle walk around the truck, the way his shoulders were proudly squared, she admired the strength in his face, in the set of his jaw. It was when her gaze dropped to his well-shaped mouth that she groaned internally. How badly she wanted his mouth upon hers.

"Jepson said he had a wrangler take a grader up into the road area earlier this morning where we'll find a tree," Kyle said, putting the truck in gear. He drove out of the plowed area, remembering the way to that hill.

"We'll need two trees today, Kyle."

"Two it is." He smiled as he drove slowly down the road covered with hard-packed snow. "How are you feeling today?"

"Okay," she lied, clasping her gloved hands in her lap.

"Dizziness?"

"None so far today."

"Good."

There was relief in his low voice, and genuine caring. In all the years, Kyle had never lied to her. He'd always been honest and straightforward with her. Anna felt as if she were sitting next to sunlight. Kyle unaccountably lifted her spirit. Fed her hope. Made her feel as if everything in the world would turn out all right. He'd always made her feel that way.

"My mother emailed me and said you'd gotten a divorce," Kyle said, giving her a glance.

"Yes. From Tom Carter." Giving him a quick look, she saw his set profile, his brows down. "Why?"

"I didn't know him."

"He was a drifter."

"Who came to work here?"

"Yes." Anna knotted her hands, staring at them.

"He must have been special for you to fall in love with him."

Wincing internally, Anna said, "I thought I loved him."

The cab went silent, just the slow grind of the engine as Kyle guided the truck up and around a long curve. Up ahead was a large hill wreathed with evergreens.

"What do you mean you thought you loved him?" Kyle moved his gloved hand a little on the steering wheel, keeping his eyes on the slippery road.

"I was…young." Her throat tightened and she didn't dare look at Kyle or she'd burst out in tears.

"I didn't know about it." Kyle took a deep breath. "Only the divorce. I'm sorry, Anna. You deserve only happiness."

Pain scored her heart. "A-after you left at twenty-two, I was lost, Kyle. I'm not blaming you. I know you asked me to marry you, but I just couldn't…I couldn't…"

He reached out and squeezed her arm for a moment. "It's all right. I understood why you didn't, Anna."

Pain increased in her heart, and she wished his fingers would remain around her lower arm. "I wanted a family…."

"Yes," he said, his voice thick, "you've always been a mother at heart. You've wanted a brood of kids since forever."

She opened her hands. "I thought when Tom entered my life, that I could love him. That we could settle down. He said he wanted kids, too." She touched her nose. A memory. "I believed him."

"We fell out of touch after I left," Kyle said, apology in his voice.

"I couldn't email you, Kyle. It was—too painful."

Nodding, he rasped, "Yeah, for both of us, but especially for you. It's okay. I understand."

"After a while," Anna whispered, "I wanted to email you. But Tom discovered all the letters and emails you had written to me over the years from eighteen until you were twenty-two…. He was furious and jealous."

Giving her a sharpened look, Kyle heard the anguish in her voice. "Jealous?"

"Very."

"I took all the letters you'd written to me and hid them from him because I knew he would destroy them. He accused me of being unfaithful to him. Of loving you, not him." Anna met his turbulent gaze. "I was twenty-seven at the time. We'd had a five-year marriage and I knew Tom wanted to leave me. I—I couldn't get pregnant. I'd suffered two miscarriages earlier and he blamed me…. He said I still loved you and not him." Anna flexed her fingers in a helpless gesture.

"Damn." Kyle's mouth thinned as he pulled up to the hill. There was a path that led up to the Scotch pine that grew on the rounded summit. Turning off the truck engine, he unbuckled his seat belt and turned, sliding his arm around Anna's hunched shoulders. Her face was filled with misery. "I wish… I wish I'd known all of this, Anna."

"Why?" She held his stare. "What good would it have done, Kyle?"

He frowned. "Because I've always cared about you, Anna. Growing up, we always talked. We were best of friends. We held one another's secrets." Kyle took his gloved finger and moved some of her long hair away from her ear so he could see her face. "I never wanted to lose that connection with you, Anna. Not ever. I'm sorry if you thought I didn't care. I always have...."

Tears jammed into her eyes and she quickly swallowed them away. Just the grazing touch of his index finger against her hair sent sheets of prickles and pleasure through her. She pulled away, unable to handle Kyle's contact. Because if she didn't remove herself, she'd collapse into his arms, cling to him and never let him go again. "I know you care," she whispered brokenly, pushing the door open, unharnessing and escaping.

Leaving the cab, Kyle picked up the saw in his left hand. The wind was chilly and he walked over to where Anna stood at the foot of the trail. "Come on," he urged her quietly, cupping her elbow. "Let's go find some nice Christmas trees."

Every foot up that winding path, Anna recalled an earlier Christmas with Kyle. By the time they entered the tree farm, tears fogged her vision and she was no longer able to drive them away. Her elbow throbbed where his hand curved around it. She found herself wanting to stop, turn and throw herself into Kyle's arms. Anna knew he would receive her. Kiss her.

"What about this one?" Kyle asked, halting. Releasing her elbow, he pointed to a six-foot Scotch pine to their left. "What do you think?"

Blindly, Anna moved toward it, not wanting Kyle to see her tears. With quick swipes of her gloved hands, she wiped the tears away. "I think it's perfect," she said. "Just the right size for that corner near the fireplace."

Kyle got down on his hands and knees, positioning the saw.

Anna stood away, watching him work, the sawing

sound filling the air around them. The snow was knee-deep and the wind was brisk. She pushed her hair away from her face, watching him make quick work of the trunk. In no time, the pine tipped and fell softly into the surrounding snow. Kyle grinned up at her.

"One down. One to go..."

Anna forced a smile. As she backed up, her boot slipped. With a startled cry, she threw out her hands, falling. In seconds, Kyle was there, catching her. He fell into the snow, bringing her on top of him, protecting her. Snow kicked up and flew all around them.

Anna's hair was showered with glistening snowflakes as Kyle rolled her on top of him to break the worst part of their fall. He was warm and strong and his arms curved around her, holding her safely against him, taking the brunt of the impact. He grunted as he hit first. Automatically, she closed her eyes, surrendering over to him entirely, knowing Kyle wasn't about to allow her injured and healing head to slam into the hillside. She utterly relaxed in relief against him.

"Anna? Are you all right?"

The urgency in Kyle's roughened tone snapped her eyes open. Snowflakes settled against her hair and across her face. She felt the length of his body against her own, her breasts pressed against his jacketed chest. She gave a short, nervous laugh.

"Yes...I'm okay...really..." She started to struggle to get off him, but then made the mistake of drowning in Kyle's narrowed gray eyes. His pupils were huge and black, reminding her of a predator that has its quarry sighted. Her heart banged violently in her chest as he eased her slowly off him, tucking her down beside his body, his arm beneath her neck and shoulder, cradling her.

The world came to a halt. Their breaths were shared raggedly between them. It was going to happen. Kyle was going to kiss her. And Anna wanted this more than anything else in her world. She reached up with her gloved hand, sliding it across his stubbled cheek, and watched Kyle's eyes suddenly grow intense upon her. Anna felt him move beside her, take off his glove and throw it aside and then curve his roughened palm against her cheek, guiding her lips toward his.

The chill of the air was warmed by his breath as his mouth moved tenderly across her parting lips. Anna heard a groan start deep within Kyle, felt his fingers grow firm against her face, angling her so he could kiss her more deeply, more fully. His mouth was strong and hungry, but not hurtful. His punctuated breath, warm against her cold nose and cheek, made Anna sink more deeply into his embrace. A small whimper caught in her throat as he coaxed her mouth open, taking her, trying to rein in his hunger for her, allowing her time to respond.

Anna's entire world melted as his mouth slid and curved fully against hers, opening her, his tongue gliding along her lower lip, tasting her. His groan met and matched her own, and she sensed Kyle shift, pulling her hard against his body, his hand ranging across her shoulders, down her spine, trapping her hips against his erection.

It felt as if a bomb had gone off low and deep within her body as Kyle worshipped her lips and kissed the corners of her mouth, urging her to kiss him in return. And she did, her hands framing his face, her lips taking his, drowning in his male scent, the cold, fresh air and the swirling fragrance of pine encircling them.

Anna forgot about the snow melting against her face or the scattering flakes falling out of the strands of her hair. She forgot everything except Kyle as a man, a man she'd secretly loved all her life. His mouth took hers more gently now, rocking her lips open, moving his tongue inside, testing, tasting her. Her breath grew chaotic, fingers tight against his face. Anna couldn't get enough of him.

As Kyle eased his fingers through her hair, sliding strands aside, he lifted his mouth from hers and pressed small, feathered kisses against her hairline, her brows and then across her closed eyelids. She could feel his breath against her skin, feel him reacquainting himself with every square inch of her flesh. Anna luxuriated in his surrounding her with his caresses, his care. Her heart exploded with love, the rippling effect moving through her, and she boldly pressed her hips against his, feeling his erection, wanting desperately to feel him inside her once more.

And as his kisses drifted near the lobe of her left ear, a little cry escaped her. Kyle knew how sensitive the region was in back of her ear, and even more so, her nape. His hand ranged across her hips, keeping her firmly against him, letting her know just how badly he wanted her. Her hair was swirling around her face as Kyle eased her forward until her head lay across his chest, her hand on his right shoulder as he teased and caressed her nape. More softened sounds, mewls of pleasure, tore out of her.

Slowly, so slowly, Kyle lightened his exploration and kisses across her slender neck and delicate ear. Easing up on his elbow, he cradled Anna in his left arm, staring down at her, raw need burning in his eyes for her alone.

Every female cell in her body took off in screaming need for Kyle. Her breath was choppy, her breasts rising and falling sharply against his chest. When he lifted his hand and gently tamed the ginger strands away from her face, he gave her a faint smile.

"It doesn't seem like time means anything between us," he rasped, smoothing a drop of water from melted snow from her brow.

Her heart was galloping in her chest. Anna couldn't think. A mass of accumulated starvation. The ache for this man so extreme, she could give only a brief nod.

"Are you all right?" Kyle looked deeply into her dazed eyes. "Your head?"

Her head was the last thing Anna was thinking of right now. The stunning fireworks going off in her lower body held her attention. She was soaking wet between her thighs, and it had nothing to do with snow melting there. Kyle's kiss had unlocked that door within her, and Anna understood the power of him as a man to trigger her into bright, burning life and need. "I—I'm okay…I think…." She managed a one-cornered smile, still lost in his turbulent, stormy gray gaze.

"That was one helluva surprise," he murmured, giving her a slanted look. "I didn't see it coming."

"I didn't either…." Anna closed her eyes, content to be exactly where she was—against Kyle.

"I'm not sorry, Anna. Are you?"

She barely shook her head, her hair mixed and coated with the snow.

"Come on," Kyle urged her thickly, "we need to get you up and out of this snow before you get wet and chilled."

Kyle gently eased her into a sitting position, stood

up and then brought her slowly to her feet. He held on to her gloved hands, making sure she wasn't dizzy or unstable. Before Anna could pull her hands from his, he began to carefully brush the snow from her dark strands. Standing so near to him, feeling his raw animal heat, sensing his care cascade over her—Anna absorbed it like the starving woman she was.

Kyle was so considerate, so careful with her. She had always felt worshipped by him. He loved her and she knew it. Right now, she'd accept secondhand love from this man because Anna had gone too long without him in her life. It was as if he were recharging her soul, allowing it to awaken once more, to dream, to want, to share with him again.

"There," Kyle murmured. Satisfaction vibrated in his tones as he nudged the clean strands across her shoulder. "You're snow free. You sure you're okay?"

"Mmm, yes, fine...wonderful..." she whispered. Searching his eyes, Anna could see his love for her, and his lust. "I wish..."

"Wish what, angel?"

Anna quivered inwardly over the endearment. Ever since she could remember, Kyle had called her his guardian angel in this lifetime. "I wish...things were different...."

He cocked his head, staring at her. "In what way, Anna?"

Her throat tightened. Tears burned in the backs of her eyes. Swallowing, she said hoarsely, "That things were different between you and me, that's all." And if she didn't pull away from Kyle right now, she was going to do the unthinkable: walk into his arms and never leave. But he would leave her. In less than thirty days.

And Anna just couldn't step across that chasm. Touching his jaw, she stepped back. "You've always known how to kiss me…."

He remained where he was, watching her, saying nothing. There was regret in Kyle's gaze. Want. Desire. Lust. She was sure she had the same expression on her face. And then, he surprised her by stepping toward her, sliding his hands around her shoulders and holding her in place.

"We have to talk, Anna. There's a lot that needs to be said. To be discussed. I was waiting for a time." Kyle lifted her chin. "I was trying to wait until you felt better. When we weren't so wary of one another…"

Anna didn't try to fight his embrace. The gesture was of a man claiming his woman. And she didn't know what Kyle's end objective was. "We never had wariness with one another until after you left for the Navy."

"Yes, it started then, Anna." Kyle gave her a pained look, his hands resting lightly on her shoulders, not trying to draw her any closer to him. Not trying to kiss her again. "I needed to see the world, angel. I felt tied down here in Montana. I didn't want to be like my father and never have adventures outside the ranch." His mouth drew into an unhappy slash as he looked above her head for a moment, trying to choose the right words. His gaze fell on hers. "Anna, this was never about you. You were the innocent victim in all of this. I didn't mean to hurt you, angel. I swear to God, I didn't. But I did and you can't know how forever sorry I am about it."

"Shh," she whispered. "Don't go there. There's nothing to forgive, Kyle. I was too young to understand why you left. But later, I did. I realized you needed to see the world, experience life, live it. I got it. I really did."

Tears slipped from her eyes. She saw Kyle's face crumple. He never could handle her tears.

He swept her into his arms, crushing her, his face buried against her hair. Giving a broken cry, Anna collapsed against him, her arms slipping around him, their hearts beating frantically against one another. He smelled of sweat, of male, of pine, and Anna dragged it into her nostrils, drinking Kyle into her in every possible way. She could feel the tension rise in him, the tightness of his shoulders, holding her close, as if to somehow protect her with his large body. The sensation was exquisite. Exactly what Anna needed.

Tears continued to stream down her face unchecked. She cried for the loss of two babies from her miscarriages; she cried for herself when Tom had beaten her; and she cried for the loss of Kyle she knew was coming. He was going to break her heart once more. A heart that had ever loved only him.

CHAPTER THREE

BY THE TIME they reached home with two Scotch pines in the back of the pickup truck, Anna had developed a blinding headache. Kyle worriedly glanced at her from time to time as he drove slowly toward the ranch. She'd become withdrawn and pale, tipping her head against the headrest. Her eyes were closed.

Had it been their blazing kiss, clinging to one another? As if to let go meant they'd never see one another again? Had her crying brought it on? God, he didn't know what to do when Anna cried. Kyle felt so damned helpless. He was a SEAL. He fixed things. That was his job. But damned if he could fix a woman's tears. And she'd wept after kissing him. Why?

The questions jammed in his throat like bitter brew, and Kyle knew this wasn't the time to ask her anything. More than likely, Anna was upset over their unexpected kiss. They eventually had to face the end of this thirty-day emergency leave. He had to return to his SEAL platoon in Afghanistan.

When they arrived at the ranch, Jepson met them with two wranglers. Together, the three men took the trees into the buildings. Kyle had wanted to be with Anna, but she'd slipped out of the truck and gone straight into the house, telling him she was going to go lie down.

When Kyle had gotten the tree ready for decoration in the corner of the room, it was nearly 6:00 p.m. The winter night had closed in quickly, and he'd built a roaring fire that would keep the entire ranch house heated.

He kept his hearing focused in case Anna was awake. He wanted to be with her. Kyle knew if he could hold her, she would feel better. It had always been that way between them. Frustrated, he got rid of his hat and gloves. Hanging his damp jacket on a wooden peg near the front door, he rolled up the sleeves on his chambray shirt and went to work in the kitchen. Kyle made a point of fixing three meals a day for Anna. She was eating better, and he wanted her to regain that lost weight. Looking through the refrigerator and cupboards, he found enough items to make a hearty shepherd's pie.

It was near 8:00 p.m. when Kyle heard the door to Anna's room open. He stopped himself from going into the hall to meet her. Sensing she needed some space, Kyle instead set the oak table for dinner.

Anna appeared.

"Hey," he called softly, setting down the flatware, "how are you feeling?" She looked wan, her eyes dark.

"Better," she mumbled. Walking slowly, Anna used her hand against the black granite island to steady herself. Motioning wearily toward her head, she said in a quiet tone, "My concussion. The doctors said I could get terrible headaches out of the blue." She grimaced. "They were right."

"Have a seat," Kyle urged, pulling out the chair for her. Anna was clearly unsteady, and he held out his hand toward her. She took it, her fingers feeling cool and clammy.

"Thanks."

"Would you like something to drink?"

"Just water."

"How about some aspirin?"

"No, docs said to stay away from them for now. The pain is pretty much gone, Kyle. I just feel bruised and beaten up, is all."

Grimacing, Kyle got her a glass of water. "You look pretty pasty."

Anna took the glass. "I feel pasty."

Kyle watched her take slow sips of the water. She used both hands to hold the glass. "I had a SEAL buddy of mine get traumatic brain injury when an IED went off too close to him. He had a helluva lot of symptoms like you do. His headaches were so bad they made him cry."

"Yes," Anna said, lifting her eyes to him, "that's about right. I feel for him. Is he better now?"

Shrugging, Kyle shoved on a pair of mitts and opened the oven door. "Chuck is stateside and still doing a lot of physical therapy. I don't get to email him often because the team and I are usually out on patrols."

He pulled out the shepherd's pie and placed it on a metal trivet on the table. Anna lifted her head and sniffed the fragrant meal. There was an appreciative expression on her face.

"Smell good to you?" he asked. Opening the oven again, Kyle retrieved some French bread wrapped in foil. Earlier, he'd sliced and placed garlic salt with butter between each slice.

"Yes, it does." Anna smiled wanly. "You're a really good cook, do you know that?"

He grinned and opened the foil up and placed the sliced bread in front of her plate. "I'm no five-star chef, angel, but I'm happy if you eat, that's all."

Reaching for the large spoon, Anna placed some of the pie on her plate. Kyle had mashed potatoes, whipped them up and covered the top of the pie with them. The top was a light golden brown, cooked to perfection. She picked up Kyle's plate and added three heaping scoops onto it. "Funny, but I am hungry. I shouldn't be, but I am."

Sitting down next to her, Kyle didn't want to go into any heavy topics tonight with Anna. She ate quite a bit and he felt heartened. After dinner, he cleared away the dishes.

"I didn't make dessert," he said. "Coffee?"

"Yes, please." She turned and gazed at the tree. "It looks nice over there, Kyle. Did Jepson get the other tree into the wranglers' bunkhouse?"

Bringing over coffee, he set a mug in front of her. "Yes. I asked him where the decorations for your tree were and he said he didn't know."

"They're in my closet." She wrapped her hands around the warm mug. "Do you remember every year how our parents would gather out here at the table? You'd pull out the colored construction paper? Cut it up for our paper loops? And I'd get out the glitter and glue gun?"

He smiled and nodded. "Yeah, lots of good times, good memories."

"I still do the same thing today." She gave him a fond look, watching his reaction.

"Seriously?"

"Sure. Why not? I've kept all our decorations over the years. And every year I hang them up. I make a bowl of fresh popcorn and string it, plus I make new paper chains."

His face softened as he reconnected with those times from their mutual past.

"So that's what we'll do tomorrow? Make paper chains and string popcorn?"

"Yep, plus hang on the tree all the old ornaments we've made over the years."

Shaking his head, he gave her a grin. "I didn't know you kept up that family tradition."

"I remember each of those decorations we made, Kyle. We'd sign the back of them. Our name, the date and year."

"Yeah…"

"You're giving me a funny look. There's nothing wrong with keeping mementos from the past. Especially if they're from good times."

He pushed his fingers through his short black hair. "You're right, Anna." He leaned to one side, pulling his wallet out of his back pocket. Opening it, he carefully pulled out a folded item. He pushed it toward her. "Check this out." His eyes darkened.

Gently picking up the folded piece of white construction paper, she gasped. "Oh, my God! This is the angel I made when I was seven years old, Kyle!" The edges were torn and frayed. The white paper had faded to yellow. All the gold glitter that had once been on the wings and halo had long ago been rubbed off.

Anna remembered painstakingly making it. As she turned it over, her fingers trembled. Emotion roared through her as she saw her name scrawled on the back of it, the month and the year. Swallowing hard, she whispered, "You've kept this all this time?" She held his soft gray gaze.

"The last Christmas we had together? Seven years

ago? When we were hanging them on the tree? Instead of hanging it up, I slipped it into my billfold."

"But…why?" Anna stared down at the poor, tattered thing that had seen better days.

Shrugging, Kyle admitted, "I wanted to take a part of you with me, Anna. Maybe because it had your energy, your love in it… I don't know. I always put it in a plastic Ziplock bag and tucked it into the pocket of my Kevlar vest when I went out on a patrol. I always believed you were my guardian angel and I wanted to take you with me into battle."

"I—I didn't know…" Her voice dropped to an aching whisper as she held it gently between her hands. Her lower lip trembled.

"One time? I forgot to put it into my vest. We went out on an op and I got shot in the right calf."

"Oh, God, Kyle—"

He held up his hands. "Sorry, I shouldn't have said anything. I'm fine now. A hundred percent, okay? Wipe the worry off your face?"

Sitting back, Anna cradled the angel in her hands.

"You are always with me, Anna." Kyle felt emotions rising swiftly in him. He forced himself to smile, but it was a poor attempt. What he wanted to do was hold her. Kiss the hell out of her again. See her smile once more. Hear that husky laugh of hers, which always sent riffles across his flesh.

Nodding, she carefully handed it back to him, their fingers briefly touching. "I'm glad to know this. Did you ever marry, Kyle?"

"No." He saw her perplexed look. "Look, I knew in our business getting married wasn't an option. And you were smart enough at twenty-two not to say yes to me even though I wanted to marry you, Anna. I kept seeing SEAL marriages fall apart, one after another. They have a ninety percent divorce rate, so I steered clear. I never got serious with a woman after you. I didn't want to lead her on." He had plenty of one-night stands, but Kyle wasn't going there with Anna. All it would do was hurt her, and he'd hurt her enough already.

"That was good of you to tell me that," she admitted quietly, sipping her coffee. "I knew I couldn't handle you being in danger all the time, Kyle. It would have killed me."

"You're a big worrywart," he teased gently. "I understand now. Back then, at twenty-two, I didn't."

"I hurt you badly by turning you down," she choked. "I always felt horrible about it."

Kyle reached out and captured her fingers. "It was the smartest thing you could have done, Anna. And like you said, we had to grow up and mature a little in order to know you did the right thing for both of us. I was kind of blind, deaf and dumb at that time." Blindly in love with her. But he always had been.

"I still feel that way at times."

"What? When you married Tom?"

Anna gave him a painful shrug and couldn't meet his eyes. Unconsciously, she rubbed her nose. "He walked into my life six months after you proposed to me. Looking back on it, Kyle, I should have realized I was on the rebound from you." She moved her finger around on the wooden table, drawing circles. "I wanted to settle down, have a family. I so desperately wanted to have what my parents had with me coming into their lives. We had been so happy as a family...."

Kyle frowned. "Anna, I don't want you getting another headache because we're getting into some serious talks here."

"My headache is gone." She managed a faint smile. "I wasn't very good at picking the right man, Kyle. I thought I loved Tom." Her voice trailed off. "I wanted kids so desperately. I got pregnant right away and then miscarried the second month. Tom blamed me."

"For what?" Kyle demanded, confused. "You can't make your body miscarry."

"That's what I told him. I got pregnant nine months later, and by the third month I miscarried again. I was devastated. I thought there was something wrong with me." She gently touched her belly.

"And where was Tom in all of this?"

"Angry. That's when he accidentally found all those letters and emails you'd written to me when you first joined the Navy. He accused me of loving you, instead. That because I loved you, I miscarried his children."

"That's a crock of bull," Kyle ground out, flexing his fingers into a fist and then forcing himself to relax.

"Things sort of fell apart between us after that. It wasn't a marriage anymore. Just two people living together, but unhappy."

"Why didn't you email me, Anna?"

She gave him a sad look. "And what good would that have done? If Tom had found me emailing you, he'd have—well—he was violent and I didn't want to stir up trouble."

Giving her a sharpened look, he asked, "What do you mean he was violent, Anna?"

She felt the tension rise between them. Kyle's face had gone stony and still, his gray eyes narrowing on her. Opening her hand, she said, "He had a terrible temper.

I didn't know it when I first married him. I only found out about it...later."

With a hiss, Kyle gripped her hand firmly. "Look at me."

Anna held his intense stare. She felt his hand warm and gentle around her coolish one. "What?"

"Your nose, Anna. How did it get broken?"

The rasp in his voice was deadly and sent a shiver down through her. Unable to look away, she said, "Tom hit me one night." She pulled her hand free of his, tucking it protectively in her lap. "I went to the police that night after it happened, Kyle. I pressed assault charges against him and they threw him in jail." She touched her nose. "I was scared, but my parents and your parents backed me up. They surrounded me, protected me and helped me through that period of my life. My father fired Tom. He was sent to prison for a year. When he got out, he left for Texas. He signed the divorce papers and I was free." She gave him an uneasy look. "It's not something I'm proud of. I made so many mistakes."

Kyle sat there wrestling with his rage over what had been done to Anna. "I wish... I wish you'd told me," he managed tightly.

"And what could you have done, Kyle?" She searched his angry eyes, saw the fury in the line of his thinned mouth. "You were somewhere. God only knows where. We weren't married. There was no legal tie between us, except that you're my emergency contact. The SEALs wouldn't have let you come home." Her voice grew thin with weariness. "I managed to get through it. I had asked your parents to not email you anything about it because I knew it would upset you. And I didn't want you distracted and maybe get you killed. That's why I never said anything to you about it."

Kyle looked away, his gut churning. His mother had emailed him about her divorce, but he didn't want to bring it up right now. "God, Anna. I wish... I wish I'd been there." And he didn't finish the rest of the sentence that if he'd married her at twenty-two, this would never have happened. Because he loved her and would never hurt Anna. He'd never lift a hand to harm her. Ever.

"You start cutting up the construction paper for the paper chains," Anna told Kyle the next evening. Today the sun had shown up after the blizzard, and Kyle had been out working all day until dusk with the wranglers, getting hay to the five thousand Herefords on the ranch. He'd come in just before dinner, taken a shower and changed clothes, and Anna made spaghetti and meatballs for dinner.

He sat down, picking up the scissors after rolling up the cuffs on his red flannel shirt to his elbows. "And you're going to string the popcorn, I hope?" He held up his hand, showing how large it was compared with hers.

Kyle had seen a marked change in Anna this morning at breakfast. It was as if getting to talk out her toxic marriage had somehow helped her. Tonight, her ginger hair was tied in a loose knot at the back of her head and she'd put some plastic mistletoe in it to look festive. He liked the gold velour sweater she wore with her jeans and bright red fluffy slippers with Frosty the Snowman on her feet. In the past, Kyle remembered Anna always dressed up for Christmas decoration night.

She wore pink lipstick and her cheeks were tinged nearly the same color. Even her eyes sparkled, although Kyle missed the gold flecks he used to see in their depths. Still, Anna was happier than he'd seen her since coming home. He knew how much Christmas meant to her. It meant the same to him.

"Yes, I'll save you from a fate worse than death," she said with a laugh. "I'll string the popcorn. You just cut, glue and make the paper chains."

He liked sitting across from Anna. She was quick and efficient with thread, needle and popcorn. Soon, she had ten-foot-long chains lying out in neat order across the length of the table. Kyle was clumsy in comparison, but he knew how to cut the colorful paper into half-inch strips and then use the glue gun to create the chains. Within an hour they had enough to encircle the tree.

There was Christmas music playing in the background and Kyle, because he was tall, got the job of stringing the lights from the top down on the Scotch pine. As soon as he had the tree swathed in lights, he helped Anna place the paper chains and then the popcorn strands around the tree.

Standing back, he smiled at her. "Looks pretty decent, doesn't it?"

She grinned. "It looks beautiful. Come on, you can help bring out the decorations." She caught his hand, gave it a quick squeeze and pulled him over to the coffee table. There was one large cardboard box sitting on it. Each year's decorations were carefully placed on sturdy, thin plastic shelves to keep them in order by the year that they'd been created.

Sitting down, he worked with her to bring out the oldest ones first, which were going around the top of the tree. The paper decorations brought back a lot of warm memories, and as they moved from their six-year-old decorations through age ten, Kyle's heart squeezed with a fierce love for Anna. Every year, there were memories, some good, some bad. They were all immortalized by two young children with color crayons, construction paper, glitter and a gold thread for hanging each of them on the tree.

Anna had carefully and painstakingly preserved each year's worth of events with both their families. Kyle remembered all of them sitting at the oak table, each of them cutting and drawing one main event that had taken place in their life that year. When the family was finished, there was a paper story of meaningful events that had occurred that particular year before Christmas. Anna had put photos with them, as well. For Kyle, it was an unexpected treasure trove, and it once more served to tell him just how important, how central, Anna had always been in his life.

For the next three hours, they talked, reminisced and then hung the oldest decorations around the top of the tree first. Some were of people, a photo with a name, who had passed on. Kyle remembered getting a black pony named Bart at age seven, and he'd drawn and colored it and then hung it proudly on the tree. As they reached the bottom of the tree, Anna handed him new construction paper, glitter, scissors and an ink pen.

She sat down opposite him. "Now you need to think about what decorations from this past year you'd like to make."

Kyle scowled. "What? An M-4 rifle? A Kevlar vest?"

"Whatever was important to you this year."

"What are you going to create?" he wondered.

"I'm going to make an image of you," she said, smiling softly. "You came home."

His heart twinged. "Then, I'll try to draw you. Not that I'm an artist," he protested.

"Okay, that sounds good," Anna murmured, giving him a wicked look. "Just get my hair and eye color right."

"Oh, I think I can do at least that much," he said, picking up some crayons. For the next twenty minutes, Kyle carefully drew Anna. Only this time, he drew a large pink heart behind her. He watched her quickly draw him, black hair and all, using some glitter for a leather belt around his waist and detailing his black combat boots on his feet.

She then drew a picture of Trevor Bates, their foreman who had died in the car wreck. Anna carefully cut Trevor's face and shoulders from a photo she'd taken of him previously and glued it in place. Kyle saw moisture come to her eyes. She wiped them from time to time as she drew the man who had been like a second father to her. Anna was easily touched by everything and everyone. Kyle thought about the two babies she'd miscarried. He couldn't imagine the pain and anguish she'd gone through twice. He tried not to think too much about it because it was obvious her husband had not offered support during her times of gut-wrenching loss and grief.

When Kyle studied the tree, he clearly saw all the events from age six through today. There were a lot of people, cows, dogs, horses and depictions of events that had affected the lives of those who lived on this century-old ranch. The last decoration with Kyle's likeness was at age twenty-two when Anna had drawn him in his SEAL uniform. And for the babies she'd lost, she'd drawn two cherub angels, their name on each one. For Kyle, this was more like a Tree of Life than a

Christmas tree. The Native Americans of old had their winter count buffalo hides on which they drew large events that had occurred to the tribe each year.

As he stood there, Anna close to him, Kyle saw the tree as much more than celebrating a holiday. It reflected both happy and sad moments for two close families. It was really about life. Every year, however, Anna had created a U.S. flag and hung it with the rest of the decorations when he'd left at twenty-two and never returned until now.

There were seven years where she made and hung that flag. Kyle wondered if it was Anna's way of remembering him. He didn't have the guts to ask her. Maybe it was a way for her to remember him but not cause her husband to get angry or jealous. Maybe someday he'd ask. But not tonight. He wanted this to be a happy event for both of them.

"Where will you go when you return to the SEALs?"

Rousing himself, he said, "Back to Afghanistan. My platoon has two more months of deployment over there before we return to Coronado." Kyle felt his heart sink because Anna tucked her lower lip between her teeth for a moment. That was a sign Anna was worrying. "It's safe," he lied. "Things are quieting in that country because of the drawdown. Most of the military is going home." Another lie. Hell, the black ops units were busier than ever now with increased patrols since most of the American forces were leaving. The black ops community was taking over the vacuum left by the military's departure.

"Those families more than deserve their loved ones home," Anna said fiercely under her breath, barely held emotion driving her words.

"Too many wars for too long," Kyle agreed somberly.

"Will your team come home for good, then?"

He heard the hope, the terror, in her voice. "Some will." That wasn't a lie. When Kyle looked over at her, he could feel her devastation. Dammit. "Tell me what's in your future, Anna. What are you going to be doing?" He wanted off this topic for many reasons.

"Just running the ranch. After I get my head healed, I intend to start looking for a new ranch foreman. It will be a long search and it will take a while. I'm hoping by spring, we'll have hired someone new. We can't operate without one."

He studied her, watching the worry leave her eyes. Thank God, Anna was easily distracted. "What about your personal life?" And Kyle held his breath, waiting.

She smiled wryly. "What personal life? I'll be here, running the ranch. I'm not about to go out and hook up with someone else. I've got a bad track record, Kyle."

"I see." He tried to keep the relief out of his tone.

"I'm taking accounting courses online," she offered. "I need to really get into running the ranch from the budget end. Trevor always did that, but I need to be more hands-on, Kyle. I have to know where we're at financially."

"That sounds like a good plan," he congratulated her.

Her eyes sparkled and she lifted up a dollar sign she'd made and glued green glitter on it. "See? Money. Accounting. All a part of my life this year and next."

Kyle wanted to reach out and pull her up from the table and bring her into his arms. "I think you ought to draw some gold coins, too. For good luck for the next year."

Tonight was so perfect. It was twenty days until

Christmas. And he wanted Anna to enjoy this time because, obviously, she'd had a lot of death and losses in her life that he'd never known about. Until now.

She laughed. "Not a bad idea. I think I'll do it." She walked forward, leaning down and touching the decoration he'd made of her. "Why did you put a heart on it, Kyle?" She twisted a look up at him.

"Because you've always owned my heart, Anna." His throat tightened. He wanted so badly to touch her. "You're important to me," he whispered thickly, reaching out, easing strands of hair away from her shoulder.

There was hope in her eyes. Wild hope. God, how he wanted to have their lives have a happy ending. He saw color come to her cheeks over his grazing contact. Anna was a woman now. She had grown up strong and beautiful. Her lips parted, as if asking him if he would kiss her once again.

Wordlessly, Kyle framed her face, leaned down, closed his eyes and felt Anna lift her chin, wanting this kiss as much as he did. Everything faded around him as he barely brushed her lips. She was so lush, warm and responsive beneath his slow exploration of her. She touched his shoulder tentatively and he slid his hand down her spine, pulling her against him. Kyle wanted to give her the choice whether she wanted this next step, this intimacy he craved so desperately with Anna.

She stepped forward, her breasts brushing lightly against his chest. He groaned as he felt her melt against him, felt her mouth open fully to his, eager, her tongue delicately touching his. Fire bolted down through Kyle, his breathing ragged as he curved his mouth powerfully against hers. He heard a soft sound in her throat, knew she liked what he was offering her. His mind dissolved, his body came online, his erection painful against the zipper of his jeans. She could turn him on in a heartbeat. Her hair swirled across his cheek as he cupped the back of her head, wanting deeper access to Anna.

Where was this going? Where did he want it to go? In the past Kyle would not have thought enough about what the woman wanted. But Anna held his heart. She always had, and right now as she sank fully against him, letting him know she wanted him, Kyle had to think. He couldn't just take her to bed. He had to know, understand, what Anna expected from him.

Tearing his mouth from hers, Kyle held her close, felt her trembling as she slowly lifted her lashes. He saw flecks of gold in her dark green eyes, saw yearning in them, heard it in her broken breathing, the way her fingers dug into his shoulders.

"Anna," he rasped, "tell me what you want." He searched her face. When he had left her at twenty-two, they'd made love one last time. And Anna had broken down in tears afterward, clinging to him, never wanting to let him go. Kyle had never felt like such a bastard. He was going to leave her and he was hurting her as he held her, weeping, in his arms. He didn't want a replay of that. Ruthlessly, he stared down at her, their hearts racing wildly against one another as the moment strung tautly between them.

"Love me?" she whispered, sliding her fingers across his stubbled jaw.

Closing his eyes, he heard the closeted grief in her voice. "You know I have to leave," he told her harshly as he opened his eyes. Kyle had to warn her. "God, Anna, I've done nothing but hurt you over the years. I've left you crying...."

She drew in a deep breath, fearlessly holding his burning gaze. "I'm older now, Kyle. Hopefully a little more realistic." Anna looked away for a moment, her hand moving restlessly across his shoulder. "I know you're going away. I accept it.… I don't like it, but I'm accepting it.…"

Just as she was accepting of her miscarriages. Kyle winced inwardly, seeing the pain in the recesses of her eyes. God, he couldn't do this. "I can't… I don't want to hurt you again, Anna." He slid his fingers through her thick ginger hair, watching her eyes close, feeling her absorbing his touch, remembering him. Remembering what they'd shared before.

She smiled sadly. "Life is full of pain and joy, Kyle. We both know that now. You make my heart come alive. I've never felt so alive as when you're near me. We have until the end of December. I want that time with you. I want to love you. Hold you. I want to sleep at your side every night." Anna gave him a pleading look. "Don't turn me away, Kyle. Let me have this much with you. It's a gift. You're a gift to me. I—I don't want to waste one more minute of it."

His heart crumbled. Just the anguish, the arousal and need of her turned Kyle inside out. When she leaned her head against his shoulder, brow against the column of his neck, drawing him forward against her with her women's strength, something broke deep within him. What was he doing? Why the hell had he left the person he loved most in this world behind? What was propelling him to make that kind of decision?

The quietness surrounded them. The Christmas music embraced Kyle. The crackle and pop from the massive fireplace made the sense of homecoming even more intense and powerful within him. He was home. He had the woman he'd never stop loving in his arms, pleading with him to love her.

Dammit.

Anna shouldn't have to ask. Shouldn't have to beg. He leaned down, kissing her cheek, sliding his fingers across her nape. His voice was low and thick with emotion. "I love you, Anna. I've never stopped loving you...."

CHAPTER FOUR

ANNA'S HEART SQUEEZED with joy and pain as Kyle's low, growling words caressed her temple and ear. He loved her! Hadn't she always known that? So much anguish from the past flowed through her in that bittersweet moment. Lifting her head away from his shoulder, she drowned in Kyle's turbulent, stormy gaze. Sensing his pain, his apology, she leaned up, capturing his mouth, rocking his lips open and giving him all those years of waiting for him in that one kiss. A groan reverberated through his chest and he hungrily met and melded against her questing mouth, as if to reassure her all over again that he loved her with a power he'd always carried in his heart for her.

In moments, he'd swept her up into his arms and she sighed, slipping her arms around his shoulders, content to be carried down the darkened hall to his bedroom. Kyle nudged the door open with the toe of his boot and carried her inside. There was a small hurricane lamp on the dresser that shed just enough light so he could take her over to the bed and deposit her on it.

Kyle sat down beside her, turning her toward him, his hands resting on her shoulders. "I don't have any condoms on me," he told her. His brows dipped as he held her upturned gaze. "I never thought this could happen, Anna." He grazed her cheek, giving her a look of regret.

"It's all right," she said, resting her cheek in his calloused palm.

"Are you protected?" he demanded.

She lifted her cheek from his hand. "No." Kyle's face grew concerned. She picked up his hand, so large and spare against her own. "I don't care, Kyle. Do you understand?" She clung to his widening gaze. "I don't think I can get pregnant, anyway."

"I'm sorry, so sorry, Anna," he growled. "I know how much family means to you."

She smoothed her fingers across the tightening flesh on his cheekbone. "Listen to me," she whispered, leaning forward, kissing him softly. "You are my family now, Kyle. I was just too much in denial and fear to admit it." She eased away, tasting him on her lips. "Don't you see? You've always been a part of my life."

He drew in a ragged breath, moving his fingers gently along her tapered ones. "Yeah," he muttered, "you're right." He gazed over at her. "I drew that heart behind you for a reason, Anna." Swallowing against a forming lump, Kyle uttered, "Just looking at our shared past in the decorations, the good times, the laughter we shared, the tough times when we would hug and cry in each other's arms."

"You were always there for me."

He slanted a glance at her. "No...not like I should have been, Anna. Not even close after I turned eighteen."

"You needed to go explore the world, Kyle."

He raised her hand, kissing her opened palm, hearing her breath intake sharply, feeling her response, watching those slender, working fingers of hers close slightly in reaction to his mouth lingering against her flesh.

"I was young. I was bored here at the ranch, Anna. I knew there were adventures out there waiting for me. I wanted to chase them."

"And you have." She tilted her head, holding his disturbed gray gaze. "Are you happy now, Kyle? I knew you were before. At twenty-two, you were high on the SEALs. You believed with all your heart in what you were doing."

His mouth quirked. "Anna, my knees are staved up. I've been shot twice. I'm twenty-nine and the old man in my platoon. I can't keep up with the younger men like I used to be able to do. I've broken my wrist twice, lost count how many times I've broken a finger, strained my ankles, torn muscles…" He held up his left hand, showing her scars from surgery on his wrist.

The silence cloaked them and Kyle cradled Anna's hand between his. He could see the small calluses across her palm and some on her fingers. She had such a delicate hand and yet she was strong internally in ways he currently was not. Anna had the guts to call him on himself. She'd opened him up by simply being herself. And God, he was hurting inside for both of them. Finally, he choked out, "We've lost so much time with one another…."

She tangled her fingers among his. "It's never too late, Kyle." And then she added quietly, "And maybe that's the idealist in me again. It's been my idealism that has distorted my life in some ways…with Tom…."

"Don't ever lose who you are," he rasped, holding her gaze. "You don't know this, Anna, but when I was shot the first time—" he pointed to his left thigh "—I was bleeding out on that damned Afghan desert between two boulders. We'd hit a large force of Taliban, and they had nearly a hundred fighters to our four men. I didn't think we'd make it out of that firefight." His mouth slashed and he held her hand more tightly. "My femoral artery had been nicked. I was trying to get a tourniquet around my upper thigh to stop it from bleeding, but my hands were bloody and slippery." He dragged in a deep breath. "I could feel myself going, Anna. Everything in front of my eyes started turning gray."

His fingers closed around hers and he wrestled with violent emotions. Forcing out the words, he said, "I knew I was going to die. And the one thing I regretted the most was not marrying you. I saw your face in front of me then. And you were calling me back home, Anna." He risked a glance up at her, saw tears glimmering in her eyes. "You told me to hang on. That help was coming. That you would be there beside me." He shook his head and pointed to his collarbone area. "I had your tattered angel in my Kevlar vest. I swear to God, to this day, there was a powerful heat that seemed to radiate out of it and flow down to my wounded leg. The heat was so damned intense, I was crying in pain. And I never cry."

The words were so hard to say, so hard to force out, but Kyle knew Anna deserved the truth. "I remembered this scalding, burning heat in my leg. I was so damned weak at that point, my hands slipped off the tourniquet. Bullets were flying all around me. I thought if I didn't bleed to death, that I'd catch a bullet in the head. It was that fierce a firefight...."

Just her quiet presence was stabilizing to Kyle. He went on in a low voice. "I passed out from loss of blood. I remember waking up on a litter in a Black Hawk medevac. There was a woman working over my leg.

I remember thinking I'd died because I'd never seen a woman combat medic before." His mouth quirked. "She told me her name—Holly. Said I was lucky. That my femoral artery had closed itself off and I stopped losing blood. She said the way the artery was cut, it closed and it saved my life."

Giving Anna a look, Kyle said, "But I knew different. I knew you or that angel had somehow stopped the bleeding." His voice lowered and he kissed the back of her hand. "It sounds crazy, but you'd healed me with the love you'd always held for me, Anna."

Tears drifted down her cheeks. There was love in her eyes for him alone. How could he have been so blind? So damned stupid? The best thing in his life was sitting right next to him. "You really are my guardian angel," he admitted, giving her a slight smile. "You saved my life, Anna, in more ways than one."

She released a ragged sigh. "Thank you for telling me, Kyle." She held his gaze. "I have a secret to share with you, too. When Tom came at me, I screamed out your name." Her voice grew hushed. "I don't know why I did it, Kyle, I just did. He'd backed me into a corner, pushed me against the stove, and I stumbled backward and slammed into the wall. I remember so clearly that as he came forward, his fist cocked, I knew I was going to die."

Anna touched her brow in a nervous gesture, risking a look into Kyle's face. A bone-chilling rage smoldered in his eyes and she understood his anger was aimed at Tom, not at her. "I tried to protect myself. I screamed and begged him to stop. And he wouldn't. He came at me again and I raised my hands, screaming out your name. He struck me here…." She touched her nose. "And the last thing I remember is seeing your face…."

Kyle stared at her, dumbfounded. "My face?"

She gave a slight shrug. "I needed you so desperately in that moment…realized all along that I'd never stopped loving you…needing you…that you and I were fated lovers. And that's why I called out to you. Tom broke my nose, cheekbone and jaw." Taking a deep breath, she said, "If my father hadn't heard my screams as he walked past our house here on the ranch, I believe Tom would have finished me off. As it was, my father busted down the door, saw Tom hunkered over me and he stopped him. I have no memory of any of it, Kyle. I was bleeding and unconscious. My father, even at fifty-seven, beat the hell out of Tom. He left him lying in an unconscious pile in the middle of the kitchen, called 911 and then tended to me."

"Jesus," Kyle rasped, passing his hand over his face. "Why, Anna? Why the hell didn't you get a hold of me? I'd have come home. I'd have been there for you."

She shook her head. "I read the emails you sent your parents. You were happy doing what you were doing, Kyle. I wasn't on your radar."

"The hell you weren't." He wanted to cry, the lump in his throat so large that he kept swallowing it back down, afraid to let it rip out of him.

She studied him. "How was I to know?"

"I didn't even know you were married." He cursed and shook his head. "I know you said Tom was jealous and you couldn't risk emailing me." His brows gathered and he held her hand tightly between his. "I should have known something happened to you, Anna. Because you stopped emailing me six months after I left at twenty-two."

"I'd met Tom at that time. When I mentioned you one time, he got angry. I knew never to bring up your name again. I couldn't email you like I'd done in the past. It wasn't until years later that I realized the depth of his jealousy toward you."

"I always asked my mom about you. She never said anything about you being married."

"Because I asked her not to talk about my private life with you, Kyle. Don't you see? I couldn't go there. I had to try and move on." Anna touched her heart, and said in a low voice, "I loved you, Kyle. I *never* stopped loving you. But your job… The life you chose…"

"I'm one selfish bastard."

"No. You were a young man full of fire, passion and adventure. You had to leave and explore the world."

"Dammit!" Kyle released her hand and stood up, slowly pacing. "I wished to hell I could do this over again." He halted, looking squarely at her. "I had heaven in my hands with you, Anna, and I walked away."

"We can't go back, Kyle. All we have is right now."

He studied her, searching her sad green eyes. His chest felt alive with angry snakes writhing within. "I've made so many mistakes with you, Anna."

"Stop it. You had to go, Kyle. If you hadn't, you'd have wondered the rest of your life what you had missed. You'd have never been happy. Always wondering what you let slip through your hands."

He stood there, absorbing her wisdom, absorbing her. "I love you, Anna. I need to know if we can make this work. I don't want to walk away from you this time." A well of emotion, so many regrets, rose in him as she sat very still, her hands in her lap, so beautiful, so alone in so many ways. She'd lost her parents last year. And now her foreman. She had no one. Nothing. And what could he offer her? More heartache and pain.

She had to be weighing everything. Was her love of him strong enough to transcend their obstacles? Never had he wanted her more. But the price was steep for Anna, and Kyle wasn't sure about the future.

"I will take whatever you can give me," Anna whispered brokenly, opening her hands. "Something is better than nothing with you, Kyle. I'll take whatever you can give me… Your time… I know you're always training, always away, but those few times when you could come home…?" Her voice grew hoarse. "Spend them here, with me."

"Don't say that," he growled. Kyle walked over and drew her up and into his arms. He held her so damned tightly he felt the air whoosh out of her lungs. She sobbed. Once. Anna buried her head against his chest, clinging to him so tightly, not an inch of space existed between them.

Kyle kissed her hair, kissed her cheek and pulled back just enough to absorb her softened face, the joy in her eyes that he lived to see once again. His heart soared with the knowledge Anna would take him back into her life. Of all people, he didn't deserve this second chance. But, God, he was grateful her generous heart and soul would allow him to return to her. He inhaled the lingering touch of oranges in her hair, the fragrant skin along the curve of her neck.

"I love you, Anna…. I need you…always," Kyle said thickly, kissing her cheek, her closed lids, her brow. "I'm going to make this work between us. I promise, you aren't going to be handed seconds anymore. You're going to come first in my life, like you should have all along." His voice cracked. Kyle crushed her against him, tears squeezing from beneath his tightly shut eyes as he held the willowy woman who had a far braver heart than he'd ever had.

ANNA AWOKE SLOWLY, as if some beautiful gossamer dream that she'd had all her life had just come true. She was naked, in Kyle's arms, his soft snore near her head, his arm protectively wrapped around her, keeping her close. Drowsily, she opened her eyes, realizing daylight was creeping around the edges of the gold drapes. She didn't want to move.

Her body was sore, but she smiled softly, luxuriating in the knowledge that they'd made love at least three times last night, unable to get their fill of each other. Kyle was a tender, considerate lover. She had felt cherished. Worshipped. There wasn't an inch of her skin that he hadn't kissed and explored.

Her eyes grew cloudy as she breathed in and out with his shallow breaths, their bodies locked against one another. Even in sleep, she could feel Kyle's erection beginning to grow, pressing against her soft belly.

She understood he would be gone soon, and not sure of when he would return. And yet Kyle had repeatedly told her last night that he'd work things out. He wasn't going to leave her again. The dark hair of his chest tickled her nose and cheek. Savoring the male scent of him, she dragged it into her lungs, always wanting to remember this night with him. He'd loved her until she nearly fainted from the intense, powerful orgasms he'd given her. He knew her body so well. Equally important, Kyle had held her as if she were a priceless gift that could shatter. Never had she felt more loved than last night.

Something told her she was pregnant. It would be her secret. Anna knew enough about SEALs to never let Kyle know about it, since the news could distract him and get him killed. She just couldn't go there. At least, not yet. And she worried about carrying a baby to full term, anyway. Would it be different this time? She didn't know. And then, gently, Anna felt her heart swell with such intense love for Kyle. She knew what pregnancy felt like and had known instantly when Tom had gotten her with child.

Anna allowed all of Kyle's whispered, growling words to fill her and give her the courage for when he left. He kept repeating that he wouldn't leave her like before. But how could Kyle make that happen? SEALs lived to fight. That was what they trained for. That was what they did for a living and wanted no other way.

Kyle awoke. She sensed it and slowly moved her head to his shoulder, looking up into his sleep-ridden gray eyes. They burned with love for her, and Anna absorbed it like a greedy miser. Their days were numbered. And so were their nights. Each moment was priceless. Never to happen again. Anna desperately wanted time to slow to a crawl so she could savor each second with this man who held her heart in his scarred hands.

"I want to wake up like this every morning," he told her thickly, lifting his hand, trailing strands of hair away from her cheek, smiling down into her half-opened eyes.

Her lips curved. "Me, too." Anna sighed, leaning upward, pressing her breasts against his chest, curving her mouth against his.

His hand ranged possessively down across her hips,

capturing her hotly against him, letting her know he was hard once more and wanting her. A low sound of anticipation vibrated in her throat as he moved his hips suggestively against hers. And as Kyle urged her thigh up and across his hip, his fingers lingered teasingly at her damp entrance, making her want to thrust herself against his hand, wanting more of that pleasure she knew he could deliver.

It was effortless to love Kyle. He made it easy on her as he melded his mouth to hers. In moments, he had turned onto his back and repositioned Anna across his hips, her wet core against the hard warmth of his erection. He lay there watching her, his hands curved around her upper arms. She smiled and leaned down and into his kiss, the scalding heat going from simmer to boil deep within her body.

Anna lifted away, her eyes crinkling. "Didn't you get enough of me last night?"

Kyle remained serious as he brushed his hands down her rib cage and across her waist and then captured her hips. "You make me hungry, angel. Only you…" He moved his hips upward, connecting solidly with her, making her moan.

Anna lost herself in the haze of his erection sliding against her swollen core, her hands splayed across his chest as she slid hotly along his length. Kyle helped stimulate the hot, sparking sensations while cupping her breasts.

"I want you," he growled. "I want to hear you cry out like you did last night…."

His gritty words cascaded through her, and Anna tipped her head back. The heat flowed powerfully through her. The years had matured Kyle as a man.

He'd been a wonderful lover when she was twenty-two. But now, seven years later, he knew how to make her body sing like a finely tuned instrument.

Kyle's cell phone rang on the bed stand.

He cursed softly, giving her a look of apology.

She eased off him. "It's all right," she whispered, knowing that even on emergency medical leave, the SEALs owned him.

Kyle got out of bed, pulled his jeans on, zipped them up and grabbed his iPhone. Giving her another look of regret, he opened the bedroom door, answering the call.

Anna lay back, her body aching for him. She pulled up the covers, closing her eyes, hearing his deep voice echo down the hall. Unable to catch anything that was being said, she sighed and moved to her side, burrowing into the goose down pillow. She felt ripe, like a luscious fruit that would soon be picked by Kyle. She'd seen the silent promise in his gray eyes as he'd turned toward her in that lost moment before he disappeared out the door. He would be back. And they would finish what they'd started.

ANNA MUST HAVE dozed off because she roused when the door to the bedroom quietly opened. Kyle placed the cell phone on the bed stand and quickly divested himself of his jeans. Slipping into bed, he pulled her against the front of his body and rained soft kisses from her temple, to her cheek and to her neck that scattered pleasant shocks of heat as he nipped her.

"I'm sorry," he rasped, pulling away. "But I've got some things going on and I have to be available, Anna." Trailing his finger across her full lower lip, he drowned in her drowsy eyes.

"It's all right," she murmured as his hand caressed her breast, his thumb trailing lazily over her taut nipple, drawing a gasp from her.

He shook his head. "There's probably going to be a few more calls," he warned her, leaning over and placing a trail of light kisses across her collarbones.

Kyle felt her arch, loving that soft sound in her throat. As he trailed his kisses down across her breast, nuzzling the nipple with his unshaven jaw, she cried out his name. A savage protectiveness washed through him when she twisted and whimpered in his arms. He placed his lips over that tight, awaiting peak.

The love he'd suppressed all those years came roaring back through Kyle, blinding him with its beauty, with its strength and resilience. As he slid his hand down between her thighs, feeling her wetness and readiness for him, he didn't want this morning to end.

IT WAS SNOWING like a picture postcard on Christmas morning. Kyle had made slow, delicious love to Anna earlier and then they'd taken a hot shower together. And he'd loved her again, unable to get his fill of her, of her lush, giving body that made him ache to always have mornings just like this one.

They had dressed and he'd made her favorite morning meal: pancakes, Vermont maple syrup and sugar-cured ham. He'd noticed she would look at the Christmas tree from time to time from the table, studying it with fondness as she sipped her coffee.

"There's something different about the tree this morning," she said finally. "Did you rearrange some of the decorations, Kyle?"

He gave a shrug, pushing his emptied plate aside.

"You don't miss much, do you?" A partial grin tipped his mouth. Anna's hair was still drying, the ends slightly curling, the light above bringing out the copper and crimson highlights among the darker strands. She had worn a soft green chenille sweater almost the color of her eyes, a set of green corduroy pants and those silly old red slippers. She'd had them since he'd bought them for her when she was seventeen. He'd purchased them for Anna as a joke because she had loved her floppy-eared Easter bunny ones until she'd worn them out years earlier.

But his Christmas present joke had turned into something special because when he saw the liquid warmth in her shining eyes as she pulled out the Frosty the Snowman slippers—with the big, wobbling white head, coal-black eyes, a carrot mouth and coal for his smiling mouth—she had cried.

Kyle remembered sitting with her and their parents around the tree as everyone eagerly opened up gifts. He had reached out, his thumb catching the escaping tear and smoothing it off her flushed cheek. Anna was so in love with things that didn't mean much to Kyle. But because they meant something to her, they were important to him. And she was still wearing those slippers to this day.

"I haven't gotten you anything for Christmas, Kyle." She gave him a worried look and reached out, running her fingers up and down his hard-muscled forearm. "I'm sorry…."

He gave her a lazy-lidded look, capturing her hand. "*You* are my gift, angel." He kissed her hand, watching her eyes go smoky as he nipped the center of her palm. In Kyle's experience, a woman's body was an erotic map, but Anna brought new meaning to this idea. She was so sensitive. Exquisitely so. And easy to please. "I never need anything else, Anna. Just you. Okay?"

She pouted a bit, more than willing to allow him to tease her palm, the delicious tingles making her nipples harden beneath her bulky green sweater. "I don't feel so bad. There are no gifts under the tree from you, either." She caught a gleam in his expression. "What? Is there something there for me? I don't see anything."

"Let's go check it out," Kyle urged, pushing the chair back and relinquishing her hand. "You have to get closer to see it...."

Stymied, Anna allowed him to guide her to the tree. The windows were frosted over, the snow thick and blowing outside the home. She smiled as they passed the window where the electric candle burned. Kyle eased his hand into hers, pulling her to the left.

Anna had placed the thick holiday quilt around the tree, all bright reds, greens and golds, to celebrate the season. Kyle asked her to kneel down on it and then came behind her, his thick, long thighs bracketing her hips.

"Now," he breathed, pulling her hair aside, tasting her nape, "take a good look at the tree."

Giving a moan of pleasure, Anna dodged his wicked mouth and sensual nips that stirred her body to instant, bright life. "If you keep this up, I'm not going to be able to concentrate."

Kyle rearranged her thick hair across her shoulders. He settled his hands lightly on her hips. "All right," he murmured next to her ear, "find your gift, Anna...."

CHAPTER FIVE

ANNA EYED KYLE warily as she gazed up at the tree. "Is this a trick? You're well-known for them." His mouth curved faintly, his eyes a light gray that told her he was happy.

"Not this time. No, this is the real deal, angel. You saw something out of place earlier when you were eating breakfast. Can you find it now?"

"It's not a trick? Because I didn't get you anything and I'll feel awful about it if you've gotten me a present, Kyle."

"Anna," he rasped, kissing her cheek, "you've had a grade-three concussion. The doctor hasn't allowed you to drive anywhere to buy me anything." His voice lightened with amusement. "And I've been really busy around the ranch with Jepson and his crew. When did I have time to go into Great Falls and buy you a gift?"

She sighed and leaned back against his hard, supportive body. Resting her head on his shoulder, Anna gazed up at Kyle. He looked like a smug, satisfied cat with a big secret. Or maybe the Cheshire cat from *Alice in Wonderland*. "You know something I don't," she suddenly accused, giving him a stern look as she sat up.

"Anything's possible," Kyle agreed, his grin increasing. He gestured toward the tree. "Figure it out? You're good with puzzles, Anna."

Snorting softly, she quirked her lips as she gazed from the top of the tree downward. "I have just about every decoration memorized, Kyle. You know that." She rubbed her palms on her slacks, her gaze skipping here and there across the upper branches of the Scotch pine.

"I know you do," he said, moving his hands gently up and down her upper arms.

"Well," she began, "there's nothing out of place on the top or the middle of the tree." And then she turned, giving him a dirty look. "Oh, don't you dare tell me you stole another decoration to take back with you. That the tattered angel is too old and beat-up. You've traded it in for another one I made. That's it, isn't it?" Her brows scrunched as she stared darkly into his innocent-looking face. Kyle could wear what he called his game face. And when he did, she couldn't tell *what* he was thinking or feeling. His gray eyes grew amused.

"I *added* something to the tree, Anna. I didn't take anything else away from it. And yes, I still have the tattered angel in my billfold." He patted his back pocket.

"You added a decoration?" Surprised, she turned, giving it a quick glance and then looked back at Kyle. "Because you felt guilty about stealing my little angel and so you replaced it with another one? I never saw you draw another one and hang it. Do you know how long I hunted for it and never found it?"

"I should have told you I took that angel," Kyle admitted quietly, grazing her cheek and dropping a quick kiss on her mouth. "But that was the day I left after you told me you wouldn't marry me."

"Oh…" All the fire went out of her and she sagged against Kyle's body, feeling his arms come around her waist, holding her gently. Anna could feel the slow, heavy beat of his heart against her back. "I didn't know."

"I didn't want you to know." Kyle nudged her earlobe, teasing it, feeling her react and seeing goose bumps form nearby. "I thought about it a year later," he confessed, "but by then, I didn't have the courage to admit I'd taken it without your knowledge. I was afraid, Anna, if I told you that you'd ask for it back." He held her glistening eyes. "I couldn't risk it. I needed a part of you with me. I wasn't sure you'd understand at that time."

"Oh, Kyle," she murmured, slipping her hands over his arms, "I would have. You must know that."

"I was hurting pretty badly about our breakup," he admitted, looking at the tree. "I'd just lost my best friend in a firefight and I felt so damned alone." Kyle gazed down at her. "But I had you with me, Anna. And you'll never know how much that tattered angel of yours got me through some pretty brutal periods in my life."

"So much heartache and loss between us," she whispered unsteadily, wiping her eyes.

"That's going to end," Kyle promised her, holding her unsure gaze. "Do you see the decoration I added yet?"

Turning, she began to mentally count the rows of decorations. Finally, she came to the lowest branches at the bottom of the pine. The most recent were always hung here. Her breath caught.

"Kyle…" Anna extended her hand toward the new decoration he'd made. It was two wedding rings overlaying one another. She gently took the decoration into her palm. Frowning, she felt something behind it. "What?" she murmured, leaning forward, carefully removing the nearly hand-size decoration off the bough. And then she gave a small cry, her eyes widening with shock.

"Remember those rings?" Kyle asked her, his voice low.

"Oh, my God, Kyle." It was the set of wedding rings he had given her when she was twenty-two. Hesitantly, Anna touched them. Kyle had tied them both to a small red ribbon and hidden them behind the decoration. Her heart twisted in her chest and she pulled out of his arms, gripping the decoration in her hand, turning around to face him.

"What does this mean?" she demanded, her voice breaking. Anna held them out toward him. "Kyle?" His eyes gleamed with tenderness and she felt a wave of powerful emotions roll off him, embracing her.

He gently took the decoration from her hand and patiently untied the rings. He picked up her left hand. "Will you marry me now, Anna Campbell?"

His face blurred and Anna pressed her hand against her lips, staring at his serious face. "But…you're a SEAL, Kyle. You're going back on December 31." A sob caught in her throat.

"Only for two months," he promised her in an urgent tone. "All those phone calls I've been fielding the past week?"

Sniffing, she stammered, "Y-yes?" Kyle's face twisted with remorse for a moment.

"After you told me what happened, losing your babies…Tom nearly killing you…I realized that you're the most important person in my life. More important than the SEALs, Anna." Kyle's mouth grew tight and he struggled to contain his feelings. The ring hovered near her ring finger. He hadn't slipped it on yet because she hadn't said she'd marry him.

"My enlistment is up in two months. I'm quitting, Anna. I'm coming home to marry you if you'll have me." Kyle searched her tear-filled eyes. "I've seen the world. I've seen too much of it, Anna. I know what's really important to me now. You. You in my arms. Waking up with you every morning, smelling your sweet scent, feeling the curved warmth of your body next to mine, drowning in that smile that makes me feel so damned good inside as a man."

She stared down at his hand holding the slender, elegant gold engagement ring with a small solitaire diamond, and then up at him. "You're really quitting? You're coming home, Kyle? For good?"

Giving a grave nod, he rasped, "I'm coming home to you, Anna. I love you. Nothing's changed about that through all these years. You've always been mine, but I've been too blind and selfish to realize it until now." His mouth thinned. "I know I'm a risk to you, but I swear, I will take care of you with my last, dying breath. I want you to carry my children, Anna. And if you can't have children, then we'll adopt. I want our family here."

He looked up at the dark, rough rafters high above the tree. "I'll help you with your family's ranch. We're a good team. We'll laugh together and we'll cry together, but at least we'll have one another to hold through it all." He smiled brokenly, his eyes burning with tears. "Will you take me back, Anna? It's only two months. And then I'll be home, for good." Where Kyle wanted to be more than any other place on earth.

She gave a jerky nod of her head. "Y-yes, I'll marry you, Kyle!" Anna sobbed as he slipped the engagement ring on her finger. "And even if you didn't leave the SEALs, I would marry you, anyway." She found herself in his arms, holding him tightly, his face buried against her neck. He squeezed her so hard she could barely breathe, but she didn't care. Kissing his shoulder, his neck, Anna pulled back before placing kiss after kiss on his face, eyelids, nose, cheek and, finally and eagerly, on his mouth.

The kiss was molten and deep, filled with unspoken promises as Kyle held her in his arms. She felt ravished by his joy as he took her mouth, a man claiming his woman forever. It was a branding kiss, stealing her breath, making her entire body leap to life, an ache surging within her.

Kyle was coming home! Her mind could barely wrap around the whole idea. It was the last thing Anna had ever expected to come out of his mouth.

Kyle felt hot tears winding down his stubbled jaw. He didn't try to stop them because they had lain like a constant, open wound in his heart for so many years. He'd loved Anna forever, wanted her so badly, and he knew he'd forced her to make a decision she should never have had to make. And because of it, she'd married that bastard who had hurt her. Her nose would be a forever reminder of what he didn't do. Kyle now realized he should have come home a lot sooner. Been Anna's bulwark, been there for her. Moving his hand across her belly, he whispered, "I want you pregnant before I leave here, if that's all right with you?"

"I—I think I already am, Kyle," she whispered, looking into his widening eyes. "I feel it. The first night... I know when I get pregnant." She saw a very proud male smile spread across his face. But then, just as quickly, it dissolved and Anna saw real concern in his eyes as he studied her. "Don't ask me how I know." She framed his face, her voice strengthening with conviction. "When we make love, it's as real as it gets and we both know it."

Kyle captured her hand, placing it between her breasts, watching her for a long moment. "You didn't love Tom. You never did."

Anna closed her eyes, feeling the pain and guilt. "Whatever I felt for him was gone in less than a year." She felt his large hand span her belly, holding her, his gaze tender with understanding. "I asked the doctor about it," she said unevenly. "I asked if it was possible that because I didn't love Tom, I had caused the miscarriages." Anna pressed her hands against her eyes, the tears falling. "He laughed at me and told me I was a silly woman. I wanted those babies so much, Kyle." She broke into tears, burying her head into his chest, needing his strong arms around her, holding her close. Holding her safe from all her withheld grief.

"Listen to me," Kyle growled, smoothing the hair from her face, pulling the wet strands aside. "Anna, your body isn't something you can control. You've got to know that," he coaxed urgently.

Sniffing, she laid her hand on his chest, his shirt wet beneath her tears. "That's what the doctor said. I went to a fertility specialist, a very nice woman doctor, Dr. Foster, and she said the same thing. She said that sometimes, after one or two miscarriages, that there are minor changes that may occur in a womb, that I might be able to carry a baby to full term with some help." She looked up at him through tear-matted lashes. "I want that so badly with you.... I know how wonderful you'll be as a father. You've always loved children."

He sighed and kissed her damp cheek. "Anna, we'll take this one step at a time. I need to talk to this doctor. I'm okay if we have to adopt. We need a plan. I need to understand, okay?" He held her wavering gaze.

There was so much guilt in her eyes, so much terror because Tom had brainwashed her, made her think that she could cause such a catastrophic event. He wanted to punish that bastard in that moment but quickly shut and locked that rage away deep inside himself. Kyle would never reveal to Anna how he felt. What he did want was for her to look forward from now on. Not back. The past was done. It couldn't be fixed, changed or repaired.

Giving a nod, Anna whispered as she closed her eyes, "Yes, we can do that. I can get us an appointment with Dr. Foster before you leave."

"Good," he said, stroking her hair, trying to soothe her. "Most of all, Anna, you can't worry about me when I'm gone." God, Kyle was more worried about that than anything else. "My team is in a safe place. It's quiet. The Taliban are far east of us, near the border. We're thirty miles inland. And usually, there's only one more patrol before we leave. The last month is cleaning gear, taking care of weapons, getting the new team coming in prepped and aware of the situation around us." He became grim. "Promise me, Anna, that you will not worry like you did before. I have email. And I have Skype where we're stationed. I'll email you every single day. Okay?"

"I promise," she said.

Kyle wasn't entirely convinced.

"DO YOU FEEL better now?" Kyle asked Anna as they left Dr. Linda Foster's office in Great Falls. He pushed open the door for her, the noontime sunlight bright and strong. Snow from the recent blizzard was piled up along the roadway and partially on the slippery and icy sidewalk.

Kyle took no chances, his arm around her waist holding her close, wanting to give Anna all the protection against the ice that he could.

"I feel much better," she said, glancing up at Kyle. He wore a black Stetson, a thick Sherpa jacket and jeans. A lot of people were out and about after the blizzard had stopped the world from turning in this part of the country for the past four days. "I'm fine." She beamed. "I'm pregnant, Kyle." She placed her hand over her belly.

The joy—and protectiveness—overwhelmed him. "I'll be home for the third-month sonogram, and we'll know at that time whether it's a boy or a girl," he reminded her.

Kyle led her into a nearby parking lot that had just been plowed free of snow. Anna's cheeks were flushed, her eyes bright. Best of all, the gold dappling was back in them. Ever since he'd slipped that ring on her finger, Kyle had experienced nonstop euphoria with Anna. It was as if his decision to finally make her first in his life had breathed new vitality into her.

Even better, Dr. Foster had said the prognosis for carrying a baby to full term was excellent. She had suggested that during the first three months that Anna do light work only. Oh, she could get up, bathe, dress and putter around the house, but nothing strenuous. Kyle would hire a housekeeper to come in and take care of the massive two-story ranch house. He wanted Anna relaxed, not stressed. And Dr. Foster had said that stress could influence a woman's pregnancy hormones. She would test Anna once a month and keep her levels normal, where they needed to be, so she could comfortably carry her baby.

The last three months, Anna would have to go to bed

and remain there. Anna said it was a price worth paying to have the baby she carried…his baby…be born at term. It was a sweet promise, but Kyle knew anything could happen. There was always adoption, but he kept that to himself.

"I feel so happy," Anna whispered, climbing into the black truck. She smiled patiently as Kyle leaned over and brought the seat belt across her and locked it in place. She'd seen his face when the doctor said she was pregnant. There had been moisture in his eyes, and he'd suddenly looked away, his jaw tight as he wrestled with a lot of escaping emotions. Already, Kyle was safeguarding her. So different from the way Tom had treated her. Pushing those unhappy memories away, Anna waited until Kyle climbed into the truck and shut the door.

"Do you feel like some lunch? Maybe do a little grocery shopping afterward?" he asked, hands on the wheel, studying her. The doctor said she could certainly do such things, like walk and easy chores. He'd grilled the doctor ruthlessly on what she meant as "light" work. He wrote everything down because he was a SEAL and SEALs memorized everything placed in front of them. It could mean the difference between living and dying.

Kyle had a hunch, a strong one, that Dr. Foster's plan would make the difference for Anna. God, he didn't want to be gone, but there was no way around it. His team needed him. He was the LPO, lead petty officer, and the men entrusted their lives to him. This one last time Kyle would be there for his band of brothers. After that, he would fill his life with his pregnant wife. Instead of taking care of his team, he would take care of his growing family. And give Anna the happiness she so richly deserved.

"Lunch sounds nice," she murmured, reaching out with her gloved hand and squeezing his hand resting on the wheel. "Let's go to Bell's. She has the best food in town."

Nodding, Kyle backed the truck out of the parking space. "Sounds like a plan, angel."

Anna smiled softly, content, and for once, not tense or worried about the baby she carried. Between Dr. Foster's maternal care, her convincing Anna that there were things she could do to minimize risk of miscarriage, plus Kyle's mother henning, Anna felt hopeful. Not terrified. Not like before.

As Kyle drove slowly through the wet, gleaming asphalt streets of the small city, Anna looked at the engagement ring on her finger. "When do you want to get married?"

"Yesterday?" He grinned over at her.

"Seriously, Kyle?"

"Nah, just kidding. Any date is fine with me." Kyle knew Anna wanted a proper wedding, inviting all her friends she'd grown up with from surrounding ranch families. He hoped that wedding planning would lift her spirits even more, if that was possible. He'd talked alone with Dr. Foster and she'd counseled that planning a wedding would be a good distraction because she was a worrywart about his safety. Furthermore, the doctor told him, to stay in touch with her as often as possible via email. Dr. Foster felt that if Anna could be given some kind of fixed, routine assurance, an email a day, that would relieve her of a lot of her anxiety. Removing stress from Anna was their mutual objective.

Kyle would never tell Anna his plan, but he was going to Chief Crawford, who ran the platoon, with a strategy to keep her calm. He would make up emails ahead of time, and because one of the three officers in the team was always there at the FOB, someone would send Anna that email on that given day. Kyle knew the officers well. They were all married and either had kids or had a child on the way. They would have his back on this tactic, understanding Anna's delicate condition. He had a handle on the situation, but this would remain one of those secrets that would hurt no one and instead was beneficial.

Kyle pulled into Bell's Diner, a local favorite. It was an aluminum dining car from a train converted into the busiest lunch place in Great Falls. They lucked out on a corner booth even though the place was filling up quickly. After giving their orders, Kyle gazed over at Anna. She sat close to him and he enjoyed her nearness. "So? A wedding date?" he teased.

"You'll be home on March 2."

"Right."

Wrinkling her nose, she said, "We get snow through May, Kyle. I wanted our wedding to be beautiful. Outdoors…" She chewed on her lip.

"Sounds fine with me. What's got you worried?"

Anna grimaced and moved her hand across her belly. "I'll be six months pregnant. I'll look like a balloon."

Patiently, Kyle picked up her hand. "Pregnant women get married right up until the moment they're going to give birth. There's no stigma these days." He squeezed her hand a little more. "We're getting married because we love one another. And no one on our guest list will think any differently about you. They'll be happy for the three of us." He burrowed into her green gaze. "Just think of it this way—that our son or daughter gets to take part in our wedding. That's an awesome memory to start your life off with." He smiled.

"You're right," she muttered, unhappy with herself.

"And Dr. Foster thought getting married would be a positive thing for you and our baby."

"Yes, she did." Blowing a puff of air between her lips, Anna shook her head. "God, I wish I'd stop worrying. It's my worst trait, Kyle. I swear it is."

"Well," he murmured, soothing her, "I feel you've got a lot of happy days stretching out ahead of you. I'll be home before you know it. You have the wedding to plan for. Your girlfriends from around here are going to keep you plenty busy with details and decisions that have to be made. And I'll take over the position as foreman for the ranch once I'm home. That's another huge concern lifted off your shoulders."

Her eyes lightened with relief. He felt the jagged edge of guilt. Anna had courageously forged ahead, trying to hold the ranch together alone. When her parents died a year ago, it had gutted Anna. How could it not? She was still recovering from their loss, coming out of that long tunnel of grief. It would take Anna a long time to work through missing them. Just as it had him when his father had died.

"It's doable," Anna said, her voice firm.

"Very," Kyle agreed. The waitress brought their orders over and he covertly watched Anna rally. She might worry a lot, but when things were in place, she released the anxiety.

He reached out, slipping her hand into his, holding her widening gaze. "I have your back, Anna. From now on, I'll be there for you...for our children." He swallowed against a forming lump, his voice dropping to a rasp. "I love you, my Christmas angel. Now and forever..."

EPILOGUE

SOPHIA MARIE CAMPBELL-ANDERSON came into the world on the fall equinox, September 21. She was born at home, at the White Sulphur Springs Ranch, where all children of the Campbell family lineage had been born. Dr. Foster, accompanied by two midwives, guided the baby's father, Kyle, to welcome Sophia as she slipped into his large, awaiting hands. She had her mother's ginger hair and her father's gray eyes.

As Kyle marveled at the red, wrinkled little being squirming and vocal in his hands, he thought back to his wife's baby pictures. Damned if Sophia wasn't nearly identical to her mother's photo at that same age. She was going to grow up strong, confident and beautiful, just like her weary mother, who gave him a trembling smile of relief and love. Sophia was born weighing eight pounds five ounces, and Dr. Foster checked her out with quick professionalism and declared her healthy and normal.

The midwives took care and fussed over exhausted Anna. Twenty hours of labor had made her weary but happy. Tears slid down her cheeks as Dr. Foster placed Sophia, all wrapped in her new pink knitted blanket, into Kyle's awaiting arms.

Her heart burst open with such love for the two of them as Kyle awkwardly held his now-quiet daughter with such carefulness. They had taken parenting and hospital courses on learning to work with a newborn. But to see Kyle's face, the tenderness and love burning in his eyes for his daughter, made Anna melt with joy. There was no question that Kyle would be an involved father. She would be a good mother. Anna knew neither of them would be perfect parents, but they would try their best because, after all, love underwrote their marriage. Love could heal any wound, small or large. Anna knew that from the way Kyle's love continued to heal her.

When her husband turned, the proudest smile she'd ever seen on his face as he held his daughter, Anna felt all the unhappy years slip away. At twenty-nine years old, Kyle Anderson held her heart, had helped salve her soul, and was there every step of the way so that Sophia could become a full-term baby. He had been her coach, her lover, her best friend and confidant. She had to spend the last three months in bed, but it had been worth it.

Anna closed her eyes, glad to have a sponge bath and a clean, white cotton gown to replace the sweaty, badly wrinkled one. She heard Kyle approach their bed, felt him place weight upon the mattress. Opening her eyes, she held out her hands to receive Sophia. The baby gurgled and waved her tiny arms as Kyle gently eased Anna up into a semisitting position, tucking pillows between her back and the wooden headboard. He moved slowly, like a cougar, turning and sitting near her hip, helping her to adjust Sophie close to her breast. Kyle moved closer, sliding his arm beneath hers.

"You're tired," he murmured, watching as Sophia's tiny mouth latched on to her mother's nipple and she noisily began to suckle. Her arm waving intensified and Kyle grinned, looking deep into Anna's dark green eyes.

"But happy. Relieved," she said, smiling sweetly down at her daughter, brushing the thick hair across her tiny head. "How are you doing?"

Kyle shrugged, his gaze never leaving his daughter. "Happy but relieved."

Reaching out, she touched his cheek. "I love you, Kyle Anderson. You've made me the happiest person in the world…."

He caught her hand, kissing it. "We'll have another decoration to add to this coming year's Christmas tree."

Rallying, Anna laughed softly. "Oh, yes."

"I'm going to let you draw it," Kyle said. "You'll do Sophie justice. You're the artist in our family."

"I'm making two this year. One for Sophie. The other—" her voice became emotional "—is you returning home with your seabag over your shoulder. You came home wearing your Stetson, your jeans and cowboy boots." Tears streamed down her face. "I never thought it would happen, Kyle."

He leaned over, kissing his wife's wet, salty lips with all the tenderness he held for her. "Because that tattered angel of yours brought me home, Anna."

* * * * *

To my military hero and husband,
Colonel Thomas Fossen

UNEXPECTED GIFT

Delores Fossen

Dear Reader,

I was an Air Force officer for nearly nine years, and some of my best memories are of my own military homecomings. For the first one, it'd been nearly two years since I'd seen my family, and I finally got leave for Christmas and was able to fly from England back to the States. There were so many people to see, hugs to give, meals to eat and stories to share. So much love.

Those wonderful memories were the reasons I was eager to write Captain Gabe Brenner's homecoming in "Unexpected Gift." Of course, Gabe's homecoming had a lot more surprises than mine. Well, one surprise, anyway, when he reunites with his best friend's sister, Kelly Coburn, and he learns that he's a father to her precious baby girl, Noel. Gabe and Kelly have to rethink everything—their feelings for each other, their lives and, most important, their future. Not easy. The globe-trotting Gabe is married to the uniform and has been on the move for over a decade, while Kelly's roots are Texas-deep. Something's got to give for Noel to have the Christmas, home and family she deserves.

Most of my stories include families going through the unexpected, and no matter how high the stakes, they always find their paths to love. Not easily. But they do find it. My latest book, *Rustling Up Trouble*, is just that kind of story, and it's part of the Sweetwater Ranch series. You can find out more about the series and all my books on my website, www.dfossen.net.

I hope you enjoy reading about Gabe's homecoming in "Unexpected Gift." I also hope you have a wonderful holiday season, filled with lots of family, hugs and, most of all, love.

Best wishes,

Delores Fossen

CHAPTER ONE

CAPTAIN GABE BRENNER figured this particular Santa assignment had the potential to turn out *bad*.

And that TV film crew sure wouldn't help things.

There were three of them in the crew. A woman with a microphone, a guy with a camera hoisted on his shoulder and the mayor, Bobby Hernandez. They were hunkered down next to some Texas sage bushes, and the woman and mayor gave Gabe rather enthusiastic waves when he brought his rental car to a stop in the parking lot.

Judging from the glittered red, white and blue sign that the mayor was holding up—Welcome Home, Captain Gabe Brenner—the trio was there for him. How the devil they'd heard about his homecoming, Gabe didn't know, but they'd obviously had time to slap together a sign, and they were waiting right next to the building where he needed to go for his "Santa" duties.

The Sugar Springs Public Library.

Gabe tucked the small Christmas present in his pocket and opened the car door, winter slamming right into him. There was more likely to be sleet than snow in this part of Texas, but it was cold enough for something icy to start falling soon. That was an even better reason for him to finish up here and make the hour-long drive back to San Antonio for a little R & R.

"Welcome home!" the reporter gushed, poking a microphone at Gabe's face before he could even take a step.

She was a thin brunette probably not old enough to drink. Her shoulders were hunched and her nose red, no doubt from the frosty wind snapping at her. He didn't know her, but Gabe knew the cameraman. Delbert Grange, once the high school football tackle who'd made an art form out of being a jerk. Delbert didn't look any happier about this assignment than Gabe did.

"Are you glad to be home?" the reporter asked, still gushing.

Since that microphone and camera were gobbling up every look and sound he made, Gabe managed a nod, a smile and a mumbled "yeah." He was plenty glad to be finished with his latest deployment. And he'd celebrate.

Right after delivering the Merry Christmas greeting, message and present that his crew partner had asked Gabe to deliver.

To Kelly.

Oh, man.

Kelly.

Forty-five hours of travel to get to his old hometown of Sugar Springs, Texas. Forty-five hours to think about what Kelly might say to him. Of course, she was just as likely to say nothing. Gabe figured the air wouldn't be the only thing that was chilly for this meeting.

"We know you're a CRO. That's an Air Force Combat Rescue Officer," the reporter said, reading from an index card. "But can you tell our viewers what that is, what you do?"

Delbert snorted, clearly not thinking much of what Gabe did.

"I get to rescue people," Gabe answered, hoping she wouldn't ask for details that he couldn't give her. Unlike this situation, his missions were classified and weren't usually caught on camera.

"And did you rescue anybody on this deployment?" the reporter pressed.

"Naw, he just flew right over them," Delbert grumbled. "Guess that's what those wings are for."

Gabe did indeed have angel wings on his CRO badge, and he was proud of them. But he got out of the car wishing he'd ditched his uniform at the airport. It would have meant digging around in his things to pull out something wrinkled and likely embedded with sand and with the smell of the desert. However, if he'd known he was going to draw the attention of a moron cameraman and a reporter out for a story of a military homecoming, then he'd be wearing civvies right now.

Or better yet, postponing this trip.

"We haven't told anyone inside about your visit," the reporter said, leaning closer and lowering her voice to a secret-telling whisper. "Kelly Coburn and the rest of library staff and patrons don't know you're coming."

"Then, how'd you find out?" Gabe tried to step around them, but the reporter just darted in front of him. She moved pretty fast for a woman teetering on four-inch heels on an ice-scabbed sidewalk.

"Kelly's brother, of course," the mayor provided. "He sent us an email. You and Captain Ross Coburn are the town heroes, and we couldn't let you sneak in without some kind of celebration."

Gabe didn't bother to mention that he'd left Sugar Springs fourteen years ago when he turned eighteen and rarely came back. But he would do some *mentioning* about it to Ross when he got him on the phone.

Hell's Texas bells.

He was doing Ross a favor by coming here, and this was how Ross repaid him?

Of course, Ross didn't have a clue that this would be the potentially bad assignment that it could turn out to be.

"This won't take long," Gabe told the reporter. "I just need to give Kelly this present from her brother and have a quick word with her."

Hopefully, a word that wouldn't involve her telling him to take a hike. A year ago she'd called him a mistake.

Well, that's what Kelly had called their one-night stand anyway.

No arguments from Gabe.

It had been exactly that—a whopping, Texas-size mistake. Brought on by four straight shots.

All right, five.

He'd been nursing the end of yet another relationship that wouldn't have lasted anyway. And Kelly had been nursing worry and fear that her brother, Ross, was off to yet another dangerous assignment in the Middle East. His fourth in ten years. Air Force CRO was pretty much a synonym for dangerous assignments, but this one had gotten to her. Bad dreams, Kelly had said. About Ross, and Gabe, not returning.

An attractive, upset woman needing a shoulder to lean on and a full bottle of Jack Daniel's were rarely a good combination.

Still, Kelly and he had set things right by agreeing it'd been wrong. They had also agreed not to tell Ross.

Gabe had jumped right on that particular "let's carry this to the grave" bandwagon since he didn't want to spend a year deployed with a man who might want to beat him to dust for sleeping with Kelly, Ross's kid sister.

A kid sister who Gabe now had to face.

"Trust me, there really won't be anything to film for this homecoming," Gabe tried again with the TV crew. "I just need to tell Kelly merry Christmas since Ross can't come home yet to do it himself."

"There'll be plenty to film," the mayor argued. "The whole state will want to see this. And Ross wants it all caught on camera so he can see the surprise on his sister's face when you walk into the library."

That didn't help the knot in Gabe's stomach.

"All right," the reporter said, her shoes tapping like a hungry woodpecker on the sidewalk as she followed him. "Everybody stay quiet so she doesn't hear us. We want to catch the happy look on Kelly's face for tonight's news."

Despite the still-gobbling camera, Gabe didn't manage to stave off a scowl that time, and he threw open the door to the library. Like just about everything else in Sugar Springs, it hadn't changed at all. A checkout desk was to his immediate right, and sprawled out in front of him were rows of scarred wooden bookcases. The place smelled like old paper, Elmer's glue and the scraggly cedar Christmas tree just to his left.

The woman behind the checkout desk was yet something else familiar. Doris Jenkins. She was eighty if she was a day, but there was nothing wrong with her eyesight. She brightened right up when she saw Gabe and the crew, and grinning, she pointed toward the back of the room.

"Kelly's back there," Doris mouthed.

Dragging in a long breath that he figured he'd need, Gabe headed in that direction to the kids' section. Even if he hadn't known the way, he could have just followed the sound of her voice.

Kelly's voice.

When he cleared the last row of bookshelves, he spotted her.

And that required yet another deep breath.

Unlike the last time he'd seen her, she wasn't dressed in the "walk of shame" wrinkled clothes that he'd been responsible for wrinkling. Today, Kelly was wearing a velvet Mrs. Santa Claus costume with white furry trim and granny shoes. She had a red ruffled bonnet plopped on bunned-up, honey-colored hair. Something that would have looked ridiculous on anyone else but her.

She looked amazing.

Happy.

She was reading *The Polar Express* to a group of kids seated on the floor around her. There were five of them, their parents and grandparents lingering back, watching. All attention focused on the kids' reactions and Kelly, the assistant librarian.

Gabe got a flash of her, naked.

Oh, man. Definitely not something he should be remembering. He wasn't here to repeat another *mistake*.

Neither Gabe nor the TV crew said a word, but their movement snagged the attention of some of the other adults. Then the kids. It went through the group like a wave, and they turned toward him. The whispers, giggles and other excitement started almost immediately, but Gabe kept his focus on Kelly.

As she lifted her gaze to meet his.

Because he was watching her so closely, he saw the recognition flash through her pale green eyes. Quickly followed by her mouth dropping open. She stood, *The Polar Express* splatting to the floor.

"Gabe," she managed to say on a rise of breath. "You're here."

"Kelly," he managed to say right back.

And he braced himself for whatever would happen next. If she ordered him out, he'd hand her the present, tell her what Ross wanted him to say and then head back to his rental car. Fast.

But nothing happened.

Kelly just stood there, looking several steps past the stunned stage while she kept repeating *Gabe,* long pause, deep breath, *you're here.*

"Gabe's really home," Mayor Hernandez announced as if Kelly needed clarification. Or to snap her out of this gobsmacked, mumbling trance she was in.

Delbert volleyed the camera between the two of them. The reporter did the same with the microphone.

All clearly waiting for something joyous to happen.

Gabe wasn't counting on that joyous part, but he would put a quick end to this very uncomfortable moment.

"I brought you a gift from Ross," Gabe said. He walked toward her, stepping around the kids and taking the present from his pocket. "He got tied up with briefings in Germany and can't make it home this week, but he wanted me to wish you a merry Christmas. He'll be home by New Year's Eve."

"Gabe," Kelly repeated.

When she didn't reach for the gift, Gabe took her hand and plopped the small present in her palm. That's when he realized she was trembling. And that she'd gone way too pale.

"I know," Gabe whispered, hoping to keep this particular message out of range of the microphone. "I'm sorry. I know you didn't want me to come."

"Of course she wanted you to come." The mayor again. Obviously, Gabe hadn't been out of range after all. "Kelly's your best friend's little sister. There's no reason on earth she wouldn't want you here."

Gabe knew otherwise.

But then, others in the room maybe did, too.

He felt the change in the air. Subtle but still there. The welcome-home and excited looks turned, well, weird. Some of the adults leaned into each other, whispering. There was even a random gasp.

Good grief.

Had folks gotten wind of Kelly's one-nighter after all? Or had something in their body language just given it away?

At least word of their indiscretion hadn't gotten back to Ross, because if it had, Ross would have *addressed* the subject with Gabe during the past year. No way would Ross have approved of his kid sister falling into bed with a no-rings-attached kind of guy like Gabe.

Heck, Gabe felt the same way.

"We have to talk," Kelly whispered. "In private."

Gabe shot a stay-back glance at the TV crew, reminding himself that this was how he'd wanted his homecoming to play out from the beginning. In private. Where Kelly could toss him out without having the details paraded on the evening news.

"We'll be right back," Kelly said to no one in particular.

She took hold of Gabe's arm, maneuvering him out of the semicircle of kids and toward the back hall, where there were three small storerooms and offices, one of them Kelly's.

"How about a welcome-home hug and kiss first?" the reporter called out to them. "That way, folks all over Texas can see how glad you are for Captain Brenner to be home."

That earned the reporter a jab in the ribs from the mayor. Kelly lost even more color in her cheeks. The behind-the-hand whispers rippled through the room again.

Yeah, nearly everybody but the reporter knew about the one-nighter, all right.

And once Ross saw this footage, he'd figure it out no time flat.

Gabe was a dead man. Or at least a hurting one, and he'd stand a serious chance of losing Ross's friendship forever.

Kelly kept up the trek toward her office despite the reporter still calling for that hug and kiss. Which definitely wasn't going to happen. But then, getting inside Kelly's office didn't happen, either. While they were still a few steps away, another familiar face popped out of the room just up the hall.

The perky blonde was Janine Slater, Kelly's best friend, and that perkiness faded considerably when her gaze landed on Gabe.

"Gabe," Janine said, "you're here."

He nearly laughed. "Yeah, I'm hearing that a lot just lately."

Kelly mumbled something he didn't catch and proceeded toward her office. This time, she might have actually gotten him in there if the sound hadn't snagged his attention.

A baby.

Specifically, one making fussing noises.

That froze Janine, and her eyes doubled in size. "Uh, she needs to be changed and the diaper bag's in your office. I was just about to get it."

"You had a baby?" Gabe automatically asked Janine.

"Uh," Janine said. Not much of an answer to a pretty direct question.

Gabe also didn't miss the renewed frozen look that Kelly was giving him.

"How about that hug and kiss so we can wrap this up?" the reporter called out again.

Worse, both the cameraman and reporter trotted toward where Kelly, Janine and Gabe were standing as if waiting for some proverbial shoe to drop.

The baby let out another wail. This time, not a fuss but a full-fledged cry. Kelly's grip melted off his arm, and she hurried toward the room with Janine.

Gabe made his way there, too. And that knot in his stomach? Well, it got even tighter.

Why would Kelly be rushing off to take care of Janine's baby? Or any baby for that matter?

Unless…

Oh, hell in a handbasket.

Yeah, that shoe dropped loud and hard.

CHAPTER TWO

EVEN THOUGH SHE clearly had some explaining to do, Kelly hurried to the bassinet and scooped up the baby into her arms. Almost immediately Noel stopped crying and even gave Kelly a coo and a smile.

Unlike Gabe.

Definitely no coos or smiles from him.

He was standing in the doorway, looking at her as if the world had just tipped on its axis. And worse, that idiot Delbert had his wide-angle camera lens right in Gabe's face, recording every second of this fiasco. A fiasco that Kelly could have diffused, some, if she'd just had a private conversation with Gabe before the hoopla of his homecoming.

"Kelly?" Gabe said with his attention swinging back and forth between Noel and her.

Noel smiled and cooed at him, too, and despite the feeling that her heart might beat right out of her chest, Kelly brushed a kiss on Noel's cheek. Even now, she wasn't immune to that smile. Never would be.

That immunity didn't extend to Gabe's shock, though. It wouldn't last. Soon, very soon, that shock would turn to anger and a whole bunch of questions.

Well, one question specifically.

Was Noel his baby?

"I need to talk to Gabe alone," Kelly told Delbert,

the mayor and the reporter, Cissy Dorman. Along with Delbert, Cissy worked for the local station over in Fredericksburg, and to the best of Kelly's knowledge, this was the first time they'd ventured to Sugar Springs for a story.

Too bad they had chosen today of all days.

"That's my baby," Gabe blurted out.

So, it hadn't come as a question after all, and like her earlier repeating bout of his being there, Gabe did the same with *that's my baby.* Except in between the repeats, he groaned, put a hand to each side of his head, and with his back against the wall, slid all the way to the floor.

Kelly didn't confirm that Noel was indeed his. Probably didn't have to since her precious baby seemingly hadn't inherited any of her DNA and all of Gabe's. The chocolate-brown hair and warm blue eyes.

That was even his smile on Noel's round baby face.

And though Kelly hadn't actually told anyone in town other than Janine that Gabe was the father, everyone was obviously aware of it now. Especially when the two were in the same room to do a face-to-face comparison.

"Gabe, you're looking a little sickly there, boy," Delbert mumbled. "You need somebody to rescue you? 'Cause you don't want to be throwing up on those pretty wings, now, do you?"

Kelly figured it wouldn't be a good idea to curse Delbert. Not with the baby in her arms and with the children looking on while she was wearing a Mrs. Santa suit. Hardly a fitting image for the assistant librarian. Still, she glared at him.

"We need some privacy, please," Kelly insisted, remembering at the last second to add the *please*. "Just give us a few minutes to settle some things."

Okay, maybe it was wishful thinking that she could resolve a life-altering situation in a matter of minutes, but she might at least be able to get some things under control.

Which could also be wishful thinking.

It was going to take much more than talk or maybe even time to get that stunned look off Gabe's face. Heck, maybe he did need to be rescued.

She didn't wait for the TV crew or mayor to comply with her request. Kelly used the door to push them back, especially Delbert, and then closed it in their privacy-invading faces.

"That's my baby," Gabe repeated.

Another groan followed. He did more head squeezing, too. He'd no doubt faced down plenty of combat situations that hadn't knocked him off his feet like this. Kelly had had a similar reaction when she'd seen that little pink plus sign on the pregnancy-test stick, but thankfully the shock hadn't lasted long.

Maybe it'd be the same for Gabe.

More wishful thinking?

Definitely.

"She's yours," Kelly confirmed. *"Ours." Mine,* she silently added. "Her name's Noel Hope, and she was born—"

"Three months ago," he interrupted, getting to his feet. "Nine months after we had that one-nighter that we were supposed to forget."

Yes, as if they could ever forget.

Even if she hadn't gotten pregnant, Kelly would have

remembered it in perfect detail. After all, she'd lusted after Gabe for years.

Still did, apparently.

Why did he have to look so hot in that uniform?

She couldn't dismiss the ribbon of heat that slid right through her again. Head to toe. But then and now, Gabe was forbidden fruit, since it would have caused a rift the size of the Rio Grande between Ross and him. It'd also caused a rift between Gabe and her, too, when they'd stumbled into bed a year ago.

The news about Noel wouldn't do much to mend that rift.

"Why—" he paused, his mouth tightening, no doubt choosing his words, ones that didn't involve too much profanity or shouting "—didn't. You. Tell. Me?"

At least this was an easy answer, though it had taken him a while to get the question out. "Because you were deployed on a dangerous assignment. I didn't want you to learn about it that way."

"And this was a better way?" Gabe flung his hand toward the hall, where the TV crew was waiting.

"No. Not this. I'd planned on telling you in private after you finished your deployment. Ross figured that'd be a day or two after Christmas. I hadn't counted on you coming here, not after what happened between us, so I was planning to tell you while you were on leave in San Antonio."

But not today.

Not like this.

This time, Jack Daniel's wouldn't have been involved, either.

"How did you even know I'd be here?" she asked.

"I did an internet search and saw that you'd be doing

the children's program at the library. Thought it would save us both time if I just came here. I had no idea I'd be walking into *this*."

Since Gabe was obviously hurtling right toward that anger stage, Kelly went on the offensive. "I figured you'd want to know," she said. "But I also figured this wouldn't be welcome news. I mean, fatherhood's never been in your career plan."

Considering she'd had nearly a year to work out how to say that, she did an awful job of it. Even though it had to be true. Still, judging from the way Gabe's nostrils flared, he wasn't happy with her pointing that out to him in such a blunt way.

"She's my baby," Gabe said, though she wasn't sure how he could speak with his teeth clenched like that. "You should have told me when you found out you were pregnant."

However, the teeth clenching extended only to her.

When Gabe's attention drifted from her to Noel, the muscles in his face relaxed. After several long moments anyway. He reached out his hand, his fingers aimed at those baby curls on Noel's head, but it was Noel who stopped him. She caught his index finger and offered another of those gummy baby smiles that could have melted every glacier on the planet.

It had a similar effect on Gabe.

"A baby," he repeated. "*My* baby."

The *my* riled her a bit. Gabe hadn't been there for any part of this except the conception. That hadn't been his fault, of course. In fact, it'd been the way Kelly had decided it would be. Still, it felt as if he was storming in, ready to claim Noel.

Since it appeared that the initial shock was quickly

wearing off, Kelly got on with what she had to say. "I know family's never been important to you and that the Air Force is what you love and want. I'd never stand in the way of that."

Noel kept her grip on his finger, and Gabe kept his attention on Noel. Except for a split-second glare that he shot Kelly.

"You should have told me," Gabe repeated.

"And risk you being killed?" She didn't wait for him to answer that. "If you remember correctly, the reason we slept together in the first place was because I was worried about Ross and you."

That, and the old attraction. An attraction that'd started around the time she was fourteen and had noticed the fit of his jeans. That attraction had steadily simmered and churned like a potent witches' brew. Of course, Gabe hadn't given her a second glance since he'd already turned eighteen by then and was busy making plans to leave for college to study engineering, football and girls.

Lots and lots of girls.

Her not included.

Well, except for what happened at the prom. But that was a memory best stored away with the others.

Like the way Gabe had looked in her bed that night.

Yes, that memory had to go, too.

"I wasn't deployed in a dangerous environment the whole year," Gabe reminded her. "Ross and I spent four months in Kandahar, then we rotated the next four months in Germany before returning to the Middle East to finish out the deployment. You could have at least told me while I was in Germany."

"I knew you were going right back out to CRO duty,"

she argued. "I was eight months pregnant when you went from Germany back to the Middle East. Would you really have wanted that on your mind while you were trying to rescue people?"

"Yes!" he snarled, then grumbled something that she didn't catch. "I needed to know," he added.

Right. But it was her judgment call, and she hadn't wanted to be the reason Gabe lost focus and got hurt. Or worse. Ditto for her brother since Gabe and he worked side by side.

"I did what I thought was best," Kelly settled for saying, and she tried to brace herself for another snarl, snap or scowl.

That didn't happen. Gabe quit volleying those glances and focused solely on Noel.

"She's so beautiful," he said. There was a different kind of emotion in his voice this time.

"She is. Of course, I might be biased." Noel was the most beautiful child who'd ever been born, and Kelly couldn't have possibly loved her any more than she did. That love had started within minutes after learning she was pregnant, and it just kept growing.

"You went through the pregnancy alone," he mumbled.

Kelly nodded and refused to think of how hard that'd been. "Janine helped me. Still does. She watches Noel on her days off from the bank, and Mrs. Saunders watches her other times. They even bring her here to work. We've converted this storeroom to a makeshift nursery."

Gabe's eyebrow lifted. "Old Lady Saunders, the woman who lives next door to you, watches her?"

Another nod. "She's really good with Noel."

Not ideal, though. Ideal would have been a day care nearby the library so that Noel could be with other babies, but Sugar Springs wasn't exactly thriving when it came to services like that for kids and families.

Noel let go of his finger, only to grab it again. It was a game she liked to play with her toes, and she laughed.

"Oh, man." Gabe practically staggered back. "She's laughing. And smiling. Is she all right? I mean, is she healthy?"

"Very. She just had a checkup in Fredericksburg, and the doctor said she's exactly at the weight and height she should be for a three-month-old."

That kept him quiet a moment. Kelly could practically see him mulling that over, and then his gaze fired around the room as if trying to figure out what to do, how to approach this.

That was Gabe.

Always looking at battle strategy. You never wanted to go up against him whether it was flag football or Monopoly. Or even foreplay. He'd approached even that with the same attitude as everything else.

"I'll cancel my trip to San Antonio," he said.

Kelly had already anticipated that. "No need. Go ahead, take some time to think this over, and we'll discuss things afterward."

"We'll discuss things *now*," he insisted. "Well, not here at the library."

Now it was her turn to mull things over. "Does that mean there'll be yelling involved?"

"Possibly. Probably," he amended just as quickly. His eyes were narrowed when they came back to her. "You should have told me."

"Then, we'll agree to disagree. Still, there's no reason for you to cancel your holiday plans. Ross said you were spending time with…friends in San Antonio."

Friends that no doubt included some of those busty, flavor-of-the-month blondes that Gabe preferred.

Friends that Kelly decided it was best not to think about.

Her reminder didn't soothe his narrowed eyes. But Noel worked a small miracle with that. When she cooed at him, Gabe gave her hand a gentle jiggle.

And he also gave her a smile.

"I'm canceling the San Antonio trip," Gabe repeated. "I'll stay here so we can have that talk."

Oh, she didn't like the sound of that. Best to just toss this out there and let the possible yelling begin.

"For the record, I don't expect you to give up your hard-earned downtime," she clarified. "In fact, I have fairly low expectations when it comes to this. Yes, you fathered Noel, but I don't expect you to be her father."

He gave her another look. One that could have withered a healthy redwood forest.

"I am her father." Gabe jabbed his left thumb against his chest. "And nothing we can talk about will change that. She's mine, and I'll be part of her life. I'm here and I'm staying put until we work this out."

"Work what out?" Kelly tossed back. "You've always known that my roots are here. I'm not leaving Sugar Springs to follow you around the world. And I seriously doubt that you want to give up being a CRO and move back here."

Silence. But those jaw muscles of his stirred and tightened as if at war with each other.

There was a soft knock at the door, barely a tap. "Kel, are you all right in there?" Janine asked.

"Fine," Kelly answered at the same moment that Gabe said, "No."

"Uh. Okay. You want me to take Noel while you two talk?" her friend pressed.

"No," Kelly and Gabe answered in unison.

At least they could agree on something.

"We'll be out soon," Kelly told Janine, though that was possibly a whopper of a lie. However, she didn't want Janine worried more than she already was.

Gabe groaned again, scrubbed his hand over his face. "Janine knows that I'm Noel's father. She knows about our night together. And she couldn't talk you into telling me you were pregnant?"

"She tried." A lot. Especially after Kelly had spilled a few of the details of her and Gabe's hot night.

Details that trickled back into her mind again. Why couldn't she just stop remembering just how good he looked out of that uniform?

Just how good he looked now?

How good he always looked?

Something flashed through Gabe's eyes, something that made Kelly's mind snap back to where it belonged. And where it belonged was on this conversation and not on memories of sex with Gabe.

"Ross…" he said.

"Doesn't know, either," Kelly quickly assured him. "The only person in town who knows is Janine. Everyone else thinks Noel's father is the guy I dated in college. And the town agreed to keep my pregnancy a secret so I could tell Ross in person when he got home."

Gabe nodded, no doubt agreeing that if Ross had known, he would have almost certainly had a major blowup with Gabe. It would have made that assignment a lot more dangerous than it already was.

"I'll tell him when he gets home next week," Kelly offered. "But if you prefer, I can leave you out of this. I can tell him what I told the town, that Noel's father is an old college boyfriend."

"That's not gonna happen." Gabe's voice took on a low, sharp edge. "She's my baby, and we'll tell Ross together. Besides, anyone who saw us just now knows that I'm Noel's father."

It happened in a flash. The thought went flying through her head, and she could see that it flew through Gabe's, as well.

Oh, God.

"The camera," he said.

He bolted across the room and threw open the door. Janine was there, her hand poised as if ready to knock again, but there was no one near her.

That got Kelly's heart thudding again, and she went past Gabe and back into the children's section. No children. The parents and grandparents were gone, too. They'd all no doubt cleared out so they could feed the gossip mill a juicy pre-Christmas tidbit of Ross Coburn's kid sister and the high-flying bad boy, Gabe Brenner.

"Where'd Delbert and that reporter go?" Gabe asked Janine. But he didn't just ask it. He ordered her to answer.

"They left a couple of minutes ago. The mayor, too."

Gabe cursed, glanced back at Noel and no doubt bit off the remaining profanity that he'd planned to dole out. He also started running toward the front of the building, his combat boots slamming against the old floor. Kelly followed him, but there was no way she could keep up with Gabe under normal circumstances, much less while she was wearing the velvet dress and clunky shoes.

"Here, let me take the baby," Janine offered, and this time, Kelly handed Noel off to her so she could try to catch up with Gabe and the TV crew.

Maybe it was the burst of energy she used for the run or else the raw fear at the thought of her brother seeing that baby bombshell captured on film. Either way, by the time she made it to the front door, Kelly was out of breath.

And she didn't regain much of it, either.

Because there was no one in the parking lot. Certainly no TV crew.

"I'll go after them," Gabe insisted, hurrying toward a black Jeep.

Despite gasping for air, Kelly managed a "yes, please."

If Delbert put that footage on TV or the internet, then Ross…

But Kelly couldn't even finish that thought.

Ross couldn't find out that way. He just couldn't. One way or another, Gabe had to stop this situation from going from bad to worse.

For his sake and hers, Gabe couldn't fail.

CHAPTER THREE

GABE FAILED.

And he really hated to have to tell Kelly that.

However, judging from the way her face dropped when he pulled into the library parking lot again, she guessed it before Gabe even stepped from his rental car. Janine, too.

Both Kelly and Janine had their faces pressed to the glass door, obviously waiting for him. Since there were smudges and breath blotches all over the glass, it appeared they'd been waiting there for a good part of the three hours that he'd been gone.

"No," Kelly said, shaking her head as he stepped inside with them. "You needed to get that film."

"Well, I didn't fail from lack of trying." Gabe had driven out of the parking lot, fast, headed after the TV van, but the darn thing had at least a ten-minute head start and had seemingly disappeared. "There was no sign of Delbert and the reporter on the farm road leading out of town. No sign of them on the highway, either."

Kelly gave him a *what the heck are we going to do now?* stare while she rocked Noel in her arms. Noel was sacked out, sleeping like, well, a baby, and thankfully oblivious to the fact that all hell could break loose if Ross learned the hard way that he was an uncle.

Gabe figured whatever went down with Ross, he

could handle it, but it'd be better all the way around if Kelly and he could tell Ross face-to-face.

Then come face-to-face with the fallout.

Gabe wasn't concerned as much for himself as he was for Kelly. Ross was more of a father to her than a big brother since he'd raised her after their parents' deaths. She idolized him, and it would cut her to the core if this put a permanent rift between them.

And it would.

Ross was a good CRO, the kind of guy who could watch your back and his own, but he was downright rigid and old-fashioned when it came to his kid sister.

"When I couldn't find the van, I went to the TV station in Fredericksburg," Gabe went on. "The reporter, Cissy, was there, but she'd already dropped off Delbert at his house, and he had the camera and film footage with him. I went there, but he wasn't home."

"Delbert," Kelly mumbled like profanity. That one word said it all.

Delbert the dirtbag would delight in using that footage in the worst possible way. It was even likely that Delbert was home when Gabe had pounded on his door and just hadn't wanted a confrontation with someone who could kick his butt six ways to Sunday.

Part of Gabe had wanted to continue the search, but the sleet had started, and he hadn't wanted Kelly leaving the library to drive home in this.

He'd also been concerned about her leaving, *period*.

As in running off so that she wouldn't have to discuss why she'd kept a pregnancy and the baby from him. Kelly wouldn't have left permanently, of course. No way would she leave Sugar Springs just to avoid him, but she might have pulled a Delbert and have been unavailable so it'd take some time for Gabe to find her.

But she hadn't done that, thank God.

Even if she looked as if that's exactly what she wanted to do. Well, tough. They were having that discussion, and this time there'd be no TV crew or anything else to distract them.

"I left voice messages for Delbert to call me," Gabe added. Profanity-laced, threatening messages. Six of them. "All I can do now is wait, and when I can, I'll get him to destroy what he filmed."

"And if he doesn't agree to that?" Kelly asked.

"Oh, he'll agree." Because he wouldn't give Delbert an alternative. That six ways to Sunday butt-kicking was still on the table.

Janine seemed to take that as gospel and blew out a breath of relief. "Then, it'll be okay. So, I'll just be getting home. Bear's coming over before the sleet gets any worse. We're doing a little gift exchange tonight."

She bobbled her eyebrows, suggesting that she had a night of hot sex planned. Probably did, too. Janine and Buddy "Bear" McElroy had been doing gift exchanges since high school.

Janine turned to leave but then looked at Kelly and him. "Will you two be okay? I mean, do you need a referee or anything?"

"We'll be fine," Kelly said, her voice crisp. "Enjoy your evening, and thanks for watching the baby while I ran the kids' program."

Maybe it was the tightness in every part of Kelly's body language and voice or the tightness in Gabe's, but Janine didn't budge.

"Go ahead," Kelly insisted. "Once Gabe and I have

talked, then he can leave for San Antonio…where he probably has people waiting for him."

"Had," Gabe corrected. "I called on the drive back here and canceled my plans so we can have that chat. Get your things so we can leave while the roads are still passable."

Kelly's eyes widened significantly. "And where are you staying?"

Good question. And she already knew the answer.

Since there was no hotel in town, and he hadn't exactly stayed chummy with anyone other than Ross, that left one option.

Kelly's.

The very place he always stayed when he was in town. She let him know that wasn't an acceptable option with her slightly narrowed eyes.

"Do you really think it'll do you any good to argue with me?" Gabe asked Kelly when she opened her mouth. No doubt to do just that—argue about him staying at her place.

She knew the answer to that, too, but that didn't stop her from trying to come up with something else. Anything else. She would have likely even suggested Janine's place if her friend hadn't already said she had hot date plans.

"After what happened the last time you came to my house, this isn't a good idea," Kelly mumbled, but she finally got moving toward the back of the library.

Janine went in the other direction. Still eyeing them as if they were sticks of dynamite with short lit fuses, she put on her coat, walked outside to the parking lot and got in her car.

After what happened last time. That was like yet another stick of dynamite. Because the last time Kelly and he had ended up in bed together, and now they were the parents of a cooing, smiling, beautiful baby girl.

His baby.

That felt like a punch to the gut and a huge warm, fuzzy hug—all at the same time.

Him, a father!

Gabe had always figured that Hades would experience a sudden ice age before fatherhood happened to him, but here she was. Literally.

Kelly made her way back toward him, turning off lights along the way. With the ice storm bearing down on them, the library had cleared out, and according to the sign on the door, it'd be closed for the next four days for the holidays.

It might take Kelly and him that entire time to hash this out.

She now had Noel bundled in a thick pink blanket. Even though Kelly seemed to be balancing everything all right, Gabe took the diaper bag from her shoulder to help lighten her load.

"Since your car probably has one of those baby seats, we'll take it, and I'll drive," Gabe said, looking out at the sleet spitting down on the sidewalk. "I don't want you driving in this."

Kelly opened her mouth again. Maybe to protest his taking charge, but she mumbled a thanks. No doubt because she truly didn't want to drive on the already slick roads.

Gabe helped her lock up the library and then got Noel and her moving to the car. It seemed to take an eternity to heat up the vehicle, and he kept checking to make sure Noel wasn't too cold. She wasn't. She was snuggled into the blanket and the thick lining of the rear-facing carrier that was strapped into the backseat.

"Nothing else can happen between us tonight," Kelly insisted as he drove out of the parking lot. "Not ever again."

Gabe nearly reminded her that the damage had already been done. But he refused to think of his little girl as *damage*. Still, he got what Kelly was trying to say, and there was a clear visual of it as he drove through town toward her house.

This was where she'd been born and raised, and a continued relationship with him would almost certainly jeopardize her staying here in her hometown.

Such that it was.

The "blink and miss it" Main Street with a handful of mom-and-pop shops that had managed to stay open over the years. The Tip Top Café—which consisted of three booths with coin-operated jukeboxes, two tables and a counter. Then there was the Snapshots and Whatnots antique store that also doubled as the town's only photographer and small-engine repair shop. It was next to the gas station and the bank that still didn't have an ATM.

To Gabe, the stagnant town always felt like dead weight that he'd been plenty happy to shed, but to Kelly this place was her anchor. However, she could find other anchors.

He hoped.

The drive was a trip down memory lane all right, and while Gabe would have preferred to use the time to figure out what the heck he was going to do about Kelly and Noel, there were things that just captured his attention.

Like the abandoned Up-Do Beauty Salon that his mother had once owned.

His dad had left months before Gabe was born, and he and his mother had lived in the back part of the tiny wood-frame house. The salon had been in the front. Just inches away from his bedroom. He'd grown up reeking of hair dye and perm solution. Not exactly welcome scents for a misfit jock.

"Do you ever hear from your mother?" Kelly asked, following his gaze to what was left of the Up-Do.

"No." She'd left town a couple of weeks after he graduated high school to run off with her current "trouble in tight jeans" boyfriend, and Gabe hadn't heard from her since.

Good riddance, as far as Gabe was concerned.

Something he wouldn't say aloud to Kelly since it definitely hadn't been good riddance for her own family.

Her parents had been killed in a car accident when Kelly was just fourteen. Ross, eighteen. Ross had raised her and lived at home while he attended college in nearby San Antonio, and he'd become as much of a father figure as a brother. Ross loved Kelly, and she loved him.

Unlike Gabe's situation with his mother, Kelly had had a home and family.

Still did.

Gabe got yet more proof of that when he pulled into the gravel driveway of her two-story house. It didn't exactly have magazine-cover curb appeal with its dark gray limestone facade and weathered front porch, but since Kelly had lived here her entire life, she probably saw only the memories.

Well, some memories anyway.

She probably wasn't hanging on to the ones that she'd made with him a year ago.

The memories hit Gabe like a Mack truck when they hurried inside. Like everything else in Sugar Springs, Kelly's house hadn't changed a bit. The mishmash of furniture and knickknacks collected over four generations. Framed family photos on the fireplace mantel and wall shelves. Some were of Ross and him in various stages of high school and their military careers.

And there was also an overstuffed floral sofa next to the fireplace.

Oh, yeah. Plenty of memories there.

That was where Kelly and he had been sitting a year ago the day after Christmas. The bottle of Jack had been on the coffee table. Ross had already left to finish up some paperwork at the base in San Antonio and would be flying out ahead of Gabe. Kelly and Gabe had talked at first. For hours. And when talk of the dangerous deployment had put some tears in her eyes, Gabe had lent her his shoulder.

Then his mouth.

It was the mouth-lending that'd gotten them in trouble because it'd led them straight to her bed.

Even though there weren't any visual reminders of that around, Gabe's imagination was pretty good, and he got a jolt of how Kelly's mouth had felt. How she tasted.

And yeah, he got another image of her naked.

That really didn't help with working out this situation between them.

Kelly eased a still-sleeping Noel into a bassinet near the sofa. She turned toward him, ditching the Mrs.

Santa hat, and she rubbed her hands down the sides of her costume.

Clearly nervous.

Still, she made a picture there with the holiday tree behind her, practically framing her. She looked like Christmas.

Except for that deeply troubled look on her face.

Kelly took the present that she'd gotten from Ross and put it beneath the tree. There were at least six other gifts, not decorated in traditional wrapping but in hand-painted paper. Kelly's doing, no doubt. She'd made Christmas here for Noel and her.

"I'll need to wake the baby up soon, or she won't sleep well tonight," she said. "Not that she actually sleeps well, but a long nap will mean she'll be up more than usual. So, if we're going to talk, it's best to do it now." Kelly glanced down at her costume. "Or at least right after I've changed."

He definitely wanted to talk, but Gabe wasn't sure Kelly was going to want to hear what he had to say. Especially when she didn't stay put. She hurried into the first room just off the living room. Her bedroom. Where she was no doubt stripping out of that velvet. Since it wasn't a good idea for him to be anywhere close to Kelly while she was almost naked, he went over to the bassinet instead.

To have a better look at his baby.

Noel was on her back, her head turned slightly to the side, and she occasionally pursed her lips as if sucking at a bottle. Everything about her was fascinating. So beautiful.

Perfect, really.

Even if that was his mouth, hair and eyes. So much of

him all rolled into that tiny, precious face. Gabe wasn't sure how he could love someone this much that he'd just met, but he did.

He'd once heard Kelly's mom say that love for a child was soul deep. Gabe hadn't understood that then.

But, man, he understood it now.

He reached down, brushed his fingers over those baby curls. Like pure silk. So was her skin, Gabe learned when he trailed his finger to her cheek.

He got so lost in the moment that he didn't immediately notice the baby monitor mounted to the foot of the bassinet. And it had a camera on it. He wondered if Kelly was on the other end, and Gabe got confirmation that she was when she practically barreled back into the living room, still tugging on a pair of socks.

"You were watching her sleep," Kelly mumbled, her tone sounding a little like an accusation. She fluttered her fingers toward her bedroom. "I have baby monitors in the house so I can keep an eye on her no matter which room I'm in."

Gabe nodded. Good idea since it was a big house. But he seriously doubted that Kelly dressed at breakneck speed when he wasn't there. Maybe she'd seen that "soul deep" look of love on his face, or maybe she was just wired too much to slow down.

Either way, she was only half put together.

Her jeans were partially zipped. Her green sweater hiked up on one hip. She bobbled around while still trying to get that sock right.

When she finally finished, she shot him one nerve-laced look and headed for the kitchen just a few yards away, where she put the kettle on the burner of the old-fashioned gas stove. For a cup of tea, no doubt, but tea wasn't going to soothe this tangle of nerves inside her.

Or the one inside him.

"You want me to fix you a cup, too?" she asked.

"No, thanks. I'd rather just talk. You should have told me about the pregnancy," he repeated and then waved her off before she could repeat her rationale for keeping it secret. "I understand why you didn't, but not telling me has put us in this position."

Too bad he wasn't exactly sure what position that was.

Gabe decided to go with the nonnegotiable part. "I want to be part of Noel's life."

"How?" Kelly immediately asked. "Her life is here with me, in Sugar Springs."

"That can change."

Judging from the gasp she made, that wasn't the answer she'd been expecting. "This is my home. I can't leave. And please don't suggest split custody. She's way too young for that."

Obviously, Kelly had given this more thought than he had. Of course, she'd had nearly a year to consider all options and angles. He'd had only a few hours to cobble together some possibilities.

And yeah, split custody had been one of them.

While looking down at Noel in the bassinet, Gabe had considered the logistics of that. Wouldn't be easy. But he could make it work.

Correction, he *would* make it work.

Kelly turned away from him, her attention suddenly fixed on the metal canister of tea that she took from the cabinets. Since he doubted the tea had captured her complete attention, she was likely about to say something that she preferred to say while not making eye contact with him.

"Besides, a baby wouldn't fit into your lifestyle," Kelly added. "You're a player, Gabe."

He groaned. No wonder she hadn't wanted to make eye contact. "You know, for a so-called player, I'm not getting a lot of action," he mumbled under his breath.

Kelly would be surprised to learn that he hadn't been with anyone since her. Probably wouldn't believe him, either. There'd been some opportunities during those four months at the base in Germany. Opportunities that he'd passed up because, well, because he just had.

Not because of Kelly.

And it was a sad day in a man's life when he started lying to himself.

Of course, it'd been because of her. Ross's little sister. That's how he'd seen her anyway until that night a year ago. That night, he'd seen Kelly exactly as he was seeing her now.

Mouthwatering.

A woman he wanted in his bed again, but that was something he couldn't have.

He had to think with his head now and not some other part of him that rarely made good decisions. He had to do what was best for Noel and give her something he'd never had.

A father.

Even if he couldn't give her what she deserved— a family.

"Well?" Kelly said, clearly waiting for an answer.

"Noel won't have to fit into my lifestyle because I'll fit into hers," he said.

She threw up her hands, one of them palm up, the other still holding the unopened canister of tea. "How?"

Gabe hoped this sounded a lot better out loud than it did in his head. "For starters, you'll marry me."

There was a moment of startled silence. Just a moment. Then, the tin of tea crashed to the floor, making a loud clanging on the hardwood floor, and tea bags inside went flying. But that wasn't the only sounds.

Kelly gasped again.

And Noel started to whimper.

Kelly didn't bother picking up the tea. She rushed past him and scooped up the baby, whirling back around toward him and holding Noel like a cuddly shield.

Despite the thick tension, Gabe smiled at Noel and his heart doubled in size when the baby smiled back.

But Kelly sure wasn't smiling, and she was almost certainly on the verge of telling him what he could do with his marriage proposal.

"Don't give me an answer now," Gabe insisted before she could say anything. "Sleep on it. In fact, take a day or two. But consider this. It'll be best for Noel if we're married. She'll be my military dependent and can get all kinds of benefits."

Kelly opened her mouth again, probably to remind him that marriage was the least of their concerns. And maybe it was.

However, it was a start.

After that, they could work out the details of visitation, shared custody and anything else that cropped up.

"Sleep on it," Gabe insisted.

He'd sleep on it, too. Well, he would if he managed to get any sleep at all, and maybe by morning he'd know what the heck he was going to do next.

CHAPTER FOUR

Sleep on it.

Even in sleep that order didn't sit well with Kelly. And it had been an order, no doubt about that. The Air Force Captain had spoken, and even though he'd given her that *sleep on it* postscript, it was still an order.

Because Gabe fully expected her to say yes.

She wouldn't, of course. And even in sleep, she knew that, too. Heck, deep down Gabe probably wanted her to turn him down anyway since there was no way a baby and a wife would fit into his life.

Still, the order repeated through her head in her dreams. Dreams of her telling him *no*. But other dreams, as well. Of that night together. The dream kiss was just as potent as the real one had been.

Scalding hot.

She'd fantasized about Gabe for so many years that the kiss, any kiss, could have been a letdown. It was hard to live up to the fairy tale that she'd spun in her head.

But that kiss had.

It had been the same for the caresses. Gentle but determined. And it was that gentle determination, and more kisses, that had sent her and Gabe stumbling for the bed.

Kelly could feel that now, too.

And as on that night, the pleasure rippled through her. So strong of a memory that she heard herself make a needy sound of pleasure that she didn't want to make. Especially since Gabe was actually in the guest room next door. He might hear it, too, and get bad ideas that would only complicate their situation.

That woke her.

Kelly forced her eyes open and sat up. She was groggy from lack of sleep. So groggy that it took her a moment to realize something was wrong.

There was sunlight threading through the partially opened curtain, and she caught a glimpse of the ice-coated window and yard. But it was worse than that. There was freezing fog drifting around like tiny bits of glass.

Good grief.

With that much ice, she'd never get Gabe out of her house and back on the road, something she needed to figure out how to do. But she couldn't drive him back to his car at the library until some of that ice melted.

Her gaze flew to the clock on the nightstand. Nearly seven-thirty. She hadn't slept that late since having Noel.

She barreled out of bed, her foot catching on the sheet, and nearly tumbled right on the floor. She hurried to the nursery in the room next to hers, grabbed on to the crib to steady herself, and her stomach went to her knees.

The crib was empty.

Oh, God. Empty!

A dozen thoughts flew through her head, none good. Mercy, where was her baby?

"Noel?" she shouted, not that the baby could answer, but someone else did.

Gabe.

"We're in the kitchen," he said.

Kelly didn't bother with a robe or her socks. She sprinted out of the nursery, across the living room, nearly taking out the Christmas tree. She skidded to a stop in the doorway of the kitchen, bracing herself to see some horrible sight. Maybe Noel had gotten sick or there'd been some other emergency.

Instead what she saw was Gabe in his uniform pants and snug tan T-shirt.

And he was feeding Noel a bottle.

Maybe because her heart was slamming against her chest or because she was practically gasping for breath, it took Kelly a couple of seconds to process that. There was no emergency or illness. Noel was in her carrier seat on the table, sucking her bottle that Gabe was holding. And he was kissing her toes as she kicked at him, smiling at him while the bottle was still in her mouth.

"What's going on?" Kelly asked.

Gabe kept his attention on Noel and lifted his shoulder. "When I got up, I heard Noel moving around in her crib. I figured you could use some extra sleep, so I brought her into the kitchen and fixed her a bottle."

It was as if he was speaking a foreign language. Gabe going into the nursery? And then fixing a baby bottle?

And she hadn't heard any of it?

"Noel was wet, too, and I changed her diaper, but I didn't do a very good job," he added.

No, he hadn't. The tapes were askew, and it was loose, gaping at the legs. Still, it was on the baby's bottom, and that was far more than Kelly would have imagined he'd tackle.

"Delbert's still not answering his phone," Gabe went on. "I tried to call him again a few minutes ago and left him another message."

Gabe looked up at her then and did a double take. His gaze slid from her face—heaven knew how rumpled and bad she looked—to her flannel pj's. Or rather to her pj top that was partially unbuttoned. There was a good deal of her right breast showing, and it had a good deal of an effect on Gabe.

She recognized that heated look.

She had been on the receiving end of it the night they'd had sex.

Kelly fixed her top and silently cursed this blasted attraction that just wouldn't cool down. It managed to get in the way of her thinking. Breathing.

And just about everything else.

"Are you sure you fixed the bottle right?" Kelly asked, making her way to the table so she could give Noel a morning kiss. "You have to mix it in the right proportions."

"Anyone who can read could have fixed it right with your notes." Gabe tipped his head to the three-ring binder on the counter. "It was a page long, typed, single spaced. There are deployment manuals not written in that kind of detail."

"I just wanted to leave specific instructions for Mrs. Saunders," Kelly mumbled, though she had to admit she'd gone a little overboard.

"You left her burping instructions," Gabe said, turning those sizzling blue eyes on her. "Since Mrs. Saunders has six kids of her own and at last count more than a dozen grandchildren, I'm thinking she knows how to rid a baby of some extra gas."

All right, she'd gone a *lot* overboard.

"I was nervous about leaving Noel when I went to work," she justified. "I think most new mothers are, and I didn't want there to be any questions about her routine and how to take care of her."

He made a lazy sound of agreement and played another round of foot kissing with Noel. This time, the baby laughed.

That shouldn't have sent a pang of jealousy through Kelly, but it did. Noel and Gabe had known each other less than twenty-four hours, and they were acting like, well, father and daughter.

"I was just glad there was a bottle around to give her," Gabe said. "If you'd been nursing, you wouldn't have gotten the extra hour of sleep."

An hour? That's how long they'd been up and she hadn't heard them? Mercy, those dreams had really sucked her in.

She headed for the teakettle and found the water already hot. Of course, it was. Gabe had had a whole hour to take care of the things she always did, and from the looks of it he'd done a good job—with the exception of that droopy diaper.

"I couldn't breast-feed," she said, glancing around for the can of formula that he had opened. She found it in the fridge, where it belonged, and Gabe had even washed out the cup he'd used to measure it. "I got an infection right after Noel was born and had to go on antibiotics. The doctor thought it best if I didn't nurse."

"An infection?" That took the smile right off his face. "Ross didn't know."

"It didn't last long, and it wasn't that serious. But by the time the infection had cleared up, Noel didn't want breast milk, only the formula."

"Well, she does seem to like it."

Yes, but she seemed to like her daddy more. Noel was doing a lot more toe kicking than formula drinking. Kelly tried not to be jealous of that, too, but failed just as much as she had before.

What she wouldn't fail at was the conversation that Gabe and she needed to have. Kelly needed to tell him no to his marriage order, but before she could get out a single word, he pointed to the trio of small framed drawings held by magnets onto the side of the fridge.

"Those are new," he said. "Like all your others, they're really good."

"Thanks." Bunnies, trees and flowers. Her favorite things to sketch, and these had reminded her of Noel.

"What about that one?" He tipped his head to a small framed drawing on the windowsill. "Are those actual dried rose petals on the flower you drew?"

They were. And it was yet something else she really didn't want to discuss.

"I was experimenting," she said. Kelly snatched up the drawing and stuffed it away in the drawer. "I drew the flower and thought it could use something extra."

Gabe stared at her, clearly not believing that explanation. Probably because it was a partial lie.

"I'm guessing those dried petals have some kind of special meaning to you," he commented. "Since you just hid it and your face is flushed, I'm guessing it has a meaning that you'd rather not share with me."

She nodded.

Good. They were on the same page.

"So, who gave you the flower?" he asked.

Okay, not on the same page, or else he would have known she didn't want to discuss it. "I've had it for a long time," she settled for saying.

She decided to have some tea before refusing his marriage proposal, and she went to the stove to fix herself a cup.

"You really should be illustrating children's books," he said before she could speak.

Yes, she'd heard that a lot over the years, but it seemed like something far off. A mirage, even. She needed to work to support Noel and herself and take care of the house. There weren't enough hours left in the day to do sketches that she might never sell.

"You sent me some sketches three years ago when I was on the other deployment," he added.

Yet something else that seemed so far off. But she had indeed sent him sketches. Prayers, too.

Always prayers.

"I figured you didn't send them this time because you were angry with me," he went on. "And maybe that was part of it, but it's my guess that taking care of Noel is a second full-time job."

She nodded. "A good full-time job."

He nodded, too. Met her gaze. "It suits you."

With everything else going on, the compliment should have made her wary, but there was something in his voice. His eyes. Something that he quickly tried to cover up with more Noel foot kisses, followed by scooping her up and putting her against his shoulder.

But burping duty didn't distract Kelly.

Even if he was doing a decent job of it.

"Was it bad over there?" she asked, not sure she really wanted to know the answer. It'd been the stuff of too many nightmares.

He looked at her again. A man carefully weighing his words. "Sometimes."

Which meant it was bad more often than not.

"Sometimes, there were children," he said, his voice suddenly raw and whispered. He brushed a kiss on Noel's cheek just as she let out a loud burp.

Gabe laughed. And Kelly was glad. She caught only a glimmer of the pain there, and it'd been enough. It was much better to hear the laughter, especially since just about everything Noel did made her smile or laugh, too.

Well, almost everything. The daddy endearment was continuing with Noel's eyes fixed on Gabe's.

"The Air Force wants me to fly a desk," Gabe added a moment later.

Kelly was familiar enough with military lingo to know what that meant. The Air Force didn't want him going back into combat. Probably because he'd already been on so many deployments.

Good.

That might save her a few prayers and some sleepless nights. He'd had four deployments in the past eight years, and she figured the majority of that time he'd either been in direct danger or else trying to deal with the effects of it.

Sometimes, there were children said it all.

"They want me to be an instructor for the next four years," Gabe went on, dragging in a deep breath. "Might not be a bad idea since it'd give me a better chance of spending more time with Noel."

Oh.

So, that's where this was going.

Desk duty not because he needed downtime from the stress of combat situations but because it would give him more opportunities just like the one he was having in her kitchen.

Since this could be the start of that conversation they needed to have anyway, Kelly sank down in the chair across from him and hoped that the attraction, his uniform and the daddy sparkle in Noel's eyes stayed out of this.

"The whole time I was carrying Noel," she said, "I wasn't thinking about you as part of this."

Well, she did think of it, but she'd shoved that particular fantasy aside. She had a lot of faults, but living in a fairy tale wasn't one of them. Gabe was a CRO, and she was a hometown librarian. Not exactly on the same grid when it came to planning a future together.

"Ouch," Gabe mumbled. He gave Noel several more burping pats on the back. "I deserve that."

Yes, but she hadn't expected to see that hurt look on his face. "It wasn't just you," Kelly explained. "My last relationship ended because I wouldn't marry him and leave Sugar Springs."

"Brent Marcum," Gabe provided. "Yeah, I remember."

Since her relationship with Brent had ended nearly three years ago, it surprised her that Gabe would even recall the guy's name. Unless he'd heard rumors or something.

"He was that lawyer, and he was all wrong for you," Gabe concluded. "Wait. Is he the one who gave you the flower that you used in the drawing?"

Good grief. Would he just not drop it? Apparently not.

"It's from your senior prom, all right?" she snapped.

Judging from the way he stared at her, he didn't have a clue what she meant. Of course, he didn't. It'd been just a little blip on Gabe's radar of life.

For her, it'd been a memory of a lifetime.

"The prom?" he repeated.

Still no clue.

Even though this wasn't on her discussion agenda, he probably wouldn't let it drop until she explained. "I sneaked into Ross's and your senior prom at the high school gym. I was fourteen and feeling somewhat left out."

"Oh, because your mom and dad had recently passed away."

They had. Just a few months before that. And yes, she was still grieving their loss after all these years. Always would, but it'd been a different emotion that had prompted her to sneak into the Midnight in Paris theme prom.

Jealousy.

"Tiffany Waters was your date," Kelly said, omitting the jealousy part altogether. "I just wanted to see how you looked dancing. Ross, too," she added because this was her version of that night and she didn't want Gabe to know that she hadn't given a flying flip about her brother's dancing skills. Only Gabe's.

Well, specifically Tiffany in Gabe's arms.

"When Tiffany saw me lurking by the retracted bleachers," she continued, "she said I needed to go home and grow some boobage before coming to a prom."

Not a shining moment for Kelly, and if it'd ended there, she wouldn't have gotten one of the best memories of her life.

Or that rose.

Lightbulb moment. "Yeah." He nodded. Smiled. Then frowned. "Tiffany wasn't very nice, and she made you look sad."

Kelly nodded. "And you danced with me."

The corner of his mouth kicked up again. "I did. Gave you my rose boutonniere, too. That's where the rose petals came from?" he asked, shaking his head. "I can't believe you kept it all this time."

She tried to dismiss it with a shrug. "It was my first dance. A girl remembers that kind of thing."

In nth detail, she remembered.

The DJ was playing the Backstreet Boys' "Shape of My Heart," and Gabe had slow danced with her on the polished gym floor. The doors had been open, and the night breeze had played with his hair. Definitely heart-throb material, and he'd done exactly that—caused her heart to throb.

Obviously, Gabe had been trying to cheer her up and hadn't realized that she had a crush on him bigger than Texas.

He made a sound of both surprise and amusement. "Funny how memories like that stick with you. I'm just glad the petals hadn't come from Brent. I didn't especially want you hanging on to any memory with him. Since he's wrong for you and all," Gabe quickly added. "Though he was right about trying to get you out of Sugar Springs. Noel needs to grow up in a town with lots of other kids. And a school."

That got her frowning. An automatic response since Brent's opinion of the town had changed somewhat. And since she had this argument with Ross every time he came home. Not about the school since both the high school and elementary schools had been closed and unified with a county district. But about her leaving and getting a job that he felt was more in line with her master's degree in library science.

"The town will make a comeback," Kelly insisted. That was possibly true.

Possibly.

Gabe's lifted eyebrow indicated that he wasn't buying into that particular theory, and he was likely about to start what would be an argument that she'd heard too many times from Ross.

But the sound of the voice stopped them.

"Get inside now!" the person shouted.

"Mrs. Saunders," Kelly mumbled.

She hurried to the window and spotted her elderly widowed neighbor in the sprawling backyard right next to Kelly's. The woman was still in her nightgown and chenille robe and was staring up at the trio of massive oak trees that divided their properties.

Gabe got up, too, and when he saw Mrs. Saunders, he handed Noel to Kelly so he could open the back door. The blast of cold air was instant, and Kelly stepped deeper into the kitchen while Gabe went onto the back porch.

"Gabe," the woman said, smiling so big that it caused her wrinkles to bunch up into more wrinkles. Her hair was almost as white as the icy ground and the fog that her breath was creating in the cold. "I saw you come in last night. Welcome home."

"Thanks. Mrs. Saunders, it's too cold for you to be outside dressed like that," Gabe warned her in a friendly voice.

"I know. That's what I've been trying to tell Doodles, but she won't come down."

Kelly groaned. Doodles, her neighbor's cat. It was always getting up that tree, but now wasn't a good time for it. She peered into the trees and did indeed spot the tabby. Not on one of the lower branches, of course, but the top one.

"Just go back inside," Gabe told the woman. "I'll get the cat down."

He came back into the kitchen, bringing some of the chill and scents of winter with him, and he immediately headed to the guest room.

"The cat won't stay up there long," Kelly explained, following him. "If you just wait a half hour, she'll get cold and go back in."

"But Mrs. Saunders likely won't budge during that time, and I don't want her dying of exposure." He took a coat from his duffel bag and slipped it on along with a pair of gloves. They looked warm enough, but this wasn't necessary.

"That tree branch is high, and it's coated with ice," Kelly pointed out.

"Worried about me?" He flashed that smile. The one that had no doubt seduced many women. "I'm a Combat Rescue Officer, remember? Wouldn't be a very good one if I couldn't rescue a tabby named Doodles."

Yes, but she was still thinking about that ice and height.

And that smile.

"Let's just hope I don't have to say Doodles's name too many times," he added. "Wouldn't be good for my tough-guy image."

She fought a smile, but Kelly knew it was a ploy to stop her from fussing about this. "Mrs. Saunders might just want some company," Kelly tried again. "So don't let her rope you into doing a long list of chores that'll keep you here."

He shrugged. "I have other things to keep me here." And he dropped a kiss on Noel's head before heading back toward the kitchen.

Again, Kelly followed him. "Just how long are you planning on staying anyway?"

Another shrug. "I have over thirty days of leave saved up. I'll stay as long as it takes you to mull over marrying me."

She blinked. "The answer to that is no."

If that bothered him in the least, he didn't show it. Instead, he opened one of the cabinets and located a can of tuna.

"Then, sleep on it again," Gabe argued. "And while you're doing that we can talk about Ross...among other things."

Ross.

Kelly certainly hadn't forgotten about her brother, but with so many other issues on her mind, she'd put him on the back burner. "What are we going to do about Ross?"

"He'll be here in a week. I'll tell him about Noel then. And us."

Just the thought of it caused her breath to go thin. "But how?"

"I got a whole week to figure that out," he said as if it would be a piece of cake. "Right now, I have a cat to rescue."

And with the can of tuna in hand, Gabe stepped out into the winter cold.

CHAPTER FIVE

THE CAT RESCUE was one of his easier *missions*.

Doodles hadn't come down for the can of tuna that Gabe had opened for her and waved around in the air, but dangling the toy catnip monkey had done the trick. The tabby had scurried down as if she had a Doberman on her tail, snatched the toy and bolted for Mrs. Saunders's porch.

Good. Nothing like a little feline addiction to save the day. It'd saved him from shimmying up the tree after her, too. With as much ice as there was on the branches, they could have snapped under his weight. Best not to add a trip to the E.R. while he was on leave, trying to work a miracle with this situation with Kelly.

And it would take a miracle since he wasn't even sure how he wanted all of this to play out.

Well, not sure except for the part about being in Noel's life in a big way. That would happen even if Kelly continued to turn down his proposal, but as with his future conversation with Ross, Gabe was still trying to work out the details about that.

Details that might include him being a married man.

That required a deep breath, and he got a reminder of the cold when his lungs practically froze.

"There you go," Mrs. Saunders said to Doodles. She

opened her back door and let the tabby in. "Gabe, come in, too, so I can properly thank you."

Gabe would have gladly settled for just a verbal thank-you, but while the cat was now inside, Mrs. Saunders still wasn't. She was on the porch, almost under the eaves where there were dozens of foot-long icicles arrowing right down toward her. Best to get her inside, and the fastest way to do that was to go with her.

Kelly was probably right about the woman just needing a little company.

He stepped into her kitchen, the scents of Christmas assaulting him. Sugar cookies, a fresh-cut tree and hot chocolate. With marshmallows. Mrs. Saunders poured him a cup and motioned for him to sit at the small kitchen table.

Her house was yet another blast from the past because it probably hadn't been updated since the seventies. Yellow cabinets with avocado-green appliances and a red-checkered tablecloth. There were pictures of her kids and grandkids everywhere, some framed and some just held on the fridge with magnets.

It was the kind of kitchen he'd always figured his own grandmother would have, if he had a grandmother, that is. His mom had never gotten around to introducing him to her folks or his dad's.

"Are your kids coming home for Christmas?" he asked.

"Three of them are. They'll be here as soon as the roads clear." She rattled off their names. Gabe had a good recollection of them, but they were all older than he was. Like him, though, they'd all left town and moved to greener pastures.

"I saw Kelly and you when you got in yesterday,"

Mrs. Saunders said a moment later. "So glad you made it home for Christmas." In addition to the cup of hot chocolate that she put in front of him, she served him a trio of shaped cookies on a saucer. A tree, a wreath and a Santa.

It was early, and he didn't usually dose up on this much sugar, but Gabe made an exception since the cat rescue, the conversation with Kelly and playtime with Noel had left him starving. One bite of the cookies and his taste buds were in heaven.

Mrs. Saunders took the chair across from him and had a sip of her own hot chocolate. Not exactly the little-old-granny type, even though just about everyone he knew called her Old Lady Saunders. Yes, her hair was gray, her shoulders hunched a little with age, but she had a sturdy build, and there was plenty of light in her weathered brown eyes.

She smiled as if she knew some kind of secret, and then leaned in closer, sliding her hand over his for a gentle pat. "I figured it was you all along. The baby looks just like you."

Oh. So, that was the secret. It made him wonder how many others knew it, as well. Or had guessed. Of course, after the fiasco at the library, there was no guessing required. Everyone in the tri-county area likely knew that the Sugar Springs assistant librarian had had a fling with the military guy who slept around a lot.

Gabe chowed down on more of the sugary Santa. "Kelly said you babysit Noel."

She nodded. "I do at that. Love that little girl to pieces. And she's a good baby, too."

Yes, but even a good baby could be taxing, and Gabe

wondered just how much longer Mrs. Saunders would be able to do nanny duty. It especially wouldn't be easy when Noel started walking.

When did babies walk anyway?

He made a mental note to download some books on baby milestones and such.

"I hope you brought Kelly a nice Christmas present," she commented.

Oh.

Gabe made a mental note to do something about that, too. "Any idea what she wants?"

"Well, she's always poring over the stuff in Snapshots and Whatnots."

"The junk store?" That didn't seem like a decent place to get a Christmas present.

"One person's junk is another man's treasure," Mrs. Saunders remarked. "If the weather clears, I'm sure you can find something up there. Herman keeps all sorts of mementos from the past that Kelly likes. Jewelry, books and toys. In his photography room, he's even got plenty of old photos that he took from when the high school was still here."

Gabe had to shake his head. He'd known the shop owner, Herman Newman, his whole life. Also knew that Herman was the town's only photographer, but Gabe had never ventured into the place.

"What kind of photos?" he asked.

"All sorts. Some of you boys in your football uniforms. Graduations. Dances. Stuff like that."

"And Kelly looks at them?"

She smiled. "Well, the football ones hold a lot of women's attention. Not mine, mind you, but younger women. Must be those tight pants and shoulder pads."

He couldn't imagine Kelly poring over old football shots, but then Ross would have been in the photos, too. Maybe this was more of that family-bond thing that she was trying her damnedest to hold on to.

"But it's not just pictures," Mrs. Saunders went on. "There's an antique rocking chair. Some pretty glass bottles…even some old Raggedy Ann dolls for Noel."

He made yet a third mental note to get Noel something, too. Something better than a Raggedy Ann doll. This was her first Christmas, and it should be special.

"She cried a lot, you know," Mrs. Saunders said, looking at him from over the rim of a World's Greatest Grandma cup.

That got his attention. "Noel cried a lot?" It felt like a punch to the gut to hear that his baby had been so upset.

"No. Kelly did."

All right. That was a punch of a different kind. With all that'd gone on, he hadn't even thought to ask Kelly about the pregnancy. "Why'd she cry a lot?"

"I suspect she had plenty of reasons. Being a single woman with money tight. Plus, she missed you."

That got his attention, too. "She said that?"

"Not with her actual words. People don't always have to use words to get their point across, but her tears said it all. I saw her once, sitting on her back porch in the rocking chair. Just staring off, her hand on her belly and the tears a-coming like spring rain."

Oh, man. Yeah, he should have asked her about the pregnancy, and maybe she would have opened up about the crying.

Or not.

Kelly was still working hard to keep her distance

from him, and she probably wouldn't have shared something like that.

"And then that fella from San Antonio came a few times," Mrs. Saunders added, "and that made her cry even more."

Suddenly, the cookie didn't taste so sweet. "What fella?"

"Brent something or another. The lawyer that Kelly used to date."

Not only had the cookie lost its flavor, but Gabe felt something he didn't want to feel. Jealousy. It didn't go that well with cookies and hot chocolate. "Why'd Brent come over? They broke up years ago."

Despite the fact they were the only two people in the entire house, Mrs. Saunders still leaned in as if telling a secret that she didn't want anyone else to hear. "I only got bits and pieces from Kelly, but it seems as if that lawyer fella wanted to marry her."

"W-what?" And yes, he stuttered.

"Marry her," Mrs. Saunders repeated. "He even told Kelly that he'd move to Sugar Springs and help her raise the baby as his own."

"When did this happen?" Gabe tried not to snap at the woman.

"A while ago. Maybe two, three weeks."

Weeks? Some scumbag ex of Kelly's wanted to marry her and raise his baby just a few weeks ago?

The answer to that would be a thousand gallons of no.

"I need to be going," Gabe said, getting to his feet. "Thanks for the cookies and cocoa."

"Anytime. I guess this means Kelly won't be marrying that lawyer fella?" she asked.

Yeah, that's exactly what it meant.

Heck, he hoped so anyway.

But it was a very long short walk back over to Kelly's. In a nutshell, Brent might be Kelly's ideal package. A lawyer willing to move to Sugar Springs and become a family with Noel and her.

Gabe heard the growl rumble in his throat.

He couldn't give Kelly that make-believe ending in Sugar Springs, but by God, he wasn't going to let some other man raise his baby, either. Or marry Kelly.

Except that last one might be out of his control.

She couldn't marry Brent. She just couldn't. But it might be the very reason she kept telling Gabe no to his own marriage proposal. And with that weighing on his mind and temper, Gabe went back inside Kelly's kitchen and ditched his coat on one of the chairs.

Kelly wasn't there, but he followed the sound of her voice and Noel's cooings to the nursery.

Kelly had changed her clothes and was in the process of changing Noel, but she looked up at him. "Are Mrs. Saunders and the cat all right?"

Gabe just skipped right over that and went to the heart of the matter. "Brent asked you to marry him?"

The surprise froze on her face for a few moments. "Mrs. Saunders told you that?"

"Yeah, that and some other things. It's true?"

The surprise turned to concern. "What other things?"

Gabe huffed. "Did Brent propose to you?"

He was riled, but it was hard to stay that way when Noel reached out her little hand and wiggled her fingers. As if motioning for him to come closer. He did, but while smiling at his baby girl, he narrowed his eyes a bit at Kelly.

"Yes, Brent asked me to marry him," Kelly finally said. And that was it. No details.

"And?" Gabe prompted.

"He's giving me to New Year's Day to think about it."

Gabe had no idea what expression was on his face, but it was possibly a mix of anger, surprise and what-the-heck? "So, you're sleeping on it, too?"

"So to speak." She finished dressing Noel and stood, meeting him eye to eye. "But I'm not sleeping with him, if that's what you're thinking."

He wasn't. Gabe figured she hadn't exactly had time for that, but if she accepted Brent's proposal, that would certainly end.

"And?" he prompted when she didn't continue. "What will you tell him?"

"I'm pretty sure my answer to his proposal will be no."

"Pretty sure?" Heck, Gabe doubted she was pretty sure when it came to his proposal. Kelly definitely seemed to be leaning to the "no way, no how" response when it came to him, but Brent got a wishy-washy kind of no.

"While I'd love for Noel to have a family as I did," she added, "I don't believe marrying for her sake is the right thing to do."

You're damn right it's not the right thing to do, Gabe nearly blurted out. However, it was sort of what he was asking her to do.

Sort of.

"The big difference between Brent and me is that I'm Noel's father." Though Gabe knew that Kelly hadn't forgotten that.

Of course, the big difference in her mind was that

Brent, the suck-up, was apparently ready to ditch San Antonio and move to Sugar Springs.

"Any reason you didn't tell me about all of this?" he asked.

"Because I was too busy sleeping on it," she grumbled, the sarcasm dripping from her voice. With Noel in her arms, she brushed past him, heading back to the kitchen, but Gabe wasn't done with this conversation.

"Mrs. Saunders said you cried a lot," he tossed out there.

Kelly didn't stop. She eased Noel into her infant seat on the table and proceeded to pour herself a cup of tea. However, Gabe moved closer, and practically got right in her face.

Not an especially good idea.

It put them practically mouth to mouth, and it was a quick reminder that her mouth was probably as sweet as those cookies Mrs. Saunders had just served him.

No, not a good time to remember that.

Or maybe it was.

Maybe if he just hauled her to him and kissed her, all the doubts about his proposal would vanish. And then he remembered that having some doubts might be good. After all, they had plenty to work out because unlike the suck-up Brent, Gabe couldn't just pull the plug on his career and move back to town.

Not immediately anyway.

He had two years left on his current military commitment, and after that he'd be just eight years away from putting in his twenty, where he could collect retirement pay. It seemed a lot to throw away, especially since he loved being in the Air Force, but he had to consider doing it for Noel.

"You're staring at my mouth," Kelly said, jolting him back to reality.

"Because I was thinking about kissing you."

The pulse jumped in her throat. "You can't think that's a good idea."

"It's not. But I'm thinking about doing it anyway."

She set her tea aside and put her palm on his chest. It was a puny attempt if she was trying to hold him back. In the swirls of all that green, he could see that she wanted to kiss him, too.

So, Gabe moved in to do just that—against his better judgment about complicating a complicated situation with yet another complication.

He touched his mouth to hers. Just a touch. But it was one of those earth-moving kinds of touches. The heat sped right through him, firing up his body and clouding his mind.

Definitely not good.

Did that stop him?

Uh, no.

He slid his hand around the back of Kelly's neck, yanked her to him and kissed her. Long, slow, deep. Just the way he liked his kisses.

But again, this wasn't his usual.

It was Kelly, and with that one kiss, his memories went back to that night when the kisses had gone on for much longer, slower and deeper until they'd ended up in bed.

"We can't," Kelly said, scrambling out of his grip.

Oh, yes, they could, but that didn't mean they *should*. Landing in bed again would be incredible. Gabe was sure of it, but it wouldn't help Kelly and him iron things out.

Unless…

"I'm not on the pill and I seriously doubt you have a condom with you," she added.

All right. That nixed his *unless*.

And it was a darn good argument, too. They'd used a condom the last time, one that he'd taken from his wallet, but clearly something had been faulty. Or maybe they were just more fertile than most people.

"Besides," she said, moving even farther away from him and to the cabinet next to the sink, "Noel's wide-awake and watching us."

She was. The baby had her attention fixed to them as if they were the most fascinating creatures on the planet. That cooled down the fire inside him, but Gabe wasn't stupid. Not about most things anyway.

And he figured a cooled fire for Kelly was only a temporary thaw.

"Formula," Kelly mumbled. "Oh, no."

Since his mind was on kisses and thaws, it took him a moment to realize she meant baby formula. "What's wrong? The rest of the can I used this morning is in the fridge."

"Yes, but that's only enough for today and tonight. I'd bought some extra cans, six of them, but I left them in my office at the library."

Understandable. She'd had plenty on her mind yesterday with his arrival and the filming of her baby news.

"The store won't be open because it's Christmas Eve," she added as if this were the end of the world. "I have a few cans of another brand, but Noel doesn't like it nearly as well as her usual."

"No problem. I'll just go to the library and get them. Anything else you need for Christmas dinner? I noticed the ham in the fridge and was hoping you were cooking that."

"I am. And no, I don't need anything but the formula." Kelly shook her head. "But that doesn't matter anyway. The roads are coated with ice. You can't drive."

"So I'll walk," he said, putting his coat back on. "Hey, I'm a Combat Rescue Officer, and I've already rescued a cat this morning. How hard can it be to rescue some formula, too?"

Since it was butt-freezing cold, and he'd have to walk the two miles and back, Gabe decided not to wait for an answer. Instead he wanted to plant a seed in her head. One that would get him a little closer to being a full-time dad to a baby who deserved nothing less.

He looked Kelly right in the eyes. "But just know that when I get back, the sleeping on it is done, and I expect an answer to my marriage proposal," Gabe told her. "And the answer I'm expecting is yes."

CHAPTER SIX

KELLY CHECKED THE time again while she paced from the kitchen to the living room and back. Gabe had been gone much too long.

Four hours.

That was a lifetime out in the cold and ice, and for some reason her calls to him were going straight to voice mail. Maybe the weather was responsible for that, too, but Kelly's imagination was causing her to think the worst.

Sweet heaven, was Gabe all right?

She couldn't help but think back to her parents' car accident. Not caused by icy roads but rather by a drunken driver. They were good people, and something horrible had happened to them.

Something horrible could be happening to Gabe, too.

Noel whimpered and looked up from the whirling butterfly mobile that Kelly had attached to her bassinet. The baby was probably sensing her mother's frayed nerves.

And they were indeed frayed.

Things weren't exactly in a good place between Gabe and her, and now he was out there. Yes, he was doing something important, getting Noel's formula, but she could have given the baby the other formula. Of course, she should have just remembered to get the cans she'd already bought in the first place. There'd been a lot going on with Gabe's homecoming, but she still should have remembered something that important.

Kelly scooped up Noel when she whimpered again, and she continued her pacing with the baby cradled in her arms. Continued looking out the windows, too, for any sign of Gabe or anyone else who might be coming up the road to deliver bad news.

"He'll be back soon," she whispered to Noel, trying to soothe the baby and herself. Gabe would be back soon, and he would want an answer to the proposal. Or rather the ultimatum.

And the answer I'm expecting is yes.

Kelly wasn't sure what the consequences of saying no would be, but it was what she'd have to tell him. She couldn't leave Sugar Springs.

Could she?

She paced, mulled that over, paced some more, and it didn't take long for the movement to put Noel to sleep. Kelly eased the baby back in the bassinet and glanced over at Mrs. Saunders's house.

Maybe she should get the woman to stay with Noel while she went out looking for Gabe.

Kelly reached for the phone to give Mrs. Saunders a call, but before she could press in the number, she saw something. At first, it seemed to be a shadow in the misting frozen fog, but she kept staring at it and finally saw something she wanted to see.

Gabe.

Not hurt and not in some ditch as she'd imagined. But here.

Thank God.

He was walking on the side of the road, a bag in each

hand. His shoulders were hunched against the cold, head slightly down, but he was keeping a steady, swift pace toward the house. Kelly grabbed a blanket throw from the sofa and hurried out onto the porch.

"You're all right," she blurted out, and Kelly made her way down the steps and into the yard so she could put the blanket around him.

"Were you worried about me?" The corner of his mouth lifted in that damnable smile that made her want to throttle him and kiss him at the same time.

Kelly went with the kiss.

The relief flooded through her. He was not only all right, but he could smile at a time like this when she was clearly worried. But one touch of her mouth to his, and it wasn't just a flood of relief.

No.

This was that fiery heat that she remembered in perfect detail. Heat that she'd longed for.

And was now getting.

Outside, in the freezing cold.

Gabe did his part to up that heat. Despite the bags, his arms went around her, pulling her closer and closer until they were slapped right against each other. Body to body, and with her own body wanting a heck of a lot more from him than just a kiss.

"The baby," he managed to say.

That jolted her back to reality fast, and Kelly untangled herself from him so that she could hurry back inside. Even though she'd left the door open a fraction, the room was still toasty warm and Noel had stayed sound asleep.

"You didn't answer my calls," she said, the frayed nerves still right there at the surface.

"My phone died, and I'd left the charger in my rental car. I stopped by and picked it up."

Gabe came in behind her, setting the bags on the floor and closing the door. He looked down at Noel, smiled and, in the same motion, took hold of Kelly and pulled her right back to him.

"I was just relieved that you were okay," she said, a split second before he kissed her again.

"I'm just relieved that you kissed me," he countered.

And Gabe returned the kiss a thousandfold.

Oh, he was so good at it, too. Just the right pressure from his mouth. The right grip of his arms around her. He was strong, muscled and pulled her right into that grip as if he were in charge.

Sadly, he was in charge. When it came to this anyway.

Probably because he fired every nerve in her body.

It was because of the heat that she didn't stop him. The kiss went on way too long, leaving her breathless, giddy and apparently stupid. The last thing she needed was to be kissing Gabe. Not with that marriage proposal lingering between them.

Talk about her sending him mixed messages.

Hours earlier she'd said no to his proposal, and now she was letting him kiss the living daylights out of her.

Heck, it was mixed messages for her own body, too, and that's why Kelly finally moved out of his grip. Of course, moving away from him didn't rid her of the heat. Not a chance. Looking at that drop-dead-hot face only made it worse.

"That was a complication I didn't need," she mumbled.

He flinched a little, as if she'd cursed at him or something. "Sometimes, complications are the spice of life."

"I thought variety was."

Gabe smiled again, obviously making his point. With her grounded roots, she hadn't been a big fan of variety, spice or complications.

The kiss had been the exception.

And he knew it.

Even if things were still unsettled between them, one thing for certain was this blasted attraction. It was clouding her head at a time when she needed clarity.

He stared at her for several long moments. Maybe waiting for this conversation to turn to the proposal, or to the possibility of another kiss, but Kelly only shook her head. That earned her a heavy sigh from him, and his face dropped a bit, but it didn't last.

"The formula," he said, holding up one of the bags.

"Thank you." And she meant it. Many men probably wouldn't have gone out in the cold for a baby's preferred formula, but she'd known her entire life that Gabe wasn't like most men.

Or maybe that was the effects of the kiss still talking.

Gabe set the formula on the coffee table and held up the other bag. "Christmas presents."

Kelly did a double take of the bag. "Where'd you get Christmas presents? Everything's closed in Sugar Springs."

"Yep, but Herman Newman opened Snapshots and Whatnots so I could do a little shopping. Well, he did after I pounded on the door for a while," he added in a mumble. "He even wrapped the gifts for me. Sort of."

She didn't want to know how much that'd cost Gabe. Herman wasn't exactly the kind of man to get caught up in the holiday spirit, and it would have taken plenty of cash—Herman didn't take checks or credit cards—

not only to get presents on Christmas Eve but to wrap them, too.

"For Noel," Gabe said, taking out a present.

Yes, it was indeed wrapped in newspaper and tied with a frayed red-yarn bow, but the shape of it told Kelly exactly what was inside. "You got her a football?"

"Not just any ol' football. It's the one from the district championship from Ross's and my senior year."

A district championship that they'd won.

Kelly had seen the football in the store, had even asked once how much it cost, but Herman had said it wasn't for sale. There were so many happy memories attached to that football since she'd been in the bleachers watching Gabe throw the winning touchdown to Ross.

"Herman said Coach Myers gave him the football after the game," Gabe added, "but I suspect somebody like Delbert took it from the locker room and sold it to Herman."

Yes, she was betting the same thing. But it was signed by most of the team and would indeed be a good keepsake for Noel. Something that family would pass down to family.

"And I got her this," Gabe said, taking out the next gift.

This one was wrapped in pink tissue paper, and the shape also gave it away.

"It's the antique angel doll." Kelly's breath caught in her throat a little. "From the top left shelf behind Herman's cash register."

Gabe made a *ding-ding-ding* sound as if she'd guessed something right on a game show.

"I always loved that doll," she admitted. "I guess Herman told you that?"

"He didn't mention it. Instead, he was trying to sell me the limited-edition rubber ducky that was still inside the box, but I figured every little girl needs an angel doll to go along with a football. Besides, the angel reminds me of the wings on my CRO badge."

Yes, it did, and that was one of the reasons Kelly had been drawn to it in the first place. That and the silk dress and blue eyes.

Eyes the same color as Gabe's.

"I'm sure Noel will love it when she's old enough to play with it." Kelly took the packages and slipped them under the tree next to the other toys she'd bought the baby and the gift from Ross that Gabe had given to her at the library.

"It probably seems a little silly to wait until tomorrow to open it," Kelly added, "since I already know what it is and Noel's too young to realize what's going on—"

"Doesn't seem silly at all. Opening presents on Christmas morning is a great tradition." Gabe took yet another present from the bag. "This one's for you."

Unlike the others, the shape didn't give this one away.

"Herman actually had a gift box to fit it," Gabe added.

She gave the eight-inch-square box a little shake. Something rattled around inside, but she had no idea what it was. "Thank you, but I didn't get you a gift."

"Sure you did. When you ran outside with the blanket and kissed me, that was a one-of-a-kind present." He paused. "Was that a limited-edition kiss, Kelly, or will there be more of those?"

There was still a trace of the smile on his mouth when he asked that, but it melted away when she just stared at him. Gabe didn't exactly sigh, but Kelly figured there was a heavy sigh somewhere inside him.

"One last present," he said and took out the small package. "But unlike the others, we're opening this one now."

Her heart jumped to her throat.

Because this one wasn't wrapped, and it was a jewelry box. The kind that held a ring.

Gabe flipped it open with his thumb.

"Now, Herman did mention that you looked at this often," Gabe added.

And there it was.

She managed a nod, but it was hard to do much of anything with her heart still in her throat.

The white-gold ring had tapered ends, folding onto each other, and making it resemble angel wings. Not the ornate ones on the angel doll or Gabe's CRO badge. This was more of a delicate swirl, the way an artist would see an angel.

She shook her head. "I can't accept this. It's too expensive."

That was the first thing that came to mind. However, there was an even bigger objection to this particular gift.

After all, it was a ring.

From Gabe.

Along with his proposal, which made this an engagement ring.

Gabe shrugged. "Herman said you'd taken a *shine* to it. I didn't have enough cash for it, so he's holding my credit card and my watch until I give him the money."

"Does this ring go along with your marriage proposal?" she asked when she finally gathered enough breath to speak.

He made another *ding-ding-ding* sound. It was light-hearted considering the seriousness of the moment. It almost seemed as if he was trying to guard his heart, or something.

"It does," he answered.

Those two words hung like a heavy weight in the air. And on her.

"I can't get out of the military right away," he continued when she didn't say anything. "Not for at least two more years, but I'll do whatever it takes to be a father to Noel and a husband to you."

She waited, in part because she lost her breath again, but mostly it was to see what if anything he would add to that.

Was there anything he could add that would change her mind?

Kelly still wasn't convinced that marriage and being a full-time dad would make Gabe happy. And making him miserable wasn't something she could live with. She cared too much about him for that.

However, there was something he could say that might sway her. Might.

The L-word.

But there was no mention of love or even his feelings for her. No verbal repeat of the marriage proposal, either. Just the look on his face that told her he'd sacrifice what he was to be a father to Noel. It was an honorable act coming from an honorable man.

However, it wasn't enough.

"I can't give you the answer that you think you want, Gabe." She closed the ring box and put it back in his hand.

He stared at the box for a long time. "Sleep on it one

more night," he finally said. "Come Christmas morning, if the answer's no, then I'll see if I can come up with something else."

She'd expected the first part but not the last. "Something else?"

He pressed a kiss on her cheek but didn't explain what he meant. However, Kelly quickly filled in the blanks.

Was he surrendering?

Was Gabe giving up on this notion of marriage and family?

Both were good questions, but the biggest one was the question that Kelly had herself.

Was this a battle that she truly wanted to win?

CHAPTER SEVEN

TRYING TO CLEAR out the remnants of a bad dream, Gabe stared out the guest room window and watched the sun lighten up the horizon. There were no real sunrise colors yet, just the darkness turning to gray. It'd be morning soon.

Christmas morning.

It'd been a while since that'd even had any meaning to him. Even when he wasn't deployed, he usually volunteered to work on Christmas Day so that other officers could spend time with their families.

Now he'd be spending Christmas with Noel. His baby girl. And while Gabe would treasure every moment of the day, it was also bittersweet.

The ice was already melting. He could see the icicles on the eaves dripping, and once the sun was up, it wouldn't take long for the roads to clear. That was winter in central Texas. An ice storm one day, and the next might see temperatures into the sixties. A clear road would add yet another level to that bittersweetness.

Because Kelly might just tell him to leave.

She certainly hadn't asked him to stay. Nor had she accepted his proposal or the ring. It was still in the box on the nightstand next to the bed.

Bittersweet indeed.

Of course, he'd never been certain that she would

accept it anyway. When Herman had mentioned that Kelly had tried it on a time or two or three, Gabe had seen immediately why she'd loved it. The clean lines of the design. Both an heirloom and modern look.

Like Kelly herself.

Even if she turned his proposal down flat, Gabe would leave it for her. One day she might just consider it a gift from him and not a ring with strings attached.

He listened to hear if there were any sounds of Kelly or Noel being awake.

Nothing.

He'd left the guest room door open so he could hear and see if Kelly came out of her bedroom, but it'd been quiet for a while now. Kelly had fed the baby a bottle about two hours earlier, around four, and Gabe wasn't sure if that meant she'd sleep later or still wake up for breakfast. He was hoping for the latter so he could spend as much time with Noel as possible.

Another piece of the dream drifted through his head again. More of a nightmare than a dream, though. These images had actually happened, fragments of rescues that hadn't gone so well.

Times he'd failed.

As bad as the failures were, and they were bad, he tried not to let them plague him to the point of PTSD. Thankfully, he'd been able to put his life into little compartments and shut the bad stuff away.

Most of it anyway.

His mother had given him lots of practice in that area.

And now that he was dredging up the past, maybe his relationship with his mother was the reason he'd drifted from one woman to another.

Great.

Here he was analyzing himself. He wouldn't mind if he could figure out how that would help him with Kelly, but reliving his past was just plain depressing.

Gabe dropped back down on the bed, the feather mattress cocooning around him, and he tucked his arms behind his head so he could think this out. Noel had brought him to this point, but there was an equally important facet to this.

"Kelly," he mumbled.

She'd been part of the dream, too. Not the nightmare part, though, but the visions of her beautiful face had worked their way into the images. It was so clear that Gabe could still see her. In fact, for just a flicker of a moment, he thought the dream had come back, but this was the real deal.

Kelly stepped into the doorway of the guest room.

She was wearing her usual flannel pj's. Hardly sexy, but she managed to make them look darn good.

Naked would look even better passed through his mind.

Gabe told that thought to take a long hike. There were lots of reasons Kelly would come into his room, and getting naked wasn't necessarily one of them.

"Is Noel okay?" he asked, getting his mind off the way the soft flannel skimmed her body and that naked thought.

While he was at it, he pulled the quilt over his midsection. He wasn't a modest man, but he was wearing only his boxers, and just in case he got any more of those naked thoughts, it was best if he covered up.

"Noel's fine. She's still sleeping." Kelly had a baby monitor that she set on the nightstand, and with her other hand she handed him something that she'd kept hidden behind her back.

A present.

Wrapped, at that. Not with newspapers or tissue, either, like the ones he'd bought from Herman. This was more of her hand-designed stuff, and once he had the paper off, he lifted the top of the gift box.

"It's not much," she said. Kelly eased down on the edge of the bed next to him and watched. "But I wanted to get you something."

Gabe liked it before he even opened it, simply because it was a gift from Kelly, but he liked it even more when he saw what she had done.

A drawing.

Part of it was a sketch of his CRO badge. A guardian angel holding the world globe in her arms, but Kelly had gone beyond the basic design on the badge. With strokes of pen and charcoal, she'd brought the angel to life, and that wasn't all. Next to it, there was yet more life.

Noel's precious, sleeping face.

Kelly had captured that deep, peaceful sleep, including the faint smile that Noel seemed to have most of the time. It was the exact image that he had of her in his head, and here it was—all caught on paper.

"When did you have time to do this?" he asked.

"Last night, when I told you I was going to bed early."

"I thought you said that so you could get away from me and have some time to think."

"That, too," she admitted. "I know it probably seems stupid, giving you a sketch of something you wear almost every day," Kelly continued, "and you can take actual photos of Noel. But I wanted to draw you something."

"It's perfect," Gabe managed to say.

Man, his throat had gone dry.

Seeing his baby together with his badge was like a gentle jolt. As if the cosmos was giving him a wake-up call, and suddenly some things that had been troubling him made a whole lot of sense.

"I love her," Gabe admitted. Even though there were some serious emotions running through him, he still risked looking up at Kelly. "If you want me to leave, I will, but please don't shut me out of her life and yours."

Kelly swallowed hard. Apparently, he wasn't the only one with a suddenly dry throat. "What you do in the military is important. It's *you*. I won't ask you to give that up."

She was right. He was a CRO and had managed to make some key rescues over the years. Rescues that'd saved lives. But he wouldn't be much of a man if he didn't give that same kind of time and energy to Noel.

Even if it meant giving up the career he loved.

And even if Kelly didn't ask.

Gabe was about to tell her that, too, but she leaned in and kissed him. He hadn't even seen it coming, but he sure as heck felt it. Oh, man. One touch of her mouth to his, and all the memories came flooding back. Memories of the kisses from the day before. And from that other night they'd kissed out on the sofa.

Memories that'd led them to her bedroom. To her bed. And then to one of the most memorable nights of his life.

"Noel," he reminded her.

"If she wakes up, we'll hear her on the monitor."

Good thing, then, that Kelly had brought it with her because the kissing just continued. Of course, Gabe didn't do anything to stop it, and he wasn't sure he even wanted to.

All right, he was positive he didn't want to, but he still did have some doubts about whether or not this should be happening.

She slid her hand around the back of his neck, pulling him closer to her. It was a dangerous move. Especially since they were already in the bed, and he wanted her more than his next breath. Another bad combination, like the one a year ago with the Jack Daniel's and her tears. There was no Jack this morning, but there was enough heat to fuel an inferno.

Too bad Gabe only made it worse.

Despite his reservations, he hooked his arm around her, snapping her closer and kissing her until all shreds of common sense were gone. But Kelly wasn't exactly fighting to hang on to her common sense, either. However, she was hanging on to him, and she didn't object one bit when Gabe deepened the kiss.

In fact, she made a silky sound of pleasure that had him wanting a whole lot more.

More that he couldn't have.

Could he?

Gabe was trying to fight through the argument that a certain part of him was making. A darn good argument, too. But he knew this couldn't continue unless...

Kelly took care of the *unless* for him.

She pulled a foil-wrapped condom from her pj pocket. "I got it from Ross's room," she said, her voice barely a whisper. "Just in case I got the nerve to go through with this."

That caused him to pause a moment. "Nerve?"

"I'm not sure this is the right thing to do."

Bingo. They were of a like mind.

Unfortunately, they were of a like body, too, since she leaned in and kissed him again before he could weigh their options and consequences. That was the problem with really good kisses. Options and consequences didn't stand a chance against them.

"You do want to do this, right?" she asked.

"More than I want air to breathe." A lot more. "And thanks for getting the condom."

It saved him from having to scramble around Ross's bedroom looking for one. Because there was no doubt in Gabe's mind that he would have done it. It no longer seemed to matter if this was right, wrong or yet another complication. He was well past that stage, and judging from the urgency of Kelly's kiss, so was she.

Maybe it was the thought that she would change her mind or that the baby would wake up, but speed suddenly seemed to matter. Or maybe speed was just because of the urgency that was burning him alive.

The urgency to have her at least one more time.

So Gabe took. Kelly did as well, and he grappled with her pj's. She didn't have much to grapple with since Gabe was wearing only his boxers, and with Gabe's help, she managed to rid him of them without even breaking the kiss.

She was clever.

But Gabe made some clever moves of his own. He went after her pj's. The moment he got her top off, he got another jolt. One of those incredible reminders of just how beautiful she was. Of course, he'd seen her naked that other time, but with the sunlight streaming through the window, she was a vision.

Perfect.

Having a baby had filled her out a little, giving her curves that Gabe couldn't wait to explore. He wouldn't have minded savoring that view a little longer, but the kissing returned. This time with her mouth on his neck. And he was lost.

Willingly lost.

They hadn't exactly had a ton of experience driving each other crazy with kisses and touches, but her instincts were pretty darn good. She was making him burn, and judging from the hot fire in her eyes, she was already there.

But *there* meant getting her naked first.

Kelly helped him shimmy off her pj bottoms, her hands sliding over him and making him crazier than he already was. Something he hadn't thought possible. The moment he got the condom on, she reached for him, pulling him on top of her. Gabe thought maybe the world had tipped on its axis when he eased into her.

Yeah, the earth definitely moved.

Mercy, the pleasure was blinding, and while it ratcheted up the urgency even more, he slowed down. Because as much as he needed Kelly—and he did need her—he also wanted to savor every moment of this.

Gabe kissed her as gently as he could manage. Looked into her eyes. There was so much he wanted to say to her. But then she adjusted their positions, lifting her hips, and the need fueled itself again.

He moved inside her, knowing this would all end too soon. Of course, a week was too soon when it came to Kelly.

Later, he might get a chance to tell her that, too.

But for now, the fire was in control, and Gabe just went with it. It didn't take long before he heard Kelly make that urgent sound, indicating her pleasure. Her grip tightened on his back, and she surrendered to the fire.

Gabe buried his face against her neck, drawing in her scent and taste at the same time when they kissed. And he surrendered right along with her.

CHAPTER EIGHT

KELLY DREW IN a deep breath and let the slack feeling of pleasure slide right through her entire body. The only word that came to mind was *perfect,* and even that didn't seem enough for what'd just happened.

Again.

Now that she'd gotten what she wanted—Gabe—she should be satisfied. Or at least worried that she'd screwed up things between them forever. But the only thing her slack brain could latch on to was that in this moment she was incredibly happy and feeling very, very good.

"I seduced you," she mumbled.

He lifted his head, located her mouth and kissed the breath right out of her. "I didn't put up much of a fight."

No, he hadn't. Not that she'd expected he would. Gabe and she had been skirting around this heat since his homecoming. Heck, even before that. Even before the night she'd gotten pregnant with Noel.

He glanced at the monitor, causing Kelly to do the same. Noel was still asleep but stirring a little. It probably wouldn't be long before she woke. That was Kelly's cue to put her clothes back on, but when Gabe moved off her, he motioned for her to stay put.

"I'll be right back," he said, heading to the bathroom.

"Then I think I owe you a snuggling session before Noel wakes up and we open the gifts."

That sounded heavenly. The perfect end to what'd already happened, so Kelly just lay there. Waiting for him to return.

Unfortunately, her common sense returned, too.

This didn't solve anything. All right, it did solve this overwhelming need she had for him. Temporarily, anyway. But it didn't work out any of the serious issues between them. Still, she hadn't been able to stop herself. After the way Gabe had left things the day before, she thought he might be ready to finish his Christmas visit and leave.

Her heart wasn't ready for that yet.

Neither was the rest of her, she realized, when Gabe came back into the room, and she got a long look at his naked body.

Good grief. No one had a right to look that good.

As promised, he slipped back into bed with her, easing her against him. The moment was perfect, and she braced herself for the serious talk that they had to have.

But no talk.

Just the rhythmic sound of his breathing and his heart beating against hers. It didn't take long for Kelly to relax again, and she might have even fallen back asleep if she hadn't heard a strange sound.

Both Gabe and she turned toward the baby monitor. She could easily see Noel on the screen, and the baby hadn't moved since the last time Kelly had checked. But there was definitely the sound of someone moving around. It took her a moment to realize the sound wasn't coming from inside the house but rather the porch.

"Someone's here," she warned Gabe, and Kelly barreled out of bed, reaching for her pj's.

She was still putting them on when she heard the key in the lock, and the door flew open. The cold air immediately rushed in.

And so did her visitor.

Except it wasn't exactly a visitor.

It was Ross.

Her heartbeat went crazy fast, and so did Kelly. She yanked the pj top closed, but she didn't manage that before Ross got an eyeful. The front door was positioned just right for him to see directly into the guest room.

And Gabe was still pulling on his pants.

It didn't take much imagination to figure out what was going on, and judging from the way Ross's eyes narrowed to slits, he figured it out right away.

"I can explain," Kelly said at the exact moment that Gabe said, "Ross, we need to talk."

Gabe pulled on his T-shirt and carried his boots into the living room. He sat down on the sofa to put them on. Too bad he didn't have a flak vest that he could wear.

"I think it's a little late for talk," Ross snarled. And there was no doubt in her mind that it was a snarl.

Ross kicked the front door shut, dropping his equipment bag on the floor. He looked around, a long, sweeping glance before his glare settled on Gabe.

Oh, no.

Kelly could see where this was going, and she didn't like the destination. Best to try to diffuse this somehow, and she knew just where to start. She needed to get Ross talking, and maybe he'd talk instead of yell.

"Merry Christmas," she greeted, hoping she sounded

more welcoming than she felt. "I obviously wasn't expecting you. How'd you even get here?"

"Well, it wasn't easy, but after seeing that footage that Delbert emailed me, I had some serious motivation to get home. I caught the first flight out of Germany."

Delbert, of course.

Kelly hadn't forgotten about the news crew at the library, but with everything else going on, she'd put it on the back burner.

Bad idea.

Because it had now simmered to an overflowing boil.

"You got here fast," Kelly mumbled.

Ross fished his phone from his pocket and kept talking. "I took a taxi from the airport into town. The road was still too icy for him to drive here so I borrowed Herman's tractor. And now that we've gotten my travel itinerary out of the way, start talking and explain this."

Ross held up his phone, hit the play button on the video and the images of the incident at the library began to move across the screen. Kelly had known it was a gobsmacked moment for her.

Gabe, too.

But it really drilled the point home when she saw their startled expressions. Probably the same reaction Ross had had, but now that surprise had settled into a tight knot of anger.

"It's true," Gabe said, stepping around her and walking closer to Ross.

Definitely not a good idea, not with Ross's temper. Besides, Gabe might allow himself to be throttled just so that Ross could get some sibling justice that her brother in no way deserved.

However, Ross did deserve an explanation.

"I slept with Gabe a year ago and got pregnant," Kelly tossed out there. "I didn't tell him, or you, because I didn't want to make the deployment worse than it already was."

She hadn't thought it possible, but Ross's eyes narrowed even more, and though he probably couldn't see well, he aimed his next glare at Gabe. "I got that part. The part I'm not getting is why you slept with my sister in the first place."

Kelly opened her mouth to attempt to answer him, but Gabe stepped between Ross and her. "It just happened. Kelly and I didn't plan it, and I certainly wasn't thinking of you."

"You should have," Ross warned, his voice a low growl.

"Maybe. Probably," Gabe amended. "But I didn't. If you're going to blame anyone for this, blame me."

"Oh, I will. And I'll blame you for that, too." Ross tipped his head to the bed in the guest room. "One mistake I might be able to forgive. *Might*. But clearly you came here to repeat it."

Gabe shook his head. "I came here to talk with Kelly and see my daughter."

Another head tip to the bedroom. "That wasn't talking."

"Oh, for Pete's sake. Quit snapping at each other," she insisted.

Despite the warning glance that Gabe gave her to stay put, Kelly didn't. She headed straight for Ross until she was practically toe-to-toe with him. She loved her brother dearly, but sometimes his pigheadedness got to her.

Still, that didn't stop her from putting her arms around Ross and hugging him. "Welcome home."

Every muscle in his body was iron stiff, and he kept his glare nailed to Gabe. "A hug isn't going to fix this."

"I didn't expect it to, but I wanted to say that before I reminded you that I'm an adult, capable of making my own decisions. Gabe didn't lure me into bed. In fact, this time it was the other way around. We landed there together, but I'm the one who started it."

Ross had to get his teeth unclenched before he could speak. "You're my kid sister—"

"And Gabe is your best friend," she reminded him.

"He *was*," Ross snapped.

Oh, that hurt. Not just Gabe, but Kelly, as well. Gabe and Ross had been best friends since preschool, and she hated that she had come between them like this. The question was—how did she undo the damage and stop Ross from riding roughshod over both Gabe and her?

Kelly didn't have time even to think of a way to approach this because she heard Noel start to whimper. She thought Gabe might volunteer to get her, and he did look in that direction, but he motioned for her to get the baby.

"Don't you two dare fight," she warned them.

But the verbal fight started the moment she stepped out of the living room.

"Kelly wasn't supposed to be one of your conquests," Ross snarled.

"And she wasn't."

"Right," Ross said with a massive amount of skepticism. "I know the way you operate, Gabe. I know you glide from one woman's bed to the other, and you should have kept your hands—and the rest of your body parts—off Kelly."

Kelly scooped up Noel, kissing her and hoping that would be enough to soothe the baby. Noel probably wasn't hungry, but she wasn't exactly used to having two men yell around her. And Kelly made sure the yelling stopped the moment she went back into the living room.

"Use your inside voices," Kelly called out to them, hoping she sounded like a determined librarian who wasn't going to let a shouting match upset her baby.

But it was Noel who actually staved off more yelling.

Ross froze when he locked eyes with the baby, and Noel, in true precious form, smiled at her uncle. No way could a man stay angry or yell after that.

Kelly hoped.

"Sweet heaven," Ross mumbled. "She's real. A real baby. I mean, I saw her on the film that Delbert sent me, but it's different seeing her like this."

"Of course, she's real." Kelly went closer when Noel reached out to the newcomer. However, the baby's attention was quickly diverted when she spotted Gabe. Noel's smile got even bigger, and she reached for him instead.

As if it were the most natural thing in the world, Gabe took her and brushed a kiss on her forehead. "Merry Christmas, sweetheart."

That renewed the anger in Ross's eyes, and he looked on the verge of cursing. Instead, he turned away from them, apparently trying to gain control of his temper.

"You can't believe you'd be a good father," Ross challenged, the moment that he turned back around to face them. However, he didn't wait for Gabe to answer. "And what about Kelly, huh? Now she's got a baby to raise, thanks to you."

"I'll help her," Gabe said, but he couldn't continue because Ross cut him off.

"How the devil will you do that? You'll either accept that instructor job at Lackland Air Force Base or you'll go to another base. Either way, you won't be here in Sugar Springs, and we both know Kelly's not budging from this house."

Gabe nodded. "Lackland's less than an hour from here. I'll take the job and can see Noel often. Maybe even commute."

"But that's not a job you want," Kelly reminded him.

Gabe's thumb landed against his chest. "Well, it's one I want now."

It was happening. Gabe was compromising a career he loved. However, she could see that he loved Noel, too.

"There's no need for you to be assigned to Lackland," Ross said like some kind of divine decree that only a Norse god or a big brother could have managed. "My commitment to the military is up, and I can refuse another assignment and get out. That way, I can be here and help Kelly raise my niece."

That was one of the scenarios she'd dreamed of when she'd first learned she was pregnant. Her brother, home.

Safe.

No more combat. No more going months and months without seeing him. They could be a family again.

But there were also flaws with those scenarios.

For one, she hadn't thought Gabe would even want to be in the picture. It was clear from his proposal and the ring that he wanted to be.

Or did he?

Despite what'd just happened in the guest room, there'd still been no mention of loving her, only his desire to be with Noel. Well, he could do that and still stay in the military.

If that's what he wanted, that is.

But there was also another flaw with Ross's plan to move back.

"There aren't exactly a lot of jobs in Sugar Springs," she reminded her brother.

"I can teach at the military academy over in Fredericksburg. I've already made a call, and if I want the job, I can start next month. As far as I'm concerned, this is a done deal."

Both Gabe and Ross looked at her. No doubt waiting to see what she thought of that done deal. However, she didn't get a chance to say anything because Ross pointed to the Christmas tree. Specifically to the present from Ross that Gabe had brought with him.

"Open it," Ross insisted. "You'll see that we can have the life you want. Right here at home."

Not exactly a welcoming invitation, but Kelly couldn't imagine what was in that little box that would smooth all of this over. Still, she went to the tree, knelt down and, despite her trembling fingers, opened Ross's gift.

It was a cream-colored business card with fancy lettering.

"Deidre McIntyre?" Kelly questioned.

"She's a top-notch agent who represents illustrators. Her nephew's a combat medic, and I met him on one of the rescues. We got to talking, and he called her for me. One thing led to another, and I emailed her some copies of your drawings, and she wants to talk to you. She believes she can get you work as an illustrator. You have an appointment with her right after the holidays."

Kelly stood there and let that sink in. It was the stuff of dreams. Something she'd always desperately wanted, and here it was. Falling right into her lap.

And she could thank Ross for it.

The giddiness rushed right through her, and giggling, she launched herself into his arms. It was yet another piece of that perfect dream scenario. Her, in her family home. With Ross. With the perfect job.

And now with the perfect baby.

It just didn't get any better than that.

Did it?

Well, it wasn't immediately perfect because Gabe was still staring at her, and Noel started to fuss. Really fuss. It took only a few seconds to turn into a full-fledged cry. One that Kelly recognized. Noel was likely wet and needed a diaper change. Since that wasn't a job that Gabe had perfected just yet, Kelly had to take the baby.

"Don't yell at each other while I'm gone, and don't continue this conversation without me," she insisted.

Did they listen?

No.

When she carried Noel into the bedroom, she could hear Ross and Gabe talking. At least they weren't yelling, though. They were speaking in hushed tones, and she couldn't make out what they were saying. However, she could practically feel the emotion and the tension.

She prayed Ross wasn't threatening to kill Gabe.

While she was praying, Kelly added another prayer.

That there'd be a Christmas miracle and that Gabe and Ross would be as happy as she was right now.

"Mommy might be an illustrator," she whispered to Noel. "And Uncle Ross is coming home for good."

And even though there was no way the baby could know what that meant, Noel grinned a big gummy grin and kicked her arms and legs. It slowed down the diapering process a bit, but Kelly was glad that Noel shared her happiness in her own baby way.

Kelly was about to head back into the living room, but she caught a glimpse of herself in the mirror.

Mercy. A train wreck stared back at her.

Yes, it was vain, but if Ross, Gabe and she were about to have a good hashing out, then she didn't want them to see her like this. She freshened up a bit, brushed her hair and put on a robe. Not exactly battle gear, but better than just the pj's.

Pulling in a long breath, she scooped up Noel and went back into the living room.

No voices.

Because no one was talking.

However, Ross was standing by the window looking out.

Alone.

That set off plenty of alarms inside her.

"Where's Gabe?" she asked, glancing into the guest room. No sign of him there, either.

"Gone," Ross said, and he mumbled it so softly that it took a moment for it to sink in.

"Gone?" Gripping Noel in her arms, she hurried to the window, practically shouldering Ross aside.

The ice was melting, creating more of that hazy mist, and it took her a moment to spot him. Gabe was on

Herman's red rusted tractor, and he was headed up the road toward town.

"Gone," Kelly repeated. "But why?"

Ross made a sound as if the answer was obvious. "Because he finally came to his senses and listened to the truth."

"The truth?" Her throat was squeezing shut, and had someone clamped a meaty fist around her heart? "And what truth would that be?"

"That he can't give you what you need," Ross quickly provided. "I made him see that he'll make you miserable if he stays, along with ruining any chance we have of salvaging what's left of our friendship."

Ross paused, added a firm nod. "Gabe said he'd call you after he's had time to cool off so you two can work out visitation with Noel."

Kelly could only shake her head. "Why?" she repeated because she didn't know what else to say.

Ross slipped his arm around her waist, pulled her closer to him. "Gabe did what he does best—he left."

CHAPTER NINE

THE TRACTOR BOBBLED over the ice-slick road, and Gabe had to fight to keep it out of the ditch. A tractor wasn't his preferred mode of transportation, especially one that appeared to be on its last leg, but if he hadn't gotten out of the house, he would have either punched Ross or exploded.

Either would have made this mess only worse.

You don't deserve Kelly and Noel.

Ross's words just kept echoing in his head. True words that Gabe couldn't dismiss. He didn't deserve them. Didn't deserve a chance at marriage or fatherhood that he hadn't earned. Besides, now that Ross was back and with plans to stay at their family home with Kelly, Gabe was just a third wheel.

Not exactly a welcome thought.

It was about as welcoming as the chilly look Kelly had given him after she realized she could have it all with her brother. Of course, that chill might have been partly shock. Gabe had to concede that, but she certainly hadn't shouted out for him to stay.

Now he had to regroup and come at this from a different direction.

That started with his getting some kind of split custody for Noel. He wasn't walking out on his baby, but he needed to clear his head and figure out the best way to do that. Hire a nanny, maybe. Accept the assignment to Lackland Air Force Base and possibly buy a house close to Sugar Springs. One way or another, he would be a big part of Noel's life.

Even if he couldn't be married to Kelly.

With her frosty looks and silence, Kelly had made it clear enough that Ross was right. That Gabe wasn't father or husband material. That's why she'd turned down his multiple proposals.

But then, why had she come to his bed?

Yeah, why?

That question pushed Ross's condemning words right out of Gabe's head, and some new ones replaced them. What if that trip to his bed had been Kelly's way of *sleeping on it?* Maybe she was still trying to decide what to do.

Except now her fantasy life had come true.

An exciting new job prospect as an illustrator. Ross safe at the home she loved. A precious baby to raise.

Perfect.

Gabe couldn't argue that in her mind it was indeed perfection, but he still brought the tractor to a stop.

Was it really perfect?

Instead of sulking over Ross's dose of truth, Gabe doled out his own truth reminder. Even if Kelly had *perfect,* it was still Christmas Day, and by God, he not only was going to spend it with Noel, but he was going to get a direct answer to his proposal.

Even if that answer was a big, messy no.

Even if it put a permanent wedge between Ross and him.

Even if Ross punched him.

He turned the tractor around. It wasn't easy, and he

darn near went in the ditch again. That wouldn't stop him, but Herman wouldn't appreciate having his tractor muddied up that way.

Gabe put the pedal to the metal and cruised back to the house at what felt like turtle speed. The moment he brought the tractor to a stop, he barreled off and rushed back inside.

Ross was there, right where he'd left him at the door. But Kelly was there, too, and she was holding Noel in her arms.

"You left," Kelly snapped, sounding as angry as Ross looked.

Gabe was certain that he looked a little confused. Kelly was clearly riled, and she had nothing to be riled about. Or so he'd thought.

"Yeah, I left," Gabe admitted. "Because I needed to cool off and wasn't thinking straight. But I'm back now."

"You left," Kelly repeated. "How could you?"

"Again, wasn't thinking straight. Am now."

That only seemed to fluster her even more. Well, his stupidity flustered him, too. Not Noel, though. She reached for him, and when Kelly didn't hand her over, Gabe went closer and got a very sloppy kiss from his baby.

He couldn't have asked for a better Christmas present.

"You don't deserve them," Ross repeated.

"No. But I'll do whatever it takes so I do deserve them. You can give Kelly this house. Your safety. Your help raising Noel. But I can give her *that*." Gabe pointed to the present he'd gotten for her.

Shaking her head, Kelly volleyed glances between

him and the gift, and she finally handed off Noel to him so she could go to the Christmas tree. Gabe got yet another kiss and the biggest smile in Texas from Noel.

Those Christmas presents just kept on coming. And the best part? He could get this every day of the year.

"Daddy loves you, sweet girl," Gabe told his daughter.

Since he'd apparently captured Noel's heart, and vice versa, he needed to try to work the same miracle with Kelly. He made a quick trip to the guest room and came back with the ring.

"That marriage proposal is still on the table," Gabe continued while Kelly picked up the gift from beneath the tree. "I'll commute to the base, or I can buy a house and move every stick of furniture, every knickknack from here to there. You'll still have your home, but it'll just be in a new house."

"You proposed?" Ross asked.

Gabe nodded and braced himself for another reminder from Ross that he didn't deserve what he was holding in his arms. Nobody deserved anything this good, but Gabe was plenty glad he had her.

"I even read your manual on diapering last night so I'd do a better job of it," Gabe added. "I'll do whatever it takes."

Kelly opened the wrapping on the present. Then, she pulled off the top of the box.

"It's a picture," she said, taking out the photo in the plain black frame. "A picture," she repeated with gallons of emotion in her voice.

Tears sprang to her eyes, and Gabe thought they might be of the happy variety since she was smiling.

She pressed her hand to her mouth, those tear-filled eyes pouring over the image.

"A picture?" Ross questioned, probably because he couldn't imagine any picture getting that reaction from his sister.

Maybe Ross still didn't get it even after he saw it.

But Kelly sure did.

It was a photo from the senior prom that Gabe had found in Herman's stash. An ordinary group shot of couples slow dancing on the gym floor under the tacky handmade Midnight in Paris banner.

Well, it was almost ordinary.

Except the camera had managed to capture the odd couple on the far edge near the bleachers.

Gabe and Kelly.

She was a good foot shorter than he was and wearing a yellow cotton dress more suited for a picnic than the prom, but she was looking up at him as if he'd given her the moon and some stars. Gabe had been too young and stupid to see it that night, but he saw it now.

The love.

And maybe even Ross finally saw that, too, because he made a grunting sound. Not of anger. This one had some surprise in it.

"If you let me, Kelly, I can give you *that*," Gabe told her, pointing to the fourteen-year-old image. "Because as much as you love me, I'm in love with you even more."

And he held his breath, waiting to hear what she had to say about that.

It was a gamble. She could turn him down flat, claiming that love wasn't enough, but Gabe figured this kind of love was enough to make just about any-thing right.

Kelly kept staring at the picture, kept swiping away tears, and she slowly lifted her gaze. Looking scared. At first. Then, just looking at him with that same ex-pression she had in the picture.

She scrambled off the floor and ran toward him. Noel obviously thought it was a game because she laughed. Gabe laughed, too, and he shifted the baby enough so he could pull Kelly into the crook of his arm. It was more than close enough for him to kiss her.

And Kelly kissed him right back.

It was probably too hot of a kiss considering they were holding their baby, but then Kelly and he had al-ways done things a little different. Her, falling in love with him when she was kid. Him, not falling in love with her sooner. He should have seen and felt this years ago.

Thankfully, it wasn't too late, and it'd be plenty of fun making up all that lost time with Kelly.

If she'd let him.

"You love me," Kelly said on a rise of breath.

"Yeah. A lot," Gabe clarified. And in case she still hadn't gotten it, he pulled her back for another kiss while trying to take the ring from the box.

Ross mumbled something under his breath. Mild profanity. "Hand me Noel so you can do this right."

Gabe looked at his old friend and passed him the baby. By taking his niece, it wasn't exactly Ross's over-whelming endorsement, but it was a start.

And everything had to start somewhere.

Kelly and he had started at the prom fourteen years ago. Now Gabe put the ring on her finger and pulled her back into his arms for another dance. There was no music, but Noel cooed, giving them the perfect sound to accompany the perfect dance.

"No more sleeping on it," Gabe whispered to Kelly. "You're marrying me because you love me. Right?"

"Yeah," she repeated, her mouth bending into a smile before she returned the kiss. "And we'll buy that house at whatever base you happen to be assigned."

That froze them all. Well, not Noel. She continued to coo, but both Ross and Gabe stared at Kelly.

"I don't have to be here for it still to be a home," Kelly said. Not in a wimpy, *I'm not certain about this* tone, either. "I can make a home anywhere with you and Noel."

Now it was Gabe's turn to get misty-eyed, and his heart felt big enough to burst.

"Does this mean we won't be getting out of the Air Force?" Ross asked.

"Yes," Kelly and Gabe said in unison.

The breath that Ross blew out sure sounded like one of relief. "And you're certain about marrying Gabe and moving off?" Ross pressed.

Kelly nodded. "More certain than I've ever been of anything."

Gabe knew exactly how she felt.

All in all, it was a darn good unexpected gift, one they could sleep on for the rest of their lives.

* * * * *

For Eugenia Kaleta with all my love

You made every Christmas special

NAVY JOY

Geri Krotow

Dear Reader,

It's an honor to be included in an anthology with my Romance Veteran (Romvet) sisters Lindsay McKenna and Delores Fossen. We were asked to write stories that reflect the intense emotions surrounding military Christmas homecomings because we've all served on active duty, and Delores and I have been military spouses.

A Navy homecoming is like Christmas, no matter what the time of year, but I remember one in particular when my husband was due home early in December. Aircraft problems meant his arrival kept getting pushed back. The days before Daddy returns after six months away are fraught with excitement (the kids plan all kinds of fun and games to share with him), anxiety (will he still think I'm beautiful?) and activity. I'd bake his favorite desserts and cookies, and have a home-cooked meal waiting.

That Christmas homecoming, I left putting up our tree until the night before Steve flew in. I'd opted for our artificial tree, as cutting and hauling a real tree was too much to contemplate with two small children (ages five and eight) and a dog (and parrot!) in tow.

My son, ever the builder, insisted on helping, and his sister joined in. Another Navy spouse stopped by, and her jaw dropped when she saw my children, who'd taken off their pajamas and were down to their underwear, thanks to the heat coming from the woodstove. The kids were working on a tree that had a gaping hole in its side. All the branches were in the wrong places. Yet it was the most beautiful tree in spirit, as it was Daddy's homecoming tree.

As I wrote "Navy Joy" I was thinking of all the military families who are waiting for their homecoming, too. Many will spend the holiday apart from their active-duty member. The Christmas Steve was deployed is as strong and poignant a memory to me as that crazy Christmas tree. Please keep our military families in your thoughts and prayers this holiday season. I wish them and you the brightest star this Christmas Eve.

Merry Christmas!

Geri Krotow

CHAPTER ONE

Angelville, Whidbey Island
December 1

"C'MON, INTEGRITY. WE'RE HOME. I hope." Chief Petty Officer Ian Cairn coaxed the powerful Belgian Malinois out of the backseat of his Jeep Wrangler. At least he still had his car, unlike his home, which had been made uninhabitable by a burst pipe.

The sable-colored dog leaped down to the gravel driveway in her usual graceful manner. Ever since he'd met her, when his best friend Gary had introduced them, Integrity's inherent adroitness had impressed him.

When Gary's death at the hands of a sniper landed Integrity in Ian's care, Ian didn't hesitate. Gary had willed Integrity to him for reasons beyond Ian's understanding, since he'd never had a dog before, but he was determined to honor a sailor's dying wish.

Ian didn't consider himself a dog person. After only two weeks with Integrity, he didn't feel completely comfortable with her and wondered if he ever would. Not only that, their short time back on American soil had been fraught with the immediate need to find suitable housing. The responsibility to take the very best care of her stressed him more than he'd expected.

He looked at his phone to verify that he had the

correct address from the selection of furnished rentals accepting pets, which he'd found on Craigslist and the *Island News*' online real-estate listings. The address was 3 Farm Lane, Angelville, Whidbey Island. Tucked along the cliffs a few miles from Naval Air Station Whidbey Island, the tiny hamlet of Angelville was quaint and the perfect place to live while he got through his postdeployment blues.

And mourned the loss of his closest friend of over a dozen years.

"Put on your best manners, Integrity. It says they allow pets." He'd thought about leaving the dog in his truck, but he didn't feel right about abandoning her, even briefly. She'd arrived on island the same time he did—eight hours ago. Since then, he'd discovered that his home had significant water damage from a burst pipe, which had occurred after the woman who was supposed to be house-sitting for him had moved out. She'd been a friend of a friend, and he'd received a blunt email from her a month before his deployment ended, saying she was transferring off-island.

A prolonged freeze two weeks later led to his home being uninhabitable. Ian's neighbor had discovered it only after the water had flowed from the upstairs bathroom, down the main stairs, through his foyer and down into his basement. The same basement he'd spent three months finishing before he left on deployment. His neighbor had emailed him, but with Gary's death and Integrity's appearance in his life, he'd hoped they'd be able to at least rough it in the house until the repairs were made.

But then he'd walked into the freezing house with its stench of mildew....

In a blink his dreams of a simple Christmas shoot-ing pool and setting up the beer-brewing kit his brother had given him last Christmas were gone. At least for the next couple of months.

His house was unlivable, and he needed a place to stay ASAP. The base was off-limits unless he put Integrity in a kennel, and some instinct, some visceral emotion, had screamed to keep Integrity with him, no matter what.

His resolve was tested as he read *no pets* over and over again in the online rental ads. The last place he'd tried, a newer apartment complex, hadn't had the edict in print, so Ian had been hopeful until the gal at the leasing office had said, "No pets, no exceptions." Ian didn't bother to tell her that, like him, his dog was a war vet and had just lost her handler. Ian wanted to find the right place for him *and* Integrity. A place where they could unwind and work on bonding with each other, without worrying about whether the dog was really wel-come. Trying to locate a pet-friendly rental for them had turned his first day back home into a nightmare.

Integrity was in mourning for Chief Petty Officer Gary Barnes, who'd been Ian's best friend since Navy A School. They were fresh out of high school when they'd met, too eager to serve their country and get on with their lives to bother with college. Stationed together for two of the following three tours, they were more than friends—they were shipmates. They'd gotten each other through the highs and lows of Navy life and during that third tour downrange, had even found themselves in the same geographical area a few times.

When he'd headed downrange for his fifth wartime deployment, Ian's spirits had lifted as soon as he learned that Gary was in Afghanistan, too, with his East Coast squadron. They'd run into each other several times over the past seven months, the final time in a mess hall in Kabul, one week before a sniper's bullet took Gary out.

And left Integrity a canine orphan.

The farmhouse was lit from within, and Ian groaned at all the Christmas decorations that hung from the door and draped the porch railing, entwined with twinkling lights. Holiday reminders weren't high on his priority list, which had a shower and twelve hours of undisturbed sleep at numbers one and two.

He raised his hand to knock on the door's threshold, because a huge wreath with big red ornaments blocked the place where a doorknocker would normally be. After he'd rapped the second time, the door flew open.

He was immediately aware of bright light, glittering Christmas bulbs on a large green shape in the depths of the house, warmth and the smell of sour milk. He took a step backward, careful not to tumble off the narrow porch.

"Ian?"

A woman almost as tall as he was met his gaze. She had brilliant blue eyes and a small smile, accentuated by a full lower lip. Her multicolored holiday sweater did nothing to hide her generous curves, and Ian's thoughts went right to his crotch as he took in her sexy cleavage. He looked closer. Was that *glitter?*

The kid on her hip extinguished his arousal as effectively as a kick in the groin. She was married? Ian didn't do complicated relationships, certainly not with married women. And why did he care what her availability was? She was going to be his landlord—he hoped. Period.

"Hey!" The kid smiled at him, her face covered in

something sticky and white. Cereal with milk, maybe? Whatever it was, it smelled. He couldn't miss the big blue eyes on the little girl, however. The exact same shade as his potential landlord's.

"Hey yourself." He gave the kid a smile before he turned back to the woman. "Yes, I'm Ian." He lowered the hand he'd raised to knock and held it out, forcing his focus on the woman's face and not allowing his glance to wander back over her body.

Seven months in the desert, seven months without the comfort of a woman's arms—it was making him feel like a rookie when it came to the opposite sex. Though this particular lady could ignite just about any man's fire.

"Hi, there," she said, clearly speaking to the dog. "I'm Wendi," she went on. "Why don't you step inside for a minute while I grab our coats and the keys. Then I'll walk you out to the guesthouse."

"How far is it? I didn't bring her leash." He'd left it in the backseat. Integrity stayed close at all times. "Or do you want me to put her in the car?"

Her eyes widened. "No! I meant both of you, of course. My pets are part of my family, and I assume she's part of yours. I've got more than one leash around here." She looked at Integrity. "At least she has a collar. That's good. Can I pet her?"

"Yes, she's friendly. Her name's Integrity. You said you have animals?" Wendi treated him as if he didn't know anything about dogs. She wasn't wrong; in truth, he knew very little—but he knew Integrity was trustworthy. The rush of protectiveness toward the dog surprised him. Maybe they were starting to bond.

"Yes, you and Integrity can meet them in a minute.

They're being good right now. They're not always this quiet, believe me."

"Hi, sweetie." Wendi petted Integrity on the head only after she'd allowed the dog to sniff her hands. Once she'd ascertained that Integrity wasn't a threat to her or her child, she crouched in front of the dog as if she'd been doing it all her life. Her hair was like a flame with deep reds and golds that twisted around every curl. And there was her sparkling cleavage again. Did she do that on purpose?

"Wen-Wen!"

"Careful, Emma. Pet the doggie nicely, just like Ranger and Lemon."

Damn homecoming libido. Even the fact that this gal wasn't his type, that she seemed bossy, and was obviously married with a kid, didn't stop her from affecting him.

"Look at her fur, Emma. She's a nice doggie, isn't she? You can pet her because I said it's okay. We only touch dogs we've been introduced to, and only after we ask, right?"

Ian thought Wendi's explanation was overkill, but since he knew even less about kids than he did about dogs, he remained silent.

The little girl, Emma, patted the top of Integrity's nose before she screwed up her courage and shoved her entire hand into the thick fur around the dog's neck.

"She's a good dog," he said. "I haven't had her long…."

"Did you get her before you left on deployment?"

Wendi stood and hoisted Emma back up onto her hip. A very nice hip, over which her dark jeans stretched perfectly.

"No, I got her two weeks ago."

"But you were deployed. Did you rescue her in Afghanistan?"

"Something like that."

Cool as the ocean, her eyes reflected doubt as she assessed him.

"It's a big responsibility, such an intelligent breed."

"Oh?" He wasn't going to explain that Integrity wasn't a German shepherd as most people assumed, but a Belgian Malinois.

"Belgian Malinois are loyal to a fault. They need you, and they need to be mentally challenged or they get depressed."

"What are you, a vet?"

"As a matter of fact, yes. Come on in."

He stepped over the threshold, Integrity at his side.

She smiled and waved her arm expansively. "Welcome to my menagerie."

He followed her gesture and took in the old farmhouse's living area. At some point it had been updated, since it boasted modern appliances in the kitchen, which he saw from across the room. A large birdcage sat on the other side of a long kitchen counter, with an indigo-blue parrot perched on top of it. That beak looked like it could give a man stitch-worthy bites.

To the side was a woodstove that glowed with warmth from the fire within. Curled up on the bricks that surrounded the stove was a big orange cat. Sprawled on the floor between the kitchen and living area were two dogs—one of an indeterminate breed and one yellow Lab. Both dogs were alert, staring at Ian or, more accurately, Integrity.

"Your dogs didn't even bark." He shook his head. "No wonder I didn't notice them before."

"Oh, yes, they barked. They let me know you were coming up the driveway. Then I put them in a stay. They're behaving, but trust me, they're dying to meet Integrity." She looked at Integrity, and her expression grew thoughtful. "You're a very good dog, Integrity. Who trained you so well?" She spoke as if to the dog, but Ian was compelled to answer.

"The Navy and then her handler. Integrity's a military working dog. Or was. Her owner was killed, and she has the option to retire from active duty. It's up to her. If she isn't happy as my companion, I'll take her to the K-9 and see if she still has the drive for active duty."

"Do you think she misses it?"

"She misses her owner, that much I know. She's woken me up at night for no reason other than to make sure I'm there. I also kind of figure she's checking to see if it's still me or if Gary's come back." He paused. "As far as the war goes, or her duties there, I think she's happy doing any task she's assigned. She still enjoys playing fetch." Not that he'd had much time to play with her.

"It would be hard to give her up, I imagine." Wendi's comment was simple, honest.

"Yes."

His immediate agreement gave him pause. He didn't want to think about another loss, not while still dealing with Gary's death.

What was it with those eyes of hers? And how did she manage to elicit feelings before he even knew he had them?

WENDI HAD EXPECTED a younger sailor after Ian Cairn's brief phone call and a few texts as he requested information about her rental.

She certainly hadn't expected such a sexy sailor. From his flight boots up to his blond crew cut, Ian was an all-American Navy guy. And he was at least her age, if not a bit older. She placed him at thirty-five or so, two years older than she was herself. Wendi wanted to giggle as she realized it was the first time in three months that she'd stopped to think about, much less admire, a man.

"I've got to get Emma bundled up before we head out."

Her hands shook a bit as she zipped up two-year-old Emma's Little Red Riding Hood jacket and hood, and put on her mittens.

"Wen-Wen, I don't *liiiike* mittens!"

"I know, sweetheart, but if you want to go see the cottage, you have to be dressed for the cold."

Emma screwed up her face in a pout but fortunately, the tears and screams didn't start.

Emma had screamed a lot over the past several weeks. Why shouldn't she? She'd lost both parents in a horrific car crash and had been adopted by her aunt Wendi as per their will.

It had been rough on both of them.

"Okay, little miss. Let's go." Wendi stood up and pulled on her fuchsia wool peacoat, jamming her matching hand-knit hat over her messy hair. Ian Cairn must think she was crazy with all these animals and a little kid.

"As I said, I'm a veterinarian. If you have any problems with Integrity or any questions, don't hesitate to ask."

"That's why you knew her breed." Ian spoke quietly, his tired voice reminding Wendi of her own grief and the emotional exhaustion that came with the whole process. He'd been through a hard time, too, she'd bet.

"Yes." Turning to the dogs, she slapped her thigh. "Come on, girls, let's go for a walk."

Ranger and Lemon jumped up and bounded through the door. Integrity looked up at Ian.

Ian looked at Wendi. "Will they be safe?"

"Yes, I'm sure they will. I have a lot of land, and my dogs know to stay nearby. They'll all check each other out and then, hopefully, play until they're exhausted." She needed all her babes, animals and Emma, to sleep well.

"Go, girl." Integrity streaked off after her new canine buds.

"By the way, the yellow Lab is Lemon and the mixed terrier is Ranger."

Ian smiled. "Cool names."

Wendi held her gloved hand out to Emma. "Walk or carry?"

"I'm walking."

"Then hold my hand, Emma."

Emma slipped her little hand in Wendi's, and Wendi grinned. It was a sad time as they both grieved. But Emma kept things lively.

"Why does she call you Wen-Wen?"

The emotional pain was sharper than the arctic wind against her face when she opened the front door.

"Shall we go?" To where the sun was quickly setting and the shadows would cover her face, which she knew reflected her broken heart.

They clambered down the steps onto the gravel path. Once they'd fallen into an easy cadence she spoke, her breath puffing out in front of her.

"I'm Emma's aunt, not her mother."

"Oh, so you're babysitting?"

"No, yes, I mean no. Sometimes it feels like babysitting because it's only been a little more than six months. But no, it's not temporary. I'm her legal guardian. Her mother was my sister, Daisy, my twin. She and Emma's father died over Memorial Day weekend. In a car crash. I was babysitting Emma, so she was safe with me. I'm still in shock—we both are."

"I'm sorry."

Two words. Polite, expected. But his tone—it was as though Ian conveyed his compassion and total understanding in this simple expression of condolence.

As if he knew.

"As a matter of fact, we were at the attorney's earlier. I signed Emma's adoption papers. As of today Emma is legally my daughter."

She wondered if he heard the catch in her voice, sensed the bittersweet joy that had overwhelmed her when she signed the papers.

"She's a sweet little girl, and I've always loved her as if she were mine. And now she is."

"Did your sister live here in Angelville, too?"

"No, they lived in Anacortes. They left me their home, but I love Whidbey Island, and my practice is only a ten-minute drive from here. With Emma, time is everything—I don't want to be making a long commute if I don't have to."

"Wouldn't the house have been a comfort to her?"

Guilt hit her sideways. All too familiar.

"Yes, to a point. I stayed there with her for the first couple of weeks. My staff took care of my pets at the clinic. But it didn't work out. Emma was too upset, missed her parents too much. We both needed a new start. This is our home."

Why was she explaining this to him? She didn't want to sound defensive but really, did this dude think he could show up on her property with a dog he obviously didn't know how to handle, and tell her where she should be living?

"I didn't mean to imply it isn't."

"Doggie!" Emma tugged free of her hand and ran after Integrity, who'd loped back to Ian after running with Ranger and Lemon.

Wendi laughed. "Do you see how tired the pooches are? And we've only been out for a few minutes."

She was rewarded with a slight chuckle.

They were almost at the cottage. She'd always planned on renting it out, ever since she'd bought the property three years ago, but hadn't gotten around to renovating the small guest lodge until this past summer. Right before Daisy and Matt died.

She shuddered.

"It's chillier than I remember it being this time of year." Ian had obviously mistaken her discomfort for cold.

"It's not too bad, and you'll be comfortable in the cottage. I had radiant heat installed. The floor tiles throughout feel great on bare feet after a long run or hike."

"I'll bet Integrity will love them."

"She should, although you know her heavy coat will make her want to stay a little cooler than we do."

He nodded. "Keeping her comfortable and hydrated is a challenge. I was worried that she'd run out of water on the flight home."

"She seems to have done just fine."

They were at the clearing in front of the cottage.

"Look, Wen-Wen!" Emma sat next to Integrity, who lay on the ground near the front door. She put her face against Integrity's neck and hugged the dog with all the love an almost-three-year-old had to give.

"Careful, she's still getting to know you, honey."

"Integrity's a good dog. She wouldn't hurt a fly unless she was told to." Ian's assessment was quick. Direct. Wendi smiled at his protectiveness. Maybe he was bonding with his new charge, after all.

Wendi walked up to the two of them while Lemon and Ranger sat down on the path, tongues lolling and tails wagging.

"She's a beautiful dog, isn't she, Emma?"

"I love her." Emma nodded as she issued her edict.

Smiling at her darling niece, Wendi felt the sting of tears. Emma's eyes were huge under her red, pointed hood, her expression earnest.

Wendi crouched beside her. "That's fine, honey, but remember, she's visiting us. Your dogs are Ranger and Lemon. Look. See how much they miss you?" Wendi nodded toward her dogs, who were lying down, gazing off into the woods.

"I want *her.*"

"Okay, but she's Mr. Ian's dog, Emma."

When Emma shook her head stubbornly, Wendi

stood up. "I'm sorry—she's never shown such interest in another dog before."

"Integrity hasn't been overly affectionate with anyone since I got her, either."

They stared at each other.

Leave it to a child and a dog to instinctively know they had something important in common.

They were both orphans.

CHAPTER TWO

IAN BOTH LIKED and felt uncomfortable with the effort-less way he and Wendi had kept up a conversation as they walked to the cottage.

Just like Emma and Integrity, he and Wendi had a common bond. Wendi was grieving, too. That was it. This instant connection he felt with her was because they'd both recently lost loved ones. Their hearts were still mending. Maybe not even close to mending—still oozing pain and misery.

He wasn't sure he liked the fact that a stranger understood his vulnerability so completely.

"Emma's certainly fond of Integrity," Wendi was saying. "If you do rent the place and you want your dog to stay with us when you're at work, just let me know. She should be fine with my dogs. I try to get home by four when I don't have evening hours."

"Do you have a babysitter for Emma?"

"No, I've found a wonderful in-home day care for her. One of the other vets has a wife who runs it. Emma didn't like it at first, but she's gotten used to it." He saw the stress lines between her brows, the frown lines around her mouth. Here he'd been bitching about having to worry about a dog, and Wendi had taken on a child. Kids were your responsibility for…well, forever in some ways. Integrity would only be around for—

"Hey, do you know the life expectancy for a Belgian Malinois?"

She looked at him sharply. "Why?"

"I was just wondering. She's four as of last month."

There was that assessing gaze again. "Big dogs, and pure breeds, are more susceptible to disease than smaller dogs or mixed breeds. But if she stays healthy, her life span could be as long as twelve years, maybe more. Although I have to add that I've had dogs who seemed perfectly healthy end up with a horrible illness and die very young, and other dogs who looked like they were on their last legs go on for years. I recently had to put down a seventeen-year-old Border collie mix."

"That has to be a tough part of your job."

"It's not my favorite." She turned to the door and unlocked it.

"Let me show you around the cottage. Come on, Emma. Integrity, you stay out here with the girls for a few minutes, okay?"

She smiled at Ian. "It's a small place, and we don't want all three dogs wrestling on the sofa and the bed."

Had her cheeks turned rosy when she said the word *bed*?

WENDI LEFT IAN at the back of the cottage and told him she'd wait in the kitchen. Ian looked around at the pine-paneled room with relief and allowed his shoulders to relax. For the first time since Gary had died, he felt he had a safe place for Integrity. And for him. As much as he missed his house and was annoyed at the inconvenience of needing to repair it, the cottage offered the solitude he craved. He wouldn't have the interruption of household chores; he could rest, work out, read and get to know Integrity. They could make do here for a while.

As long as he didn't have to see much of his new landlord. Wendi had already proved to be more of a distraction than he wanted at the moment. Thinking she was married hadn't stopped his instant attraction to her. Now that he knew she was single, he was having a hard time keeping his head out of his crotch. Wendi was an instant turn-on to him. Even with a kid. And a house full of animals. And that parrot—he had to ask her about it. Did it bite?

He wondered if he'd started to get through his grief over Gary. But then pain sucker punched him, and he blinked back the bitter tears he'd grown accustomed to downrange. He'd understood there were never any guarantees, and Gary wasn't the first friend he'd lost to combat. But he had been his closest friend.

"Get a grip, buddy," he whispered to himself before he went into the kitchen. And looked right into Wendi's killer blue eyes.

"Is this your first tour on Whidbey?"

Her melodic voice was as effective as strong hands on his shoulders, grabbing him back from the brink of despair.

"Yes, but I'm over two years into it. I've got ten months left on this tour, then I'm up for transfer."

"Any idea where you'll go next?"

"None. I could stay here, get another degree, but I've been thinking an overseas tour might be a nice change."

Her eyes met his. She blinked.

"Where? Wait—let me guess. If you're single, you probably want to go where there's great nightlife, like Southeast Asia or a big city in Europe."

He laughed.

"I am single but no, the city lights aren't my style. I'm more of an outdoors type. I've been thinking about asking if there's a spot available in Korea, since the hiking and surfing there are spectacular. And it would only be for a year. I could transfer back wherever I wanted stateside."

"Don't you have that choice available now, after being downrange so recently?"

She might be a civilian, but Wendi had a better sense of Navy life than most of the women he'd dated.

Why was he comparing her to them? He hoped it was just postdeployment lust, nothing more.

Renting from her might be a big mistake. If it became too difficult to keep his mind off Wendi, he'd have to get out of the lease. He could put Integrity in the kennel for a couple of nights, until he got his living situation straightened out. Not a good solution, but...

"Yes, I suppose I do have choices," he said, replying to her question. He wasn't going to share with her why he really wanted to leave Whidbey. That there were too many reminders of the young sailor he'd once been. The man he'd never be again, not after so much loss, so many wartime deployments.

"And what about Integrity? Can you take a dog with you on an unaccompanied tour?"

"How do you know so much about overseas tours?"

Her eyes glistened for a second before he saw her stiffen and place a smooth expression on her face.

"I dated a Navy guy for a bit."

So that was all she was going to give up, and frankly, he was relieved. He didn't need or want to know anything about Wendi's love life.

How the hell had *love* slipped into his thoughts?

IAN WASN'T FITTING neatly into the box Wendi figured all military men lived in. She'd dated a few since living on Whidbey, and while going to military balls and big events could be fun and exciting, the guys she'd met had wanted all fun and no commitment. Wendi didn't have a problem with that. Or she hadn't in the past. But she'd refused to be anybody's go-to buddy for sexual release. The men had loved her when they returned from each naval exercise, each deployment. But then she'd been left with days, months, between dates, with no promise of a future relationship.

It got old.

The last guy had been a pilot, and they'd been together almost a year before he pulled the "I've met someone else" routine.

A relationship wasn't a priority for her since Emma had come to stay.

Judging by her body's reaction to Ian, it wasn't listening to her current life plans.

"How can you be so certain you won't deploy again?"

Ian's eyebrows rose—a signal that she'd crossed some invisible boundary, perhaps.

She held up her hand. "No, wait, I'm sorry. It's none of my business. I'm not sure where that came from."

"Let me guess. You've seen guys come and go. You and your girlfriends have all experienced that, right? And been around to deal with the wreckage?"

"You're pretty wise," she said with a smile.

Ian laughed. She liked his laugh. Quick, belly-deep and infectious.

"What makes you think I haven't faced the same thing, but from the other side?" His green eyes sparked with challenge, and she suspected plenty of women had been charmed by his manner.

"I don't see how having a warm bed waiting for you every time you come home could be viewed as disadvantageous for the active-duty sailor."

Ian shook his head. "That's not how it usually goes, Wendi, at least in my not-so-vast experience with women." He ran his hand over his crew cut, and she wondered if the blond hair in which she caught glimpses of red would grow out curly or straight.

What would he look like with a beard? Kris Kringle? Not so much, but she needed to find a Santa.

She met his eyes again; their deep green had turned stormy. Those weren't Santa eyes, either. They were eyes that made her want to kiss him.

"What?" He must have seen her staring like a teenager.

"I'm sorry, I was just... I mean, I'm in charge of a huge Christmas celebration for Angelville, and I volunteer at the base. They want to have a Santa visit for the kids of the guys and gals who are deployed. Would you be willing to play Santa Claus?"

"I can't say I've ever thought of myself as a Santa type, and I'm positive I wouldn't be good at playing him. Christmas isn't my favorite time of year, and this year it's even tougher."

"You might surprise yourself. Helping with the Christmas Spirit Committee has kept a lot of our volunteers from being lonely over the holidays."

"How did we get from the sexual politics of Navy relationships to me dressing up as Santa? And who says I'm lonely?"

"I'm sorry." She cast a quick glance at Emma, who

seemed content leaning against Integrity, stroking the fur around the dog's throat.

Ian followed her gaze. "Integrity is loving the attention, let me tell you."

Integrity chose that moment to give Emma's hand a gentle lick.

"I'd say they both are." Her tears threatened to overflow, and Wendi dabbed her eyes while Ian's attention was on the pair of fast friends.

She envied Emma and Integrity their ability to forgo all boundaries and seek comfort from each other.

"Back to the original discussion, uh, yes, I've had a few relationships with Navy guys. No, most have never progressed past the stage of a few weeks with the exception of the last one. But I don't blame the Navy. I'm just as wrapped up in my civilian career as people in the military are in theirs, and so far I haven't been willing to reduce my work hours or give up any of my pets to make room for someone else."

"You're saying you get everything you need from your animals?" His lips twitched, and a flare of anger—or was it awareness?—made it hard to keep her foot square on the kitchen tiles and not stomp on them.

"Just about, yes." She offered him her best smile, the one that said, *Mind your own business, buddy, you're not even close*.

Ian slapped his hand on the counter and laughed.

"I like you, Wendi. You've got backbone."

Backbone? It was all she could do not to roll her eyes. This was how a guy who'd been downrange for seven months and back for only a day saw her? Not as sexy or pretty, but strong-willed? She might as well face the fact that her thirties were upon her.

She might very well spend the rest of her life with her animals.

And Emma.

CHAPTER THREE

A FURTIVE BARK, more like a yip, woke Ian from a deep, warm sleep. It'd taken a good hour to stop fantasizing about Wendi Cooper, but he'd slept solidly since then.

A cold, wet nose pressed his cheek.

"In a minute. It's still dark out!"

Ian burrowed under the comforter on the surprisingly comfortable cottage bed. Integrity wanted out, and he couldn't blame the poor dog. She'd slept in front of the main door, no doubt from her training as a security dog. He supposed she felt it was her job to protect him now that Gary was gone.

Ian was dead tired. After he'd taken over the cottage and Wendi had handed him the key, he'd unloaded everything he'd shoved into the back of his car. When he'd found out he couldn't stay at his place, he'd packed a few things in a hurry. His king-size comforter dwarfed the double bed he lay in, and he'd brought too many things for the kitchen, but he'd make do for now. He didn't have a choice.

Integrity's high-pitched whine and her earnest expression stirred his guilt.

"Okay, okay, I'll let you out."

She gave another of her little yips as if to say, "Yes, that's what I mean!"

"You're the smartest dog I've ever met, girl."

He got up and fumbled in the darkness before he remembered where the switch for the overhead light was—next to the door. The sudden glare of yellow light from a circa-1970s fixture seemed to shoot right through his eyes and into his brain.

Had he remembered to pack his coffeepot?

"We'll go for a quick walk, and then we're coming back in for more sleep, dog."

Integrity thumped her tail on the tiled floor.

Once he had his jacket, hat and gloves on, he opened the door and motioned for the dog to run out. She didn't need her leash on; he'd observed enough of her these past couple of weeks to know that she obeyed every command without question. And she never left his line of sight.

More good training.

The early-morning air cut through his layers, and he pushed his hands into his jacket pockets, grateful he'd taken the time to put on his flannel-lined jeans. The air felt heavy, and he was disappointed that no stars were out. Only a swath of gray light to the east indicated that the sun had begun to rise.

He watched Integrity find the spot she needed to do her business, and walked partway up the path that led to the main drive between the cottage and the house.

The kitchen light was on in the house, and he could make out the rectangular shape of the parrot's cage through the large window. It still had a cover on it.

So Wendi was up before the bird woke. Did she get up this early every morning?

None of your business, bud.

The sound of Integrity's clean trot pulled him out of

his thoughts as she came up next to him. She sat and issued one bark.

"Shh! You'll wake people up, dog."

She looked like she was going to bark again. He really didn't want Wendi thinking he'd let the dog out by herself, or wonder if he was doing something stupid.

Not that he really cared about Wendi's opinion of him.

"Tell me what you want, girl."

Integrity jumped up and bolted for the cottage door. Ian walked behind her and opened the door, watching as the dog went directly into the kitchen and sat down in front of her food and water bowls. And barked. Once.

"Are you hungry?"

Two short barks.

Ian laughed.

"I can help you with that, girl." She was hungry. Of course she was—he didn't remember feeding her last night. He'd been jet-lagged and in a typical first-day-back fog. He might have fed her five times for all he knew.

The image of Wendi standing at the counter reminded him that he hadn't lost his memory at all. In fact, every minute with her and little Emma yesterday afternoon seemed seared into his brain.

He shook his head.

"Coming back from deployment is never easy, Integrity. Don't worry, we'll get through it together." As he said the words, it hit him—he was definitely going to keep Integrity. Somehow, in the midst of the shock, grief and chaos of Gary's death, followed by Integrity's being shipped to him, and bringing her back to the United

States with him, he'd bonded with the Belgian Malinois. Even though he hadn't realized it until now.

"Next step is to get you to bond with me, gal. Let's see, where's your food?"

He found the empty Ziploc bag he'd filled with pre-measured food before they'd boarded the flight from Afghanistan, and groaned. He'd meant to get her more food yesterday, before he'd walked into his unlivable home.

Who would've known a burst pipe could destroy an entire house?

He could have opted to take his postdeployment leave right then and there. But he enjoyed having a break at Christmas, and the squadron was still on postdeployment reduced hours, so he saw no need to waste his leave days. He'd be able to go back and forth from the base and his house throughout the day, as the contractors started the repair work. Once he'd had a chance to make the arrangements…

He had ninety days of leave on the books, a full three years' worth. He'd only taken ten days last year due to deployment. He'd hoped that by now he'd be dating someone to take on a vacation with him, but it hadn't panned out.

The last several tours had included five deployments to either Iraq or Afghanistan. Not the best circumstances for a dating life.

Woof!

Integrity's plea ended his brooding.

"I'm sorry, gal." He patted her head. "I've got to run out and get you some food. Want to come with me?"

The dog answered with another bark and ran to the door. Her ability to understand freaked him out at times.

He knew military dogs were well trained, but the way she grieved Gary's death and appeared to intuit whatever was said to her astonished Ian. The memory of Integrity lying in front of Gary's coffin before it was carried to the airlift for Gary's last flight home from Afghanistan still brought tears to Ian's eyes.

All Integrity had left of Gary was one of his old T-shirts that she slept with. Ian didn't doubt that she'd never forget Gary.

He eyed the leash that Wendi had left on the counter and stuffed it in his jacket pocket. Integrity didn't need it for this trip; she loved the Wrangler, and he wasn't going to take her into the grocery store with him. But it didn't hurt to be prepared for any and all contingencies.

"Come on, girl." He opened the door and stepped out, waiting for her to follow. She did—and as soon as she got outside, bolted.

But not for the Jeep.

"Integrity!"

He ran after her. His gut told him where she was headed, and he groaned.

"Integrity!" His quiet call grew more insistent. All he needed was for her to get Wendi's dogs going.

He couldn't see her in the dark, but the sound of dogs barking reached him just as he made out her silhouette on the porch of the main house. She'd activated the motion detector light and stood at Wendi's door, her ears up and happy, her tail wagging.

The front door opened, and he saw Wendi's silhouette in the door frame. Ian slowed to a walk for the last hundred yards as he approached the house.

"I'm sorry, she's hungry and I was taking her with

me to the grocery store. She took off before I could get her in the car."

He was at the bottom of the steps, his breath puffing out as the weight of cold, damp air settled around them.

"Come on in. I have some food you can give her." She balanced Emma, who looked less than thrilled to see them, on her hip. The child did, however, reach her hand down toward Integrity.

"No, that's okay, I need to get her some, anyway."

Wendi turned to go back into the house, ignoring his remark. The glance she threw him over her shoulder conveyed how unimpressed she was with his inability to feed his own dog.

"Just come in and shut the door behind you."

Integrity had already followed her inside, so Ian had to go in to at least take control of the situation.

The unmistakable scent of cinnamon reached his nose before he'd even crossed the threshold. Once in the living room with the door firmly closed behind him, he took in the scene before his eyes.

The woodstove was going, as it had been yesterday, with Ranger and Lemon in the front hall to greet their friend Integrity. The dining room table was covered with piles of packaged food, from microwave popcorn to pasta. Tall stacks of large baskets occupied the corners of every room he saw.

"Do you run a gift basket business on the side or something?"

Wendi laughed. "It looks like it, doesn't it? No, I'm a full-time vet. These are the community Christmas Spirit baskets. I need to have them filled and wrapped over the next two weeks."

"Who are they for—economically challenged folks?"

She nodded and turned back toward the kitchen, and he noticed her profile, backlit by the soft holiday lights. Wendi was a beautiful woman, and he wished they'd met at a different time for both of them.

The Christmas tree lights were on, as were strands of twinkling lights all over the main room.

"Do you leave these on all night or did you just plug them in?"

"No, I plugged them in to keep things cheerful for Emma. We've been up most of the night."

She turned back to him, raking her free hand through her long, curly, red hair. It was a cloud of chaos around her head, and she looked…tired. He studied Emma, whose cheeks were bright red, her eyes bright.

"Is Emma sick?"

"She's been awake since two with a fever. The Tylenol's brought it down. I think it's just a cold, but I'm going to have her ears checked as soon as the doctor's office opens."

"Darn, I'm sorry. And now you have your new renter barging in with his dog at four-thirty. You don't need to worry about feeding my dog, Wendi. I'm wide-awake, still on Kabul time. It's no problem for me to go get her food."

Wendi's look was stern. "This is your first dog, isn't it?"

"Yes." He braced himself for what was certain to be a lecture.

"What kind of food are you going to get her?"

"Um, dog food? In a big bag."

Wendi sighed, then motioned toward the sofa. "Sit. Watch Emma while I feed Integrity—I don't want to risk my dogs bothering her while she's eating. Then I'll explain the science of dog food."

She placed Emma at the end of the sofa with a small pink blanket and kissed her forehead.

"Okay." Did he have a choice?

Emma stared up at him from the depths of the sofa. She clutched a worn stuffed something-or-other in her right hand; her left thumb was in her mouth.

"Hi." He sank down next to her, surprised that they still made footed pajamas. Emma's were red with snowmen all over them.

"Wen-Wen."

"She's over there." He pointed to the kitchen, but Emma didn't bother looking. The poor kid had obviously been through the wringer.

And taken Wendi with her.

"Here." Wendi handed him a steaming mug of coffee. "I assume you drink it—you're a Navy chief. I left it black, or do you want some cream?"

"No, thanks. You're right on target. I take it black and strong." The coffee was rich and tasted wonderful. "Ah, nectar of the gods."

"It's my survival at the moment." To his shock she sat cross-legged on the sofa beside him as if they were old friends. Her red flannel pajama bottoms had candy canes printed all over them. Her thermal top was a solid red and didn't hide the soft curves of her breasts.

"Is anything in this house not decorated for the holiday?"

She smiled. "As the community Christmas Spirit Committee chairperson, it's my job to keep the downtown and local vendors all in the holiday spirit. So I have to do my bit here at home."

"Are you baking cookies now?" The heavenly scent was making his stomach grumble and groan like a hungry bear.

"No, that's a slow cooker full of steel-cut oats. The oatmeal's almost done. Would you like to try some?"

"Oatmeal's one of my favorites. But it's, um, awfully early for a social visit, and I'm your renter. You're not required to provide room *and* board—for me or my dog."

"My dream is to turn this into a bed-and-breakfast specifically for pet owners," she said.

At what must have been his blank expression, she explained. "I've been on the road with my dogs, and it's difficult to find a dog-friendly place. I'd hoped to have it going by the summer. But work got busy, and then…"

"Emma?"

"Yes, Emma."

They both looked at the little girl and with a start Ian realized Integrity had finished eating and was sitting on the floor in front of Emma, her head resting on the couch. Emma lay next to the dog's head, her eyes closed.

"Finally. She needs to sleep, but her fever wouldn't let her."

"You're not worried about Integrity being so close to her?"

"How can I be? Look at them."

Ian couldn't take his eyes off Emma or Integrity. Their bond was palpable.

"I'm happy to let her sleep here, but if you're nervous I'll put her to bed."

He turned to her.

Her face was so close, only inches away, her eyes bare of makeup.

"No, leave them. You might wake her up if you move her. Can I get anything for you at the grocery store when I go?"

"Thanks, but no, I'm okay for now. Oh! About dog food. You can't change her food suddenly, because that will upset her stomach. And a dog like Integrity requires a higher-protein food. I have a few different brands we get in at the clinic, and I'm happy to give you samples until you figure out which she likes."

"Cans?"

"Oh, no. Just dry food. I gave her a very basic potato and fish formula that most likely won't upset her system. She's had a long journey, and it's best to keep her stomach calm. She should thrive on a lamb-based or bison-based diet."

"Wow. I thought dogs ate anything."

She smiled as she sipped her coffee—with cream, he noted—and he was mesmerized. She looked pretty spectacular for no makeup, and at zero dark thirty.

"Well, a lot of them will eat whatever they can find, but they shouldn't. I have to keep all our food up and behind closed doors, or Ranger will help herself to it. She's been known to indulge in walnuts, which most dogs are very allergic to. Fortunately, she only needed some Benadryl to treat her hives, but it could have been much worse."

"Even the animal expert makes mistakes."

"I never said anything else."

He glanced into his mug, then up at the Christmas tree. "It's so weird. Three days ago I was in a war zone, and now it's like I've been dropped into Santa's workshop at the North Pole. The only thing you don't have here is Rudolph."

"Oh, but we have reindeer food. Emma's class made some, and we're going to scatter it out the back door on Christmas Eve. It's her birthday that day, too, so it'll add to the festivities."

He didn't miss the wistful note in her voice, the sadness over what Emma had been through. Maybe Wendi needed a break from her grieving, too.

"My family used to throw a carrot or two out there. What do they do now?"

"The preschool teacher had bowls of oats, birdseed and sparkling decorator sugar. The kids put scoops of each into paper bags that they decorated as reindeers."

"Sparkling sugar?"

"Magic dust to help them fly."

"Ah." So that was where the "glitter" on her breasts had come from. He smiled.

"What's so funny?"

"You had sparkles on your, um, chest earlier today."

"Did I? You must have wondered about that." She giggled. "It's fun having Emma here. I'm not going to lie—I've always wanted kids of my own, but I didn't think they'd happen for a while yet. Emma's been a big surprise. It's been the best of surprises, though, considering the awful circumstances."

Her voice lowered at her last two words, and he knew what had caused the almost undetectable quaver. Grief.

"We're never ready to lose someone so young." He still couldn't fathom a lifetime ahead of him without Gary's chiding and friendship.

"Your friend, Integrity's handler—he was young, too?"

"Yes. My age."

"Which is?"

He smiled. "Thirtysomething."

"I'm thirty-three."

"I've got three years on you, lady."

"Thirtysomething is too young for anyone to go."

"It sure is." He didn't want to move, reluctant to break away from the warmth of their proximity and conversation. But he didn't want to give Wendi the wrong impression, either.

He wasn't interested in a hookup.

"I should go. Do you want to put a blanket on Emma?"

"No, it's warm enough here, and I don't want to encourage the fever."

"Oh." He knew quite a bit about battlefield trauma and wartime first aid, but next to nothing about little kids.

"You can leave Integrity here while you go out."

"It's not your job to babysit my dog."

"Actually, I think it's the dog doing the babysitting."

Wendi was right. Integrity had curled up on the rug, her face and ears cocked toward Emma as if waiting for her to wake up from her nap.

Anxiety shot through Ian. This was too cozy, too fast.

CHAPTER FOUR

"DON'T GO YET. The oats will be done in fifteen minutes—have another cup of coffee." Wendi hated to
sound so eager, but Emma had finally settled down
after a rough few hours. Integrity soothed her.

"You think Integrity's helping Emma sleep, don't
you?" Ian's eyes tilted up with his smile.

"You've caught me."

"Okay, then, I'll stay for another coffee. Meanwhile,
let me help you with something. What about filling
those baskets?"

"The baskets? Oh, no, you don't have to do that."

"No, but I want to." He stood up and headed toward
the dining room table.

With a quick look at Emma, who slept with the peace
of an angel, Wendi followed him.

She tried not to stare at Ian's butt in his jeans, but
it was such a fine example of American military in-
genuity, she didn't want to be unpatriotic by ignoring
the view.

Too bad they'd met now, when dating was out of the
question for her. She wasn't ready to fall into a relationship after her last disastrous liaison with the naval avia-
tor who'd left her feeling like a fool. And now, with a
child, it wasn't going to happen with anyone. Not until

she figured out what was best for Emma and if she even wanted a man in the mix.

"Do you put the same things into each basket?" He took one from the stack and turned to face the table.

"Yes, at this point. As it gets closer, we add different nonperishables to each one, depending on the recipient. If the basket's going to a family with young kids, they get enough for Christmas breakfast and dinner, as well as toys for the children. If it's for a senior, we choose gifts according to their health and dietary needs."

Ian let out a low whistle. "That's a lot of planning."

"Good morning, Vietnam!" Blue followed his greeting with a whistle that matched Ian's.

Ian's eyes widened. "I take it that's your monster bird."

Wendi laughed. "Blue? He's not a monster, just a very large psittacine. He's a Hyacinth Macaw, named for his color. He looks all tough and his beak is scary, but he's a big softie. He's not supposed to get up for another hour and he knows it—he's taking advantage of the change in routine."

"Helloooo!" Blue's call was louder.

"I'd better try to quiet him down before he wakes Emma."

She left Ian and went to feed Blue. Emma remained dozing, Integrity snoozing softly. Lemon and Ranger lay not far from Integrity, and Bubba the tabby cat watched it all from the top of the sofa.

Ian must think she lived in a crazy house, she thought—not for the first time. She doubted he was used to so much activity and noise in his home. His life was his. No attachments, no kids.

The same life she'd led until a few months ago. It

was hard to imagine a time without Emma here, as hers, but Wendi had enjoyed many years on her own, only needing to care for herself and her animals. Having a child meant she hadn't had a chance to dwell on her lack of a love life.

Until yesterday when she'd met Ian.

She shook her head as she emptied Blue's water dish and rinsed it. No sense going there.

Her best friend, Shelly, begged to watch Emma for her on an almost daily basis, so finding a safe person to babysit wasn't the issue.

The issue was Wendi's heart. She didn't have the energy to entertain any kind of permanent relationship with a man. Emma took all her effort and focus these days.

Of course, her interest had been dormant, no doubt due to her new-parent exhaustion. Ian had shown up as she was adjusting to her new routine. He could look like an ogre and she'd probably consider him attractive.

But Ian was attractive, the kind of guy she could imagine spending a few sexy nights with, no question.

But she wasn't a one-night type of woman. And Ian was fresh back from not only deployment, but losing his closest friend, too.

"Here you go. Now keep quiet." She handed Blue a large piece of banana.

"Kiss kiss." The bird punctuated his reply with smooching noises, which made Wendi grin even though she thought she was too tired to do anything but go back to bed.

With Ian.

It had been a long time since she'd reacted this way to a man.

She stirred the oatmeal and was glad it was ready. The sooner Ian left, the sooner she could get her mind back to the reality of her life—and stop lusting after a relationship that wasn't going to happen.

Ian had filled ten baskets in her absence, and was working on another one as she walked into the dining room.

"You're a natural at this! You want to be on the Christmas Spirit Committee. Come on, admit it."

"Ah, no. But I was happy to do this." He placed the last item in the basket he held and added it to his finished pile. "Do you need more nonperishables for these? I'm happy to donate whatever you think would be good—I can get it while I'm out."

"Trust me, I've got a garage full of food for the baskets. You've done so much already. It'll be easier for me to keep the momentum going now that you've begun the process."

"Well, let me know." He didn't look at her as he straightened up the piles of cans and packages.

"Before you go, try the oatmeal."

"Twist my arm." His smile was as sexy as his butt.

"It's in the kitchen."

The mess on the counters—used medicine droppers, wet washcloths, the half-full cardboard canister of oatmeal, dirty plates—looked ten times worse as she saw it through Ian's eyes.

"It's been a long night. Excuse the mess."

"Didn't even notice."

"Liar."

"Maybe. Just a bit. Where are your bowls?"

"Second cupboard to the right of the sink. Here's a spoon." She handed it to him, and their fingertips touched. It was the lack of sleep, the early hour, the Christmas lights twinkling, that must have caused the spark arcing between their hands. And continuing up her arm and down her body.

Ian turned away and opened a cabinet door.

"All your dishes are red and green. With snowflakes on them." He held up one of her cereal bowls as if it were a rare art piece.

"They're my Christmas set. Don't you have plates for the holidays?"

"If I'm having company they're lucky to get paper plates with *ho ho ho* printed on them."

The thought of Ian serving a meal to a group of people he cared about proved as enticing as his touch.

"That's a joke, Dr. Wendi."

Was she that transparent?

She smiled. "I know."

"Do you?" His eyes narrowed. "Have I offended you? Jeez, you invite me in, feed my dog and now you're feeding *me*. And here I am, making fun of your plates."

He took the few steps between them. He was so close she felt his heat, saw his chest move with his breath.

"I'm sorry. You've been nothing but kind and generous to me and Integrity since we showed up."

"There's nothing to apologize for. I'm not myself— I've been up all night, and it's a busy time of year to start with."

He reached up and stroked her hair, then rested his hand on her shoulder for a long moment before he continued down her arm and clasped her hand in his.

"I know what it's like to feel overwhelmed. You look the way I do when the world's closing in. But you're obviously doing a great job here. Emma's resting, and she'll get better. You've saved Integrity from the loneliness of a kennel, not to mention a bellyache. And you've given me a place where I can decompress without any fuss."

She couldn't take her gaze from his. Ian was one rugged sailor, all right. His strength and fitness were evident even in his rugged jeans. The lines that fanned from his eyes and around his mouth proved that he had a good sense of humor, but when was the last time he'd been able to relax with no worries? She wished she could keep looking at his lips but didn't want to give him the wrong idea, so she looked up. And *ensured* he'd get the wrong idea. His green eyes were unexpectedly kind, so full of compassion—and something else, which she knew was reflected in her eyes, too.

"Ian, I don't—"

"Too late."

She'd already closed her eyes, anyway. Why *not* let him kiss her?

You're a mother now.

Being a mother didn't preclude feeling desire....

His breath was on her face, warm and sexy. He brought her body closer. Anticipation flared, and she relished the throbbing between her legs.

The sound of something crashing onto the kitchen floor pierced the lusty haze she wanted to stay in, and she pulled back.

Wendi opened her eyes to find that Ian had taken a step back, his eyes narrowed, a wry twist to his mouth. His hand still held hers.

"I broke your bowl." His voice was throaty, full of sex. He wanted her, too.

The intensity in his eyes was enough to make her

feel like shoving him against the counter and climbing all over him.

Instead, she shook her head.

"What now?" She glanced down. Shards of shattered green ceramic lay on the floor, contrasting with the light blond pinewood. "Oh. The bowl. No problem. I keep meaning to get more plastic dishes with Emma here, but I haven't had the time. Let me get this cleaned up before Emma or the animals cut themselves."

"I'll do it." Ian let go of her hand and bent down.

"Don't pick up the pieces with your bare hands."

"Trust me, I've handled worse."

She grabbed the brush and dustpan from under the sink and handed them to him after he'd dumped his handful of broken bowl into the garbage.

"Here." She brought the wastebasket out from under the sink and tipped it toward him so he could dump in the remaining shards and pottery dust. "That was as much my fault as yours," she said.

He paused at her words, and their eyes met. Both on their knees, she was a full head shorter than he was. That small fact delighted her, as her height usually made her equal in stature, if not taller, than the men she dated.

You're not dating him. He's your tenant.

Tell it to the earworm in her head, Mariah Carey's "All I Want for Christmas Is You."

"Let's call it a wash." Ian was on his feet in one smooth motion and reached down to grasp her elbows and ease her up. She noted that he dropped his hands and took a careful step back the minute she was on her feet.

"I apologize. I'm not normally one to…make unwanted advances."

"Trust me, that wasn't unwanted—or even what I'd classify as an *advance*."

"What would you call it, Ian?" Anger surged, and she was certain he could read through her as easily as she could see through the sheers she'd hung over the front windows.

"An almost damn wonderful kiss." At her stunned silence, he smiled. "Brought on by exhaustion from your long night nursing a sick baby and my jet lag, combined with stress from looking for a place to live all day yesterday. I'm sorry if I offended you, Wendi."

Wendi shook her head. Offended *her*? If anything she was sadly disappointed that they hadn't followed through with the kiss.

Not that she'd tell Ian that.

"Don't misunderstand me, Wendi. I still want to kiss you. It's not the best idea for either of us, though, is it?" His green eyes blazed with a sincerity and candor that made her want to simultaneously run out of the room and wrap her arms around him.

She sighed.

"No, you're absolutely right."

"No harm, no foul?" Ian's voice was gruff.

"Sure." What else was she going to say?

"I need to go." He moved out of the kitchen.

"Don't buy any of that cheap grocery-store dog food. I'm serious. I'll get you some food from the clinic in time for Integrity's dinner tonight."

They were at her front door. Ian's face had the tight look he'd worn when he arrived with Integrity.

"I'll leave it by your door." She didn't want him to think she was jonesing for a way to see him again.

"I appreciate it. Let me know how much it costs. Integrity, come." He pulled her leash from his pocket, and Wendi had to give him credit. He was a quick learner for a jet-lagged, brand-new dog owner, especially one still grieving the death of his best friend.

Integrity reluctantly left Emma's side, obedient to her master. She sat in front of Ian and patiently waited for him to clip the leash to her collar. She blinked at Wendi, and Wendi imagined the dog saying, "He'll be fine once he gets used to me."

Wendi giggled; she couldn't help it.

Ian looked up at her. "Am I doing this wrong, too?"

"No, not at all. It's obvious that she adores you."

Ian straightened with a grunt.

"We'll see." He gave her a nod, and then he was gone. She waited until she heard his Jeep clear the driveway before she went back to the sofa and sank down on the floor next to the still-sleeping Emma.

"What was I thinking, baby girl?" she whispered to her darling niece and allowed Bubba, her orange tabby, to settle on her lap. Ranger and Lemon stayed closer to the hearth. The dogs had learned quickly that they'd lose in any tangle with Bubba, who ruled the roost with his claws. Except on Blue, whom Bubba had been raised to respect and leave alone.

"Good morning, Vietnam!" Blue let out a wolf whistle and Wendi grinned. Who needed a man? She had all the love she needed right here.

Emma didn't need the confusion of a new male coming into her life, anyhow. Wendi had finally hit a decent stride with her and their new life together. Adding a partner—temporary or more lasting—wasn't advisable.

All Wendi had to do was to get her mind off her new neighbor.

CHAPTER FIVE

IAN WENT TO the supermarket after he left Wendi's, but first he treated himself to a coffee at one of the drive-through coffee shacks that were unique to the Pacific Northwest. He wasn't one for the fancy stuff, but he did enjoy a hot, strong coffee. Just as Wendi had guessed.

As good as the take-out coffee was, he wished he was back in her house sipping her coffee.

Stop fooling yourself. If you were still there, you'd be doing more than tasting her coffee.

She had a kid, a sick kid, on the sofa, and he'd still almost kissed her. Ian had never wanted to be involved with a woman with a child. Didn't want to have his own kids—because he didn't want to ever cause a child the pain he'd gone through at too young an age.

His exhaustion was messing with his judgment. He finished the coffee and looked into the backseat at Integrity.

"Sorry, gal. You've got to stay out here while I go inside. Keep the car safe." He leaned over and scratched Integrity between her ears, but she wasn't paying much attention. She was in full-alert mode, watching every person who walked through the parking lot to the store entrance.

He didn't think dogs were allowed in supermarkets in the United States, and since Integrity was no longer a working military dog, she didn't wear the vest that indicated her privilege. No one would mess with his car while she was in it, of that he was certain. As sweet as she was, he'd seen military dogs in full offensive; they were fearsome fighters and didn't hesitate to risk their lives for their handlers.

"We're family, Integrity. You and me. I'll be right back."

He locked the doors after he exited the vehicle.

Wendi had convinced him to leave the dog food to her, but he planned to get Integrity some biscuits. He needed to be able to give her treats.

The bright fluorescent overheads glared down at product after product on the store shelves. He'd forgotten about this part of coming back home. The choices.

Overseas, and especially in a combat zone, life got down to the basics. One type of soap served as shampoo, body wash, hand soap and laundry detergent as needed. Ian grew exasperated by the sheer number of choices on the shelves. Did he need scented or unscented detergent? He'd noted that the washer in the cottage was front load, like the European washers he was used to overseas. He needed detergent for that; at least he had a clue there.

"Lavender?" he murmured to himself. Was that what had made Wendi smell so good? Did her pajamas carry the scent of her fabric softener?

He sighed and pulled the nearest bottle of soap from the shelf. Wendi was off-limits. He was a mess, relationship-wise. He didn't need a woman, not longterm. Particularly one with a kid. He wheeled down the main aisle of the huge store, noting the cacophony of colors and garish displays at the end of each aisle.

His gaze caught on sets of small holiday-themed plates. For kids. The packages consisted of a plate, bowl and silverware, lined up like gifts, with themes for boys on one side and girls on the other. He noticed the green plastic set with red Santas, and immediately thought of Emma.

Wendi had mentioned that she wanted plasticware for Emma. And he'd broken one of her ceramic bowls. Not on purpose, but he felt responsible since his mind had been on the things he'd love to do with Wendi. He hadn't been so careful about where he placed the dish.

That little girl, Emma, was adorable. Something in her expressive eyes made his gut go weak. Integrity had warmed up to her quickly, which wasn't typical for her. A trained military dog was usually reserved around strangers.

Although being at the cottage and at Wendi Cooper's home wasn't anything like being downrange.

Ian rubbed his neck, standing in the middle of the aisle. He'd slept like a baby last night—as if his body knew it was safe, that he'd come home.

He didn't allow himself to think as he placed the toddler dish set into his cart.

He pushed the cart around the end display and came face-to-face with an eight-foot-tall, inflated snowman. Ian blinked. He wasn't dreaming. They were actually selling the snowman, and several similarly sized seasonal figures, including Santas and reindeer. He looked at the price—for less than the cost of a full tank of gas, he could have his very own blow-up snowman. Did people really put these things on their front lawns? Santas, reindeer and even a blow-up snow globe replica were lined up along the main artery of the store.

Wendi loved Christmas in a way he wished he could. He didn't have a problem with people who liked Christmas; at one time, he had, too. Until he was six years old and had come home to his dad crying at the kitchen table.

It was the last day of school, the afternoon that meant the beginning of the long holiday break. He'd held his Christmas gift for his mother in a brown paper lunch bag. It was a Christmas tree—different kinds of pasta glued to a cardboard cone, then spray-painted gold. He'd wanted to paint it green, but the art teacher had said gold was all the school had that year.

It didn't matter; Mom would love it.

His father had looked up at him as if Christmas wasn't coming in five days.

"Son, I have some bad news."

Ian would remember that sentence as long as he lived. It signaled the end of his childhood and the end of happy Christmases forever after. His mother had been taken to the hospital in agonizing pain, eight months pregnant with what would have been Ian's younger sister. Neither had made it.

As the youngest of four, he'd sat by his dad in the kitchen until his older brothers and one sister came in from middle and high school. He'd watched his dad tell the same awful story to each of them, and their reactions.

It was as if he had to feel the pain through them. At six, he hadn't completely understood that he'd never see his mom again.

He made a note to call his father, let him know he was back in the United States. Dad was remarried and busy with his second family during the holidays, but they'd arranged to get together after New Year's.

"Can I help you find something, mister?" An eager college-age boy stood in front of him, wearing the store's bright green vest with his name tag prominently displayed.

"No, thanks, Jeb. I'm just looking."

"Those will be gone before Christmas—they go quicker every year." The boy nodded at the snowmen.

"I'll bet they do." As he pushed the cart toward the food aisles, he vowed never to end up in the holiday section again.

CHAPTER SIX

"WHAT IS IT about the holidays that makes so many pets sick?" Amy DuPont, the new vet tech, looked as tired as Wendi felt. It'd been a nonstop Monday, including three emergency surgeries and several episodes of indigestion or allergic reaction from ingestion of inappropriate substances. Including candy canes and a fruitcake that was heavy on the walnuts.

"It happens every year." Wendi kept entering her surgical notes into the office computer. "People have more food in the house than they can store properly, there are decorations all over the place that any dog or cat would consider a toy, and pet owners are too stressed or busy to recognize the potential for a dangerous situation."

"That makes sense, Dr. Cooper. But the last cat ate tinsel. Why would anyone with a cat think tinsel was even an option? And who uses tinsel these days, anyway?"

Wendi eyed her young assistant. Was she serious?

"Tradition, Amy. Tradition is important, no matter what holiday you celebrate. My family always had tinsel on our tree."

"But you don't, do you, Doctor? You have Bubba. And Blue can't be trusted around any decorations, can he?"

"Bye, you two." Dr. Tom Lassiter, the owner of the

clinic, stopped by Wendi's station and smiled. "See you in the morning!"

"Night, Tom."

"Good night, Dr. Lassiter."

Wendi stood up and stretched her lower back. She touched her toes, and when she straightened she plucked her Santa hat from her desk and put it back on her head. She'd had to remove it for her surgical duties.

"You're right, Amy, I don't have tinsel in the house, but I've found all kinds of garlands and lights to make up for it. Not everyone has the resources or the inclination to go to that much effort, though. And not every cat eats tinsel. Bubba, by the way, ignores the Christmas decorations as long as he has a decent toy of his own to play with."

"I hope we don't see another tinsel patient. That was just plain nasty!"

Wendi laughed. "I'm glad we were able to save Pepper," she said, referring to the tuxedo cat who'd ingested three strands of tinsel.

"That cat's lucky you were here. How did you know it was tinsel?"

"Mrs. Anderson is on the Angelville Christmas Spirit Committee with me. I happen to know that she prides herself on using tinsel she's had since the seventies. All of her other cats are older and they've never shown an interest in it, but this is only Pepper's second Christmas with her. Last year he was a kitten, and she watched him more closely. She left him in her bedroom with the door closed whenever she had to leave the house."

"This year she got lazy?" Amy's black-and-white view of clinical situations was a direct reflection of her age.

Wendi shook her head. "Not lazy. Just full of Christmas spirit. Speaking of which, I've got to get a move on—I'm due to pick up Emma in ten minutes." She was grateful to have a flexible child-care situation, but six o'clock was the absolute latest she could get Emma.

More important, she missed her. Emma had become part of her life the minute she'd popped her confident little self into the world. It had been around this time three years ago that Emma was born, on Christmas Eve. Wendi had never known a more magical Christmas. Her parents and her sister's husband's family had all been present in the waiting room at the hospital. They'd all gotten to meet Emma within the first hour of her birth.

Had that only been three years ago? In those few years, both sets of grandparents had experienced physical setbacks that meant they were unable to care for Emma.

Not that it mattered. Daisy had left Emma to Wendi because, as identical twins, she knew Wendi would be the best mother for Emma, the person who would most effectively preserve Daisy's legacy.

"I'll see you in the morning, Amy. Have fun tonight."

"We always do. My book club reads the latest romances, and we spend the time talking about how we wish we could meet a guy like the hero."

"Don't be so hung up on fictional heroes that you miss out on a decent real-life guy, Amy. You do realize those are just characters in a book, right?"

"This coming from a self-appointed elf." Amy added a sly smile to her comment.

"Touché."

"Don't forget your dog food, Dr. Cooper. Here, let

me help you." Amy hefted one of the forty-pound bags while Wendi carried the other.

"Why do you need so much dog food? Didn't you buy some for your dogs last week?"

"Yes, but this is for my new tenant."

"Oh, you rented out the cottage? I really wanted to live there, but it's a bit out of my budget right now."

"I understand. Yes, a Navy air crewman who just returned from Kabul needed a place to stay that allows pets."

"Is he single?"

"Um, yes."

"Hot?"

Wendi couldn't stop the heat that rushed up her face. "Not my concern. He's my tenant. And considering everything I've been dealing with, a cute guy is the last thing on my agenda." She felt comfortable saying this to Amy; the entire clinic had pitched in and helped with her adjustment to single parenthood these past few months. Not much of her personal life was private to them.

"But, Dr. Cooper, you're forgetting what you told me a minute ago."

Wendi's exasperation threatened her patience. She heaved her bag of dry dog food into the trunk and moved so Amy could do the same.

"What was that, Amy?"

Amy smiled. "You wouldn't want to miss the real-life hero right in front of you. Who knows—you might have your very own Christmas romance going on at home."

Wendi couldn't keep from laughing. "Amy, I want to see how you feel about all these topics when you're my age."

"We're not that far apart, only about ten years."

"I've done a lot of living in the past ten years, and you've got a lot ahead of you. The next decade's going to bring you all kinds of insight."

"Maybe so, but what good is your insight if you won't take your own advice?" Amy's words put a wrinkle in Wendi's careful composure.

"You know how full my life is at the moment, Amy. Romance isn't on my radar."

"Humph." Amy was young and idealistic. *Wait another ten years,* Wendi wanted to add—but didn't.

"See you bright and early tomorrow." She opened her driver's side door.

"Bye, Dr. Cooper!" Amy walked into the clinic, and Wendi fought the urge to call her back and explain that she was serious. Ian Cairn was not the man of her dreams. He was simply the answer to her prayers for a way to increase her cash flow. He was the means to an end; his rental payments would help fund her vision of turning the cottage into a pet-friendly bed-and-breakfast.

No, he wasn't an answer to her romantic hopes—if she'd had any. Emma had been her entire focus since the end of May, and now she had Christmas to deal with.

A man wasn't necessary to her holiday happiness.

WENDI BARELY MADE it into her car before she had a text from her child-care provider, asking her to text back if she was going to be late.

"I'm coming, I'm coming. I still have five minutes," she grumbled to herself in the car. Since the center was less than five minutes away, she'd get there just in time.

Ignoring the tense knot in her stomach, which she'd

had, on and off, since Emma arrived, Wendi backed out of her assigned parking spot at the clinic and turned onto the main highway.

Luckily for her, she was on her way back to Angelville, so traffic wasn't bumper-to-bumper like the lane heading off-island. It was hard not to wish *she* was heading off-island for the holidays, too, and that her sister was still alive. Her family was all from either Seattle or Whidbey Island, which had always been a comfort. At least until recently. Her parents' aging had come with a host of health problems that left them unable to drive up to Whidbey for quick visits like they used to. Daisy's loss hadn't helped their outlook on life, either. Wendi understood—she was still struggling with it herself—but she missed seeing them as often as she had. Her work schedule precluded going down to Seattle with Emma more than once a month. She'd never felt lonely on Whidbey, but lately the remoteness of island living had demonstrated its drawbacks.

Was she doing enough for Emma? Would Whidbey give Emma everything she needed?

What about what *she* needed?

Eager for a distraction from her worries, she found the memory of Ian in her kitchen this morning a welcome relief.

Ian had needed a safe place to stay with his dog. Now that he was living in Angelville, she hoped she could get him to enjoy some of the town's Christmas festivities.

Not that she was invested in Ian's happiness, or how fast he got through his grief over losing his best friend.

The compassion she felt for him was because of his status as a newly returning sailor—and because of the grief they both experienced.

Two Weeks Before Christmas

"I CAN STILL get the baskets put together. Actually, they're all done, except for the nonperishables we voted to purchase. I'm going to need some help delivering them. I've got Emma this year, and I don't want her stuck in the car while I make the rounds." She paused, glancing around at her fellow Christmas Spirit Elves during their Saturday meeting. "I've got some baby-sitting lined up, but we also have a lot of baskets to deliver."

Wendi always enjoyed dropping off the Christmas baskets, especially to homes with children or to elderly shut-ins. Each basket was personalized; their community was small enough that they could ascertain who needed what to make their otherwise potentially dreary holiday a little brighter.

"I'll ask my grandson if he can give us a hand this year," octogenarian Dolly Roberts spoke up, her reindeer antlers bobbing as she nodded. One rule of the committee—enthusiastically followed—was to dress in holiday garb every day after Thanksgiving until Christmas. And it didn't have to be all about Christmas, either. All symbols of winter celebration were welcome. Anything that might cheer up the island during the often gray-skied season.

"Can you let me know by Tuesday, Dolly? If he agrees to it, I'll get him a dozen baskets by Thursday."

Wendi looked over at the corner of the community room in the library. Emma sat with five other toddlers, playing with blocks and books. They'd been reasonably quiet so far, playing with a couple of teenagers who'd volunteered to sit with them during the meeting. Wendi

figured she had about ten more minutes before Emma
started getting antsy. The library was only a few minutes from home, so she planned to go back, let the dogs
out, eat lunch and then work on basket-delivery planning while Emma took her nap.

As the meeting wrapped up, Shelly White, her best
friend and fellow committee member, walked up to her
and grinned.

"What's up?" Wendi was tired. Emma had recovered
from her virus last week, but with Christmas and all its
preparations, Wendi's sleep was taking a hit.

"You haven't said anything about your new tenant
since you told me he's a single sailor. Do you have time
for coffee? My treat."

"Oh, Shelly, I'd love to, but Emma needs lunch and
her nap." This was one of the adjustments Wendi had
faced when Emma became her priority. Her Saturday-
morning talks with friends like Shelly were put on hold.
That life seemed so long ago, much longer than six
months.

"I totally understand. You're a mommy now. But I'd
be lying if I said I didn't miss our time together on the
weekends." Wendi felt a surge of affection for her high
school classmate.

"I know you do. I miss our coffee talks, too."

"One day you'll be married and your husband can
watch Emma." Shelly's dimples deepened. She knew
how other's matchmaking attempts wore on Wendi.

"Don't hold your breath on that one, Shelly."

"Hey, it probably seems crazy now, but things will
balance out for you. As a matter of fact, you haven't
let me babysit in weeks. You need a break. Not just for

Christmas Spirit events, either. You need to start getting out."

Shelly was going to watch Emma next Saturday so
Wendi could deliver the Christmas Spirit baskets.

Wendi gave her a brief hug and smiled. "I'm really
grateful, Shelly. And believe me, the minute I need a
break, I'll call you. At the moment, though, I still find
it hard to leave Emma all day while I'm working. When
I get home I want to spend my time with her." Shelly
nodded. She understood; she was a school counselor.
"Of course. Just know that I won't stop offering until
you take me up on it more often."

"Thanks, Shelly. I will." With a final wave, Wendi
walked over to Emma.

"Wen-Wen!" She didn't think she'd ever tire of Emma's
voice calling out in sheer exuberance whenever they re-
united.

"Hey, sweet pea." She swooped her up and swung
her around. "Want to go get some lunch?"

"Pea butt jelly?"

Wendi laughed. "Yes, you can have a PB and J."

She felt the stares of a couple of the mothers and
looked over at them. "I cut the sandwich up in tiny
pieces, and I know she didn't have any peanut butter
before she was two."

"You're amazing, Wendi." Serena Delgado, a new
member of the Christmas Committee, beamed at her.

"How are Snowball and Cami?" Wendi had made a
house call to see Serena's alpacas earlier in the week.

"They're fine, and stop avoiding the compliment.
You *are* an amazing woman, Wendi. We're not looking
at you because we're worried about what you're feeding Emma, you know."

"No?"

"No. We were all just saying what a wonderful mother you've become—you *are*—to Emma."

"You're a natural!" Joyce Patterson chimed in, holding her two-year-old son, James. "And I wanted to tell you that a group of us have started to get together for playdates once a week. We know you work during the day, but if you can ever attend with Emma, we'd love to have you. Have you got a pen? I'll give you my number."

Wendi took the information from Joyce in a bit of a daze. They thought she was a good mother?

Maybe she should rearrange her clinic hours so that she could go to the playgroup with Emma. A new mom needed all the support and nurturing she could get.

She ignored the feeling that insisted the woman in her still needed to be nurtured, too.

AT HOME WENDI made Emma the promised peanut butter and jelly sandwich, and within an hour the child was sleeping peacefully in her room. Wendi let out a sigh of relief once she was sure Emma was down for the count.

The delivery maps for the Christmas Spirit baskets had to be finished. She could drop some of them off practically in her sleep because many of the recipients had been on the list for the past several years. But she wanted to make sure she gave Dolly's grandson all the information he needed for his deliveries.

Last year and the years before that, she'd never thought twice about having the baskets and their various contents laid out all over the house. Emma was a well-behaved child, but she was a toddler with a toddler's curiosity. Wendi had to take extra care to keep her scissors and other sharp tools out of sight and in cabinets with childproof locks.

Ian had been a huge help, filling the baskets for her the morning Emma was sick.

She sighed and twirled a red-and-green-striped ribbon between her fingers. All thoughts led to Ian, it seemed, although he'd only moved in a couple of weeks ago. Was this a sign that, as Shelly had said, she needed to get out more? Or was it Ian? Did they have the connection she felt they did? A connection that, despite her claims to the contrary, was about more than their shared grief.

The maps occupied her mind for the next hour, and after she'd replaced the color ink toner on her office printer, she printed them out.

As she stood to walk upstairs to retrieve the final maps, Lemon and Ranger gave several sharp barks to let her know she had a visitor.

"Shhh!" Emma usually slept through the dogs' noise when she was tired, but Wendi didn't want to take any chances. If she was lucky she might catch a thirty-minute power nap herself.

She immediately recognized the two figures through the glass panes that framed the sides of her front door. Worse, the fluttering in her stomach didn't feel odd but familiar. Too familiar—and not unpleasant. As if she was excited to see Ian again.

His intense eyes captivated her the moment she opened the door.

"Hi, Ian, Integrity. Emma's napping." She didn't want him to think she was whispering to be seductive.

"Sorry, I was afraid of that. I wasn't going to ring the bell, just knock. But you beat me to it."

"Well, Ranger and Lemon make the best doorbells."

"Sure do," Ian said with a grin.

"What can I do for you? Is everything at the cottage okay?"

"Yes, it's fine. I wanted to thank you for all your help, and for dropping off the dog food last week." He brought his arm from behind his back, extending a huge poinsettia and a red foil gift bag.

"It's gorgeous! You didn't have to—thank you so much, Ian." She took the plant and gift from him.

"I asked the gal at the flower shop about the poinsettia, and she assured me it's safe for pets and Emma to be around it. They're not as toxic as commonly believed. As long as none of them makes a meal out of it. I looked it up on the internet, too. Your bird won't want to munch on it, will he?"

Wendi laughed, shaking her head. "Blue will eat anything, but he sticks to his cage and his own toys for the most part. I have the perfect place for this, on the mantel near the woodstove. The cat doesn't go up there."

"Good. Well, thanks again for your support."

"How are the repairs to your house coming along?"

Ian grimaced. "Not so great. It's too close to the holidays. I've been guaranteed the contractors will redouble their efforts after the first of the year."

"I'm sorry."

"I may have to stay here until spring."

Spring? Three more months? That cheered her, and it wasn't because of the incoming rent money.

"Whatever you need. That's why we left the lease open. You and Integrity are great to have on the property. Have you thought any more about leaving her here during the day, with my dogs?"

"Yes, and yes." He scratched the light beard growth on his chin. Ian went from stern Navy chief to sexy neighbor in a blink.

She'd noticed he didn't shave when he didn't have to go to the base.

That was a detail she shouldn't notice, or at least shouldn't be so…interested in.

"It's been fine for now, keeping her at the cottage. I can go back and forth every couple of hours. But after my break's up mid-January, I'd be relieved to know she's with her pals."

"Sure, just tell me when, and I'll leave the back door unlocked. That way you're not dependent on my work hours."

"That'd be great, Wendi." He turned and stepped off the porch, slapping the side of his thigh to command Integrity to follow. He looked back over his shoulder. "Thanks again."

She watched them walk back toward the cottage. She'd felt like this before. This feeling that, in some ways, Ian had always been part of her life.

It was similar to the feeling she had about Emma; it now felt to her as if she'd always been Emma's mother.

Her feelings for Emma made sense; she'd known her since birth, and she and Emma shared the same blood. From the very beginning, she'd been a surrogate mother of sorts, and Emma had been—and still was—her link with the twin sister Wendi adored.

Ian should by all rights feel like a complete stranger.

Instead, she couldn't remember a time she didn't wake up thinking about him. And he'd only been in her life for two weeks.

"Shelly's got a point. I need to get off the island

more, make new friends." She spoke to Lemon and
Ranger, and Blue chimed in with one of his whistles.
Bubba gazed down at her from his perch on the kitchen
counter, where he wasn't supposed to be.

The poinsettia looked perfect in the living room,
and she sat on the sofa to admire it and open the gift
bag. She pulled out a set of toddler dishes. Christmas-
themed.

How could she *not* feel as though Ian was more than
her tenant when he made such a thoughtful gesture?

CHAPTER SEVEN

One Week Before Christmas

WENDI LOVED EARLY Saturday mornings on her property, when the birds were starting to chirp and the quiet of the weekend, with its peace and serenity, enthralled her. She worked efficiently, loading the Christmas Spirit baskets into her trunk and the backseat of her car. A few had to go in the front passenger seat, too. The only empty space left was for Emma's car seat.

Emma hadn't awakened yet. She still had another half hour or so before the little girl's voice sang through the house.

Much as she *felt* like Emma's mother, she sometimes despaired over whether she had what it took to be the parent Emma needed, especially with the trauma of losing both parents at once. Yet as the days and weeks went on, Emma felt more and more like her very own daughter. They were a family now, and Wendi would do anything to give Emma the childhood she deserved.

She wondered if Ian was feeling the same way about Integrity as he grieved his friend Gary's death. Granted, a dog wasn't a child, but the emotions weren't dissimilar.

Wendi recognized the grief and exhaustion on Ian's face—and she sensed that it wasn't all attributable to postdeployment fatigue. He appeared to be quite stable, in fact. Their almost-kiss and his honest reaction to it wasn't what a guy suffering from overt PTSD would have had. Ian had been fully present.

She was the one who wanted to wish their attraction away. Well, not really. It was the timing she wished she could change.

Life doesn't happen on our terms or on our timetable.

Her sister's refrain echoed in her mind. Daisy had been a big believer in fate and soul mates.

Wendi grunted as she hoisted two baskets into the trunk. Ian would end his lease and disappear if he ever guessed her thoughts. A soul mate, showing up as a renter?

Or maybe it was a Christmas miracle, just like Amy had suggested....

Christmas miracles do happen!

Again, Daisy's voice echoed in her memory. When they'd found out she was pregnant with Emma after three years of trying, and that the baby was due at Christmas, there was no stopping Daisy's miracle theories.

As Wendi loaded more baskets into the trunk, she was grateful that Dolly's grandson had taken over a number of the deliveries. This was going to be a long day as it was.

The sound of Ian's Jeep reached her as she arranged the last two baskets on the backseat. She lifted her head from the cramped space and looked up. Ian slowed the vehicle as he neared her, obviously on his way out for the day.

He rolled down his passenger window. "Hi!"

"Hi." She'd successfully avoided him since he'd

dropped off his gifts last week, and hoped to keep their contact minimal. She didn't need Ian thinking she was some kind of desperate single mother out for fun with her tenant. Or with any Navy guy, for that matter.

If the timing had been different, Ian would've been the perfect man for her, Navy or not.

Squaring her shoulders, she drew herself up to full height, trying to ignore the tingles that danced over her skin.

Integrity placed her snout against the rear passenger window, ears quizzically perked, as if making a face at her, mocking her. Wendi laughed.

Ian followed her gaze, and she saw him reach into the backseat, petting the dog.

"She's so starved for attention. Like I didn't just walk her for the past hour."

"You've been up that long?"

He looked away, through his windshield. "Yeah, well, it takes a while to adjust to a new time zone. Not just me, but Integrity, too. She likes to get up before the crack of dawn."

"Maybe it's what she's used to—patrolling during a night shift." She walked closer to the car, stopping inches from the front passenger door.

Ian nodded. "You're probably right. I chalked it up to her grieving for Gary, but she's eating more now and has started to get friskier on our walks. She brought me a stick to toss for her this morning."

"That's wonderful!" Wendi couldn't stop the joy that bubbled through her. She remembered how worried Ian had been about Integrity's spirits when they'd arrived. "Where are you two going?" Immediately she wanted to take her words back. It wasn't any of her business. The less she knew about Ian Cairn and his life, the better.

"We're going for a quick run, then I'm picking up groceries for this storm we're supposed to be getting. Do you need anything?"

"No, thanks." She looked into his eyes and felt the sudden urge to lean in and touch his cheek.

She shoved her hands into her pockets instead.

"Emma's still asleep. I'm taking her to stay at a friend's while I run some errands." She didn't want to talk about her charity mission, even though Ian had helped with the baskets. It was one thing for the Christmas Spirit Committee to be aware of what she did every year, but she liked to keep her service work quiet. It wasn't about her.

"Is there anything I should know if we lose power?" His voice was low, almost gravelly, and it only increased her awareness of him.

His face showed military-man concern, and his energy was palpable. She didn't remember ever meeting such a sexy, powerful, full-of-life man.

"We rarely lose power, so I wouldn't worry about it. But if we do, you're going to get really cold in the cottage, really fast. Come knock on the door if that happens. If I'm not back, you can let yourself in the kitchen door. I'll leave it open, just like on workdays, because Ranger and Lemon are here and will guard the place fine. They know you, so you'll be safe, especially with Integrity at your side. They love her. The two of you can take over the upstairs guest room and bath. You'll even have your own office up there."

She and Emma lived totally on the bottom floor, with the small bedroom next to her master bedroom perfect for the little tyke. Wendi expected that Emma would eventually move upstairs. As she grew into a teen, she'd relish the personal space. For now Wendi wanted her new charge nearby.

"I've survived some pretty cold nights downrange. I'm sure Integrity and I will be fine if the power goes out. Thanks for the offer, though."

"Don't turn it down yet, Ian. Like I said, it can get unbearably cold because of the damp. But the odds are minimal that we'll lose electricity."

They gazed at each other for a moment, and Wendi took a deep breath, wanting to run away but not wanting him to see how he affected her. "Well," she said, shrugging off the enchantment he seemed to cast over her, "I've got to wake up Emma and give her breakfast. Have a great run. And don't worry if you forget anything—I keep a pantry stocked for bad weather, or for when Emma gets sick and I can't make it to the store." She'd learned that the hard way when Emma first came to her and developed a cold within days.

She stepped back as she waved at Ian and Integrity, who stared at Ian with total attentiveness. Wendi understood; she felt the same way, and it wasn't entirely willing. Ian waved back. "See you later, Wendi."

After he drove off, she got into her car and again tried to ignore the physical reactions Ian stirred in her. Her lips actually tingled as if he'd kissed her. And the way he said her name—as if it meant something to him. As if he cared about her.

Ridiculous.

Yes, it was a very good idea to avoid any more interaction with him than necessary. After the holidays she had to find out exactly when he'd be able to move back into his house. Maybe one of the other veterinarians knew a good contractor who could speed up the repair work.

Because if she spent too much time around him, she didn't trust herself not to touch him—and more.

"THANKS FOR HELPING me out today, Shelly." Wendi sat at Shelly's kitchen table sipping a cup of coffee before she was due to leave with the three dozen Christmas Spirit baskets.

"Are you kidding me? I adore Emma, and this lets me contribute to the committee's work, too." Shelly smiled, her short red hair framing her petite face, making her look a bit like an elf.

"I'm sorry about Tony, Shelly." The relationship had been on the rocks for a while, but Shelly had confided that Tony had broken up with her last night.

"Please. He's just one more to add to my list of practice frogs before my true hero shows up." Shelly grimaced as she sipped from her mug. The last time they'd talked about Tony they'd had a bottle of cabernet to share.

Wendi didn't press Shelly on it, but she knew how hard the breakup was on her friend. Shelly had been the one to comfort her through the worst of the failed relationship with the last Navy guy. Another reason she needed to cool her jets when it came to Ian—Navy guys went away and broke women's hearts.

"We've always had fun doing the baskets together. Maybe next year we'll be able to tag-team it again." When Shelly looked after Emma, she often took her to the local coffeehouses. Emma's favorite treat was a steamer—warm milk with a flavor in it. Emma's flavor of choice the past few times had been marshmallow.

"You'll get it done more quickly this way. The storm isn't due to hit until late tonight, but you never know. The sooner you're finished, the sooner we'll all be able to hunker down."

"Do you really think the storm will be that bad? You know how these things go. The weather forecasters throw dire warnings around, we get a couple of feet of snow instead of a few inches of rain, and it all melts tomorrow. Not quite the apocalypse."

Shelly laughed. She was a native Whidbey Islander, too. "You're probably right, but this system might bring an ice storm. What if you lose power?"

"That's what my woodstove's for."

"You're braver than I am." Shelly's home was a modern bungalow in the middle of Oak Harbor. She'd grown up in Angelville, however, and her parents still lived in a farmhouse like Wendi's.

"You and Emma are welcome to stay here if the weather gets too dicey, or your power goes out. Remember that storm a few years ago? I never had more than a flickering of the lights, but you were without power for days."

"Yes, I remember." Wendi silently prayed that wouldn't happen again. As a single person, she'd been able to go out for food, eating at restaurants downtown until her power came back. She'd showered at her gym. With Emma, she really would have to cook on the woodstove, and maybe even heat water. Neither of which appealed to her.

"I'll get back in time so I can make it home before Highway 20 turns into a skating rink."

"It shouldn't take you more than half the day to deliver everything, should it?"

Wendi stood up and grabbed her jacket. "Hopefully not. Give me a hug, Emma."

"Where you goin', Wen-Wen?"

Wendi hugged her and breathed in the sweet smell of her blond curls.

"I'm headed out to bring Christmas to some of our neighbors. Have fun with Shelly and be a good girl, okay? When I come back, we'll go home and make dinner together."

"Bye-bye!" Emma ran back into the family room and sat down with the box of bright toys Shelly kept specifically for her "Emma visits," as she called them.

"Thank goodness for our routine at her preschool. She doesn't freak out anymore when I leave her."

"You've done a great job with her, Wendi. Now get out of here. Treat yourself to a fancy cup of coffee while you're at it. Have fun!"

"Will do. See you." Wendi put on her Santa hat and walked out to her car. As she turned the key in her ignition and drove out of Shelly's driveway, her mind went back to this morning and Ian's concern about the weather.

Was she foolish to hope it wasn't *just* about the weather?

CHAPTER EIGHT

IAN WAS IMPRESSED with how well Integrity kept up with him. He'd thought he'd run a mile, walk a mile, run a mile, to get the dog conditioned. Instead he had the distinct feeling that Integrity was conditioning him to her superb level of fitness.

The air was cold and thick—snow was on its way. He'd caught the last of the local news station's report last night on television before he'd fallen into the deep slumber he'd been experiencing in the cottage. He was starting to feel a little spoiled.

"Good girl." He puffed out the words as Integrity adroitly leaped over a log that lay on the rocky beach. He'd been happy to see that the tide was low this morning, allowing them to take the shore run. By tomorrow, the water would be white-capped and the wind too strong to exercise outdoors.

Another runner passed him. They nodded at each other, and he noted that the dude was wearing a Santa hat.

Like Wendi's.

He'd replayed that near-kiss a thousand times in the past few weeks, evidence that he needed to be with a woman after so long away. If he'd had a girlfriend through deployment or struck up a relationship with any of the women he'd known who had no problem with the "friends with benefits" arrangement, he wouldn't still be hard over a woman he'd never kissed.

Or would he?

There was something different about Wendi. As much as her exuberant love for Christmas had initially put him off, there was a sincerity to her enthusiasm that disarmed him. Not only that, Wendi appeared to take everything in stride, accepting loss and change as part of life.

His breathing quickened as he thought of her full breasts and the way her ass filled out her jeans.

Wendi was not the "friends with benefits" type and that was all he could handle at the moment. Adding a family to the mix when he might still have more deployments in his future, more high-risk missions, wasn't in his plans.

He watched Integrity lope along the wet sand beside him, her face regal, her ears back. She might be the only female he'd be spending his nights with for a while.

"HERE YOU GO, Mrs. Vandyke." Wendi placed the heavy basket on the side table in the elderly woman's small entryway. Helen Vandyke was the sixth of nine residents at Oakwood Manor receiving a basket. The senior living community comprised seniors like Helen who still lived relatively independently, as well as those who could no longer care for themselves.

"Wendi! It's so good to see you. Come in, come in. I want you to see how Misty's doing."

"I don't have much time today since I'm not on a house call, but I'd love to see her." Inwardly Wendi groaned. She came out to the community once a month to see the various small pets owned by the residents as so many of them were unable to get their pets to the clinic. Helen's cat, Misty, suffered from diabetes, but with minimal training Helen had learned to administer daily insulin injections.

"Here she is." Helen placed the plump gray Himalayan cat in Wendi's arms.

Wendi grinned at Helen. "She's not having any problems eating, I see."

Helen giggled. "I'm watching her every move, don't you worry. Only the dry food and no more than what you prescribed. She doesn't seem bothered by the shots anymore, either."

Wendi petted the sweet cat, who purred as she rubbed behind her ears. Truth was, Helen had gotten used to the needles, so Misty, in turn, no longer reacted to her owner's stress.

"You're doing a great job. Are your children picking you up for Christmas?"

Helen's face clouded. "Well, yes, I think my daughter will. But my son is still between jobs, and it's tough at his house. I don't want to be a bother."

"I'm sure you're not a bother, Mrs. Vandyke. And you always enjoy your time with your daughter. Remember the story you told me last year? How your granddaughter tried to make your favorite Christmas cookies?"

Helen chuckled, obviously remembering how hard the cookies had turned out—so solid that Helen had broken one of her dental crowns on it.

"Oh my, yes! None of us will forget that."

"Hopefully, she'll stick to helping your daughter in the kitchen this year, and maybe bake a cake or choose something easier."

"Yes, something much softer." Helen took back Misty, who allowed her mistress to hold her over her shoulder like a baby.

Wendi looked at her watch. "I'm trying to beat the weather today, Mrs. Vandyke. I'll see you in the New Year, all right? Merry Christmas." She gave Helen and Misty a hug.

"You, too, Dr. Wendi."

Wendi walked out of the apartment and back to her car for another basket. Her heart ached with every story she heard about seniors who didn't have family to celebrate the holiday with, but she couldn't help everyone. She'd learned to focus on the positives. Helen had said she'd be with one of her children at Christmas, and that was a good thing, even if it necessitated another trip to the dentist. She grinned to herself at the story.

Her cell phone rang, and she pulled it out of her jacket pocket.

"Hey, Shelly. Is everything okay?"

"Oh, we're great. Emma's such a joy. How many more baskets do you have to deliver?"

"Eight. I started with twenty-seven, so I'm almost there."

"Well, the weather's getting worse. We're supposed to get ice pellets in the next two hours."

"Three of my remaining deliveries are here at Oakwood Manor," Wendi said, "and the last five are nearby. Remember the trailer park we delivered to last year? I'll be back soon to pick up Emma, don't worry."

"I'm not worried about me—or Emma. She can always camp out here with me. I'm more concerned about you being on the road when it ices up—you know how bad it gets. You're closer to your place now. If it's icy, just go home and stay off the road until it passes."

"Do you really think it'll come to that?"

"Can you see the scary clouds from where you are?"

Wendi looked up and northwest. The sky was an unusual mix of heavy, dark cumulus clouds.

"Yes, and it *is* getting colder. You may be right."

"I am. Like I said, do *not* fret about Emma. She's having a blast at Auntie Shelly's. Take care of yourself."

"I will. Let me get off the phone and finish here. Thanks for the heads-up, Shelly."

Wendi put her phone back in her pocket and walked through the parking lot more quickly. If she could postpone the basket deliveries, she would, but each basket included perishables meant for the holidays. If the storm ended up being as bad as predicted, the recipients might not get them in time to plan for their own holiday shopping. The thought of being alone at her house without Emma panicked Wendi. She completely trusted Shelly, and Emma was actually safer at Shelly's if there was a power loss. As well, in the middle of Oak Harbor there weren't the trees that posed a threat to the farmhouse in a windstorm.

It was more than Emma's physical safety that worried her.

She might not have given birth to Emma, but she was Emma's mother now, and had the same instincts as her sister always had. A storm was coming, and she wanted to be with her child, both of them safe and secure.

The baskets would be done in an hour, an hour and fifteen minutes, tops.

She could do this.

CHAPTER NINE

IAN GRABBED THE last half gallon of milk left in the dairy case and hurried to the checkout. He'd stocked up on a month's worth of nonperishable food when he'd come out a week ago, so all he needed for the duration was what was in his basket—milk, eggs, bacon, steaks, apples and bananas.

While he waited in line, his gaze landed on a display of Christmas baked goods. He wasn't one for sweets, but the dark chocolate cupcakes looked tasty, even if they were decorated with red-tinted cream frosting and green sprinkles.

You could always take a couple to Wendi and Emma.

Where the hell did that come from? He wasn't the neighborly type, and Christmas still reminded him of the lost little boy he'd once been. He'd never gone out of his way to make it the special time for himself that it was for so many—like Dr. Wendi Cooper. He couldn't take one step in her place without hitting a wreath, hanging snowflake or stuffed reindeer.

Besides, he'd brought over the plant and dishes for Emma as a peace offering because of that almost-kiss. He didn't need the temptation of Wendi, didn't want to deal with her any more than necessary.

He didn't need the sugar rush the cupcakes prom-

ised, either. And he'd bet Wendi wouldn't want Emma
eating anything so sweet or junky.

You loved the cupcakes your mom used to bake.

What was it about Wendi that made him think about
Christmas past?

The customer ahead of him at the cash register
started yelling at the cashier about a discount price, and
Ian was tempted to leave his basket and just go home.

His anxiety had lessened thanks to his run, and his
muscles were pleasantly fatigued. Otherwise, he might
want to put his fist in the belligerent customer's mouth.

But he was back on Whidbey, not in a combat zone.

The store manager walked up to the register to calm
the customer down. As the clerk finished the order a few
minutes later, Ian forced himself not to get involved. He
looked around at the checkout displays again, set up for
impulse buyers. Ian never considered himself impulsive
about anything. He took his time, measured every action before he acted.

*Gary had always done the same thing. It didn't do
anything to keep him alive.*

Ian groaned.

And put the package of cupcakes into his basket.

A MIX OF rain and tiny ice pellets fell on the Jeep's windshield as he made his way out of the grocery parking lot.

He was an imbecile. Did he really think he'd eat all
those cupcakes and not take them to Wendi's?

He'd noticed the baskets in her car this morning, all
topped with a bright red-and-white-striped bow. She
obviously hadn't wanted to tell him she was delivering the packages to families who needed an extra holiday boost, but he remembered the stacks of supplies

scattered about the farmhouse when he'd first arrived. When he'd filled the baskets he had that morning, he'd barely made a dent in her workload.

There must've been a couple of dozen baskets in the back of her car. Delivering them was going to take her long enough that she'd arranged to have her friend watch Emma.

Did Wendi realize that the bad weather had the potential to bring everything on-island to a halt? Not for a few hours, but possibly a few days?

"It's none of my business, Integrity," he said. "I need to get a grip."

The dog looked at him in the rearview mirror as he drove onto the main highway. Was he nuts or did the dog think he was crazy?

"Oh, all right." He put on his signal flasher and pulled over to the wide shoulder. With a few quick touches to his phone, he made contact with Wendi.

"Ian?"

"Yes. Wendi, are you home yet?"

"No, I'm delivering the last of my—"

"I know, your Christmas baskets. Look, there's a mess of a weather system coming in, and I'm still out. The roads are getting icy already. Can your car make it back to the farmhouse?"

"You're nice to be concerned, Ian, but I've lived here my entire life. I'm used to this. I'll be finishing up in the next hour or so, and I'll be home way before the snow starts to pile up."

"I hear you, Wendi, but the snow isn't the problem at the moment. It's the ice." As he spoke, he watched two cars slide into each other as if they were on an ice rink. "I have a four-wheel drive, and I have snow tires. Where are you, exactly?"

The silence on the line made him fear he'd lost their connection, until he heard a soft sigh.

"I'm in a neighborhood at the end of Winding Road. Do you know it?"

He swore under his breath. That was a long stretch of narrow, unkempt road that led to a dilapidated trailer park. Ian's gut tightened at the thought of Wendi being anywhere near the run-down, transient neighborhood. He'd had to pull one of his junior petty officers out of there after an ugly domestic altercation last year, and had been relieved when the police showed up.

"I do. I'll be there as soon as I can. Sit tight, and don't even try to get back to the main road."

"Ian, it's not necessary for you to—"

"It is. You need to get back to Emma, and you're going to need my car to do it. And Wendi?"

"Yes?"

"Stay in the car with your doors locked."

WENDI CALLED SHELLY as soon as she'd disconnected. Shelly assured her that she and Emma were still totally safe; in fact, Emma was napping.

"I'm sorry this has turned into a longer day for you than we planned, Shelly."

"We can't predict the weather, hon, and this storm is hitting eight hours before they'd originally estimated. I'm glad Ian's coming to get you. My car and driveway are covered with a solid sheet of ice. Emma's fine with me, and I honestly think you're going to have to get to your place and stay there. Who knows—this could be the date you've always dreamed of."

"Give me a break." Wendi knew she didn't mean it, knew she was already thinking of Ian as more than her friend.

She hadn't fooled Shelly, either. She was wildly attracted to the man, and cursed the fates that had thrown them together at the most inopportune time for both of them.

"I understand your reasons for not wanting to get together with anyone right now, and I understand your resistance to a Navy guy, trust me. But Ian's not Tony, and you're not me. You deserve to be happy, Wendi, and if it's happening too fast for you, just look at tonight as a one-time, um, date." Shelly didn't use her usual salty language in front of Emma, even when the two-year-old was napping. Wendi appreciated that.

"He's a horny guy back from deployment," she said. "He'd pay *any* woman the same attention."

"Sure. Click your heels together three times and we'll all be in Tahiti instead of on this stormy island."

Wendi laughed. "Well, that's not my concern at the moment. I just wanted to be in the house with Emma and my animals. This will be my first night away from her since…"

"Understood. But it's not worth driving back to my place, Wendi. Stay where you are until Ian shows up, and take your time getting home. I'll see you in the morning."

"Thanks. We will."

As she hung up she realized she'd said *we*.

Wendi lightly pounded her head against the headrest. A noise drew her gaze toward the trailer park she'd just left. Two young men, maybe even teens, were there, arguing. They wore only T-shirts, and their clenched fists and red faces underscored the tension between them.

Wendi sank down in her seat. She hoped they wouldn't notice her, and that they'd resolve their disagreement without violence.

She pulled up the weather app on her phone. Switching to the radar picture, she cringed. It looked like a hurricane was going to smash into the coast, even though hurricanes were more typically East Coast events. This storm had the potential to dump a large amount of snow on the island in a short time, fueled by the current of arctic air that had dipped into the temperate Pacific Northwest airflow.

As ice began to pelt her windshield, her gratitude toward Ian grew. How had a man she'd known less than a month figured out she was in over her head? He'd instinctively realized that she'd need help getting home.

Headlights approaching on the road behind her cut her musings short. Instead of Ian's Jeep, however, they belonged to a behemoth pickup truck that had been outfitted with giant tires. Wendi sat up straight and prepared to move her car; the gargantuan vehicle could drive right over her sedan and never notice.

The two men who'd been fighting ran toward the truck, slipping and sliding on the icy gravel.

As soon as she put her car into Drive, they looked over at her.

"Don't mind me, I'm leaving." She said the words to herself, praying she'd be far down the access road before the men had a chance to follow her. Her suspicions about this being a drug deal of some sort were confirmed when the blackened window of the monster truck rolled down and the male driver gave her a hard stare.

Where was Ian?

She'd put the truck well behind her on the side road and could see the highway when a rabbit ran in front of her. She tried to stop but her brakes went into anti-lock mode and she lost control of the car. Only after it slid to a stop right before it would have ended up in the ditch did she peel her hands off the steering wheel.

Thank heaven she hadn't been going any faster.

Headlights coming from town slowed, and she recognized Ian's Jeep.

"Thank God."

She flashed her lights to ensure that he knew it was her vehicle.

He made driving on ice look simple as he maneuvered onto the side road and parked on the shoulder, close to where she'd stopped in the frozen field. Once he'd parked, he hopped out of the Jeep and walked around to the driver's side of her car.

She lowered the window. His green eyes were the best thing she'd seen since she'd left the house this morning.

"What's wrong?"

"I had to leave the trailer park. I think I was witnessing a drug deal going down, and the participants didn't look too friendly. The driving wasn't bad until here. Now I can't get my car off this grass."

Solid crystals of ice stuck to Ian's eyebrows, lashes and the collar of his jacket. She had to consciously keep her hands from reaching out to brush off the icy mess.

"Get out and let me see if I can move it. Go wait in the Jeep with Integrity."

"But—"

"Go." In mission mode, Ian opened her door and reached in to take her hand.

Wendi complied. She'd deal with her offended inner feminist later.

Once in the passenger seat of the Jeep, she turned to Integrity and scratched her neck, rubbed her chest.

"You are the best dog, aren't you, girl?"

Integrity responded with a quick lick to Wendi's chin.

Wendi hugged the dog from the front seat and turned to watch Ian's progress.

He'd managed to get her car moving. It looked like he was driving an inch at a time on the sleet that had built up on the shoulder of the side road. Wendi didn't care how long it took; Ian had succeeded at what she'd thought was impossible.

How did he manage that?

It didn't matter, as long as the end result got her safely home. Shelly had been right; it was too treacherous to consider picking up Emma. She was all Emma had left—she had to stay in one piece.

After ten minutes or so, Ian had her car up onto the shoulder of the main highway. He got out and strode back to the Jeep. She took advantage of being able to watch his sexy form move like the military man he was; there was nothing unnecessary in any of his movements, no frills.

Only solid, war-proven Ian.

Reality washed in with the cold air that hit her cheeks when he yanked open her door.

"The main road's been treated with salt. I think you'll

be okay if you take it slow the entire way back. I'll follow directly behind you in case you run into trouble."

"That's not necessary."

"Save it. We're going back to the same place, anyway. We can argue about it once I get you home in one
piece."

"Okay. Wait—home? Emma's at Shelly's. My friend's
place. I know it's crazy to still want to get there, in this,
but..." She ignored the hand he'd stretched out for her,
hopping down to face him.

"Where's Shelly's?"

"In Oak Harbor."

Ian's chest visibly rose and fell as he absorbed her
words. "Is Emma safe with Shelly?"

"Yes, of course."

"Then you'd better focus on getting back to *your*
house this afternoon. The roads are closing as we speak.
If we move now, we'll be lucky to get back to your place
before we're stopped by the highway patrol."

"Shelly said much the same thing. Okay, I don't have
a choice. Let's go." She turned to head back to her car.

"Wendi?"

"What?"

Ian stood next to his Jeep, only a foot behind her,
his grin so wide she could see it through the dimming
light and increasingly heavy snowfall.

"You'll need these."

She squinted her eyes to make out the keys he dan-
gled from his gloved hand.

"Thanks." She held out her hand for the keys. But
Ian didn't play fair. He tugged at them the moment she
grasped them, forcing her to step closer.

They were mere inches apart, and the falling snow

made it feel as if they were the only two people inside a giant snow globe.

"It'll be okay, Wendi. Emma's safe. You said so yourself."

She nodded. "I know. It's just that…just that…we haven't been apart since…since…"

"Since your sister died."

"Yes."

"It's hard, I know. But isn't it good that she has a safe place, that she's with someone you trust?"

She nodded, then swiped at the tears that had squeezed out of her eyes. "I'm being overly protective. I can't seem to help it."

"Listen to me." He raised her chin and she met his eyes.

"You're being a good mom. You wouldn't be you if you found it easy to be apart from your daughter. Emma's your niece, I know that, but let's call it what it is. You're her mother. She needs you. And you need to stay safe, in one piece. For her."

"You're right." She smiled at him and for the first time since Shelly had suggested she might not be able to reach Emma tonight, relief relaxed the tight knot in her chest.

"Let's go back to my place. Hopefully, the storm will be short-lived, and I'll still be able to get Emma tonight."

"Probably not tonight, but tomorrow morning we can four-wheel it over the snow in my Jeep."

Ian's body heat soothed her. Wendi could almost forget she had bigger responsibilities than staring at the single most attractive guy she'd met in a long while. Never mind the storm. She had her own storm churning in her mind, her heart. It wasn't logical that she could be falling for a man she'd known for a matter of weeks. There was an unspoken yet real connection between them. Realization struck Wendi. The practical, responsible community Christmas Spirit Elf, the dependable veterinarian, the motivated new mom, could still have strong feelings for a man. Grief took away a lot, but time gave it back.

Was Ian the man she could let into her life?

IAN KNEW HE was playing with fire. Teasing Wendi was flirting, and flirting led to other more enjoyable activities. With any other woman, at any other time, he would welcome them without reservation. If only they weren't both so damned vulnerable and grieving. She was the wrong person for him, just like he was for her.

And yet... Wendi's hand in his felt anything but wrong. It was warm, firm and fit perfectly in his. He pulled her closer, so close that he felt the tips of her boots hit his. With one small move of his hips or hers, they'd be nose to nose. And then...

He couldn't hold back the rumble of laughter that forced itself through his chest and up his throat. "You have ice crystals and snowflakes all over you." She looked like a glitter fairy.

"So do you." The breathlessness in her voice told him she was as aroused as he was. That this thing between them wasn't just his postdeployment loneliness.

He didn't want to kiss any other woman like he wanted to kiss Wendi.

"Ian."

"Yes."

"This is a bad idea."

"Yes, it is. We already decided that the first morning I was at your place, didn't we?"

They looked at each other, and Ian saw curiosity, doubt, maybe even dread in Wendi's eyes. He also saw flickers of desire and a tiny fleck of hope.

He felt that he couldn't come this close to kissing her again and not go through with it. Wendi took the decision out of his hands as she placed her hands on his biceps and stood on tiptoe to reach his mouth.

Ian told himself to be responsible, to step back and end the moment. He lifted his foot to do just that, but then her lips touched his. Followed by a quick wet lick of her tongue.

He was a goner.

He groaned and wrapped his hands around her waist, bringing her pelvis up against his. Wendi responded by pressing herself close to him in a way that made it clear that she wanted him, too.

Ian leaned against the side of the Jeep, his legs spread, all the while maintaining contact with her. As their kiss deepened, he reached down, cupping her bottom, wishing he could feel her bare skin. It would be even softer than the skin on her face, her neck. Thinking about it drove him mad.

The blare of a horn broke through his lusty haze, and he placed his hands on either side of Wendi's face as he lifted his lips from hers. Her eyes were open, her pupils dilated.

"We'll finish this later."

He looked over his shoulder into the headlights of a monster truck.

"Ian, that's the truck that I told you about."

"Right. Get in your car, and I'll pull up behind you."

Ian made a point of waving at the truck driver as if he thought the dude was just another friendly face and not the criminal Wendi suspected he was. There was nothing either of them could do about it right now, and he wanted Wendi home, safe and secure. He got into the Jeep and was behind Wendi's car within seconds. The big black truck turned in the opposite direction, onto the highway toward Deception Pass Bridge.

Ian let out a sigh of relief and flashed his lights to tell Wendi he was ready to go.

As he tailed her the entire way back to the farm-house, he went bayonet-to-pistol with his emotions.

CHAPTER TEN

AS PROMISED, IAN followed her the entire way back to the house. In good weather the trip took no more than ten minutes, tops.

They'd been crawling along Highway 20 for the past hour and had another mile to go. Still, she hadn't spun out, and no other cars had hit her.

She blew out a breath and tried to relax her shoulders, her neck, her back. Her thoughts clashed with her attempts to focus on the road. This wasn't the time to fantasize about a man. But once she'd accepted that she couldn't get to Emma, her mind had shot straight to Ian.

Getting to her road necessitated a left-hand turn. Flicking her blinker on, she caught a glimpse of Ian's Jeep behind her. They were alone on the highway, which according to the radio reports had now been closed to all but emergency traffic.

Was it only Ian's calm presence that comforted her? A friend who'd stayed with her while she fought her way through rough weather to a place of safety?

Or was it more?

She ordered herself to concentrate on reaching the house. The driveway wouldn't be too bad, since the snow wasn't sticking yet, and she hoped the gravel would provide the traction she needed to get over the ice. But it was half a mile to the driveway.

She glanced at the dashboard clock and groaned. Delivering the baskets had taken less time than driving on ice. It wasn't turning out to be the Saturday she'd wanted to spend with her new daughter. As much as she loved her work with the Christmas Spirit Committee, she'd have to rethink her participation next year. Delivering baskets was out.

Ian had seen the baskets strewn all over her house and hadn't missed a beat. Instead, he'd offered to help. The memory of him bent over her dining room table made her insides vibrate with anticipation. Ian was attractive, plain and simple. It wasn't just her lack of a partner or a regular sex life, it was a fact.

She sensed that he'd be a wonderful lover and a dedicated partner. Their chemistry was unmistakable. As a veterinarian she'd learned to judge pet owners by how they treated their animals. Ian treated Integrity in the best possible way and asked for help if he needed it.

He cared.

Crunch.

The steering wheel lurched out of her hands, and she felt her car sliding across the road toward the ditch. The logical part of her brain ordered her foot off the gas and the brakes as the car continued on its out-of-control trajectory. It seemed like an hour but couldn't have been more than a few seconds....

Ian was with her. It'd be all right.

Her head hit the back of the headrest when she did eventually stop—in the ditch. The front of her car pointed toward the snowy sky like a rocket.

She tried to move her fingers, her toes. All working and intact. The air bag hadn't deployed, and the actual impact hadn't been any rougher than she'd get from a sudden stop at an unexpected red light. It was her lack of control over what had happened and the awkward angle of the car in the ditch that she found disconcerting. Nevertheless, the car could be towed—tomorrow. Once the storm had passed.

She unlocked her driver's door and tried to open it. It didn't budge.

Wendi handled animals in life or death situations every day. She'd helped many clients, both pets and their owners, deal with anxiety. Nothing prepared her for the panic that overwhelmed her at the thought of being trapped in this car. So close to home, but so far away.

Her heart raced—she felt the pounding of blood in her ears. She held on to the useless wheel, clenching and unclenching her hands. This was the worst time for a panic attack.

Within seconds she saw Ian's figure at the top of the ditch and watched as he slowly lowered himself onto the ground next to her car.

Ian. He'd save her.

His face was up against the driver's side window, and he gave her a thumbs-up. She responded the same way, still trying to catch her breath.

"I can't get the door open." Her words were barely a whisper.

"Lower the window." Ian's voice was loud and firm. He knew what he was doing.

With a start she noticed that the car was still running. Maybe she'd hit her head harder than she realized.

Her fingers felt for the buttons and miraculously the window rolled down.

She felt Ian's breath on her face. She closed her eyes, relishing the warmth and security he represented.

"Are you okay, Wendi?"

She opened her eyes and looked into his. There were lines between his brows, and concern shone from his irises.

"Can two people know each other this well after only two weeks?" What had happened to her normal voice? She sounded like…a waif.

"Wendi? Everything's fine. I'm here." He kissed her firmly on the lips before he leaned in and turned off the engine and unfastened her seat belt. All the while he maintained eye contact with her. His gaze was her anchor.

"I'm going to pull you out of this window. Can you move everything? Does anything hurt?"

"No, no, I'm fine."

"Great. Then help me by pushing with your feet and legs if you can. We'll have you out of here in a minute. Ready?"

She nodded.

"Here we go."

She felt Ian's shoulder and chest against her as he reached down and under her arms. She tried to push against the floor of the car but couldn't get purchase as both she and Ian were wedged in the window.

Her sob flew into the night.

"It's okay, Wendi, we're getting out of here. Let me back off and see if you can do it without me crowding you."

She cried out when he let go of her and grabbed at his hands. Ian grasped hers and squeezed.

"Come on, Wendi. You can do this. Get your foot on the seat."

Wendi listened to his voice, her lifeline, as darkness fell.

"I'm on the seat." With a few more movements she was standing on it, her body hanging out the window, in Ian's arms.

"I've got you. Relax and let me pull you out the rest of the way. Trust me."

She nodded against his chest. "I do."

IAN SAW HIS life flash before him when Wendi said those two words.

I do.

As if her reply had a deeper meaning than her willingness to let him pull her from the car.

His military training took over, and seconds later he had Wendi up on the road. When they both stood on the icy pavement he drew her against him.

"You're safe. Come here."

The Jeep headlights illuminated them, and he stepped back to look in her face.

Wide eyes stared at him in the dark, her bottom lip trembling.

"You're okay, Wendi. Good job!" He gave her a slight shake, trying to coax her out of her panic.

She blinked, and he saw her come back to the present. Snowflakes as big as quarters fell between them and on them, the quiet night broken only by the hum of the Jeep's engine.

"I would've been in a lot of trouble if you weren't here."

"That's not an issue, is it? Because I *am* here."

"Yes." She licked her bottom lip as she stared at him again. At his eyes, his mouth.

Ian stopped worrying about whether or not Wendi was in shock. He kissed her.

Her lips were cool under his, so his first mission was to warm her up. Shock and hypothermia were real concerns, whether on the battlefield or home on Whidbey.

He nipped and sucked on her lip until she gasped, opening her mouth fully to him.

Ian relished the pure sensuality of their tongues meeting, sparring, stroking. Her hands moving from his waist up to his neck, her gloved fingers caressing his nape.

She had too many layers on—he couldn't get close enough to her. He appeased his need by grasping her buttocks and bringing her closer, against his erection.

Which put them right where they'd been earlier, up the road.

Wendi pulled back, and the desire shining in her eyes sent a bolt of satisfaction through him.

"Ian, this is crazy."

"Crazy good."

They laughed, and he kissed her again. This time he lingered, memorizing every nuance of her reaction.

Her throat was so soft, her scent uniquely her own.

Reluctantly, he took a step back. "I'm supposed to be helping you get home."

"You saved me from a frozen night in the car." A shudder ran through her, and he held her close.

"Let me take you home."

THE HOUSE WAS dark, and only the light from the motion detector on her porch spilled out to welcome her home.

Ian stood behind her, Integrity at his side. Slipping

and sliding, they'd made it up to the porch, and Wendi fought for balance as she tried to unlock the front door.

Her fingers shook, the adrenaline from her time in the ditch still coursing through her system.

Ian took the keys, and with one smooth twist had her front door open. Lemon and Ranger were waiting for them, wagging their tails and barking.

"Go ahead, doggies. Slow, slow." She knew they didn't understand what the words meant, but they recognized the cautionary tone in her voice. She and Ian laughed as they greeted Integrity, and all three dogs went off to find a place to do their business.

"Can I make you a cup of coffee? Or even dinner? I can't promise anything gourmet, but I'm stocked up on canned soups and tuna."

"No, I'm fine. You could probably use some time to relax. I think I'll walk down to my place. It's not worth driving any farther than necessary tonight. I'll come and get my car in the morning, and if you need me to drive you to pick up Emma, we can go to the grocery store then. You'll have to call a tow truck at some point, as well."

Disappointment she'd have to examine later welled up and she nodded, fighting tears of exhaustion.

"I can't thank you enough for getting me back safely, Ian."

"No thanks needed. I'm glad I could help. Lock up, and I'll see you in the morning." With that he walked back out into the storm, the snow whirling about him. She called to her dogs, and they returned immediately. Both she and the dogs stood on the porch watching the tall man with his dog walk down toward the cottage.

As if all three of them wished they'd stayed.

WENDI FELT BETTER after a long, hot bath and glass of
red wine. She'd talked to Shelly and Emma over the
phone, and Emma was being completely spoiled by her
adopted auntie.

The morning was going to come quickly and with
it, the potential for a lot of snow, so she thought making up a pot of steel-cut oats in her slow cooker would
be smart.

"Hellooooo, Mommy." Blue, her Hyacinth Macaw,
spoke to her as she worked in the kitchen.

"Hi, Blue Baby. You haven't had enough attention
lately, have you, my pretty boy?" She sliced up a banana
and went over to him, holding out a large chunk, which
he took in his big black beak with a gentle dexterity that
always surprised her.

"Mmm." The bird verbalized his approval of his favorite fruit.

"It's good, huh?" She laughed and went back to mea-
suring out water and oats.

The grueling drive and icy roads already felt like
memories. She'd only been home two hours, but it
seemed like far longer.

Lemon and Ranger alerted her, their nails clicking
on the hardwood kitchen floor before they stepped onto
the carpet of the living room and sat by the door.

She knew who it was because they didn't bark. Both
dogs looked at the door expectantly, tails wagging.

Wendi glanced down at her cozy but worn pajamas.
It wasn't as if Ian hadn't seen her at her worst before.
And this wasn't her worst, by far.

She pulled open the door; dog and man entered her
home in a huge gust of icy snow and cold wind.

"Quick, close the door!"

GERI KROTOW 293

Ian complied and shut out the elements. Integrity and her dogs greeted each other as if they hadn't just played together a couple of hours ago.

Which left Wendi staring at Ian.

He smiled and held up a bottle of wine and a clear plastic tray of grocery Christmas cupcakes.

The man who acted as though he was allergic to Christmas had brought Christmas plates for Emma, a poinsettia and now silly cupcakes.

"I'm sorry I took off in such a hurry. But I wanted to bring this. I thought you could use something sweet."

She accepted the bottle and the cupcakes while keeping her eyes on him.

"I've already opened a cabernet and had a glass. Do you mind having some of mine before we open this?"

He reached out and held her face in his hands. His intent was unmistakable, and her knees turned weak again, the way they'd been when he kissed her earlier.

"I told you we'd finish up what we started."

His lips came down on hers, and Wendi let go of her doubts, worries and hesitation. Ian was as real as anything in her life. He made her feel alive like no other man had in a long time, if ever.

Making love to him wasn't foolish or crazy. It was what she wanted, what felt right.

He lifted his head. "Can we go to your room and save the wine for later? Otherwise, I'm going to make love to you here on the sofa in front of an audience."

Wendi giggled and stepped back. "You mean you don't want three dogs, a parrot and a cat watching your moves?"

"If I have my way, you won't be seeing anything, either. You'll be feeling how much I want you."

Her breath caught, and she put the wine bottle on the side table and pulled Ian farther into the house.

"Take off your jacket, your boots."

"Yes, ma'am."

She walked away from him, into her bedroom.

She suddenly realized there were piles of Emma's toys, clean clothes and stacks of books in every corner.

What could she do in two minutes?

"Are you hiding?"

His arms slipped around her, and he pressed his front to her back, dropping a warm kiss on her neck that sent tremors through every part of her. "My room's a mess."

He turned her to face him, his fingers riding up the hem of her pajama top.

"You worry too much about messes. It's about to get very chaotic in here." He smiled when her breath hitched, and she groaned as his hand covered her bare breast.

"Hurry, Ian." She struggled to get her shirt over her head, and he laughed.

"We have all night."

He tortured her with his gentle caresses, alternating soft bites with sucking at her earlobes, her neck, her nipples.

She grabbed his T-shirt and pulled it over his head, glad he'd worn the minimum under his cold-weather gear. As her fingers touched his bare chest for the first time, she registered how smooth his skin was, how tight his muscles were.

All Ian. And he made her feel like she was the only woman on earth.

"Wendi, I don't want you to think I'm doing this just

for fun. It means more to me. *We* mean more. It can't be a coincidence that we found each other this Christmas."

"I know. Either we're both crazy, or we might really have something here."

He stopped her hands, which were caressing his belly, and held them.

"Let me touch you, Ian."

"Are you absolutely positive about this, Wendi?"

She met his gaze. They'd both faced pain and fear, but when she was with him, she felt something better, and it wasn't just desire.

Hope.

Ian gave her back hope she thought she'd lost.

"I'm sure, Ian. Take your pants off, okay?" She broke free of his grasp and a moment later reached down to hold his erection in her hand.

Ian tilted back his head, and she smiled at the growl of arousal in his throat.

Once his pants were around his feet, he put his attention on her.

"This is going to be fair and square. Your turn." He tugged down her flannel bottoms, and they stood naked with each other.

Wendi's nerve endings screamed with desire, and she gave in to whatever these hours with Ian would bring. This time when he kissed her, she pulled his head toward hers and leaned back, forcing them both onto the bed.

"I want this to be perfect for you, Wendi."

"It *is* perfect, Ian. We have all night. Can we stop talking, and will you please take me? Now?"

She reached over to her nightstand and yanked open the small drawer.

Ian didn't comment or react other than to grab a condom and open it.

Wendi put the protection on him. She stroked him while whispering how much she wanted him.

"I can't wait any longer, Wendi." With one thrust Ian filled her, and Wendi cried out as he moved inside her. She wrapped her legs around his waist, urging him to move faster, deeper. They reached their climax together as if this was the thousandth time they'd made love and not the first. Words ceased as they both focused on the pure joy of being together, at last.

CHAPTER ELEVEN

Christmas Eve

WENDI PUT THE last touches on Emma's third birthday cake while Blue continued his monologue next to her.

"Blue's a pretty bird. Merry, merry Christmas!"

"Merry Christmas, Blue. Emma, have you worn Auntie Shelly out yet?"

"No! Auntie Shelly likes stringing popcorn!"

Shelly laughed from her spot on the living room floor, a large bowl of popcorn and cranberries between her and Emma.

"Auntie Shelly's funny."

A knock at the door broke through their merriment, and Wendi looked over to where Lemon and Ranger normally sat guard.

"How long have the dogs been out?"

"I let them out five minutes ago."

"They usually tell me if someone's coming. Unless they aren't worried about whoever it is." She had a feeling she knew who that *someone* was and delighted at the anticipation rippling in her stomach. She and Ian were spending a lot of time together, but they were taking it day by day. No commitments.

Not yet.

She brushed a curl away from her face and walked

to the door. It wasn't fair to impose her expectations on Ian. He hadn't said anything about the long term.

The door opened before she could get to it, and Lemon and Ranger ran in, along with Integrity.

"Missing two dogs?" Ian's smile seemed to fill the room, and it included both Emma and Shelly. Wendi had told her best friend she was dating Ian, but hadn't expressed how much he meant to her.

It was too soon, wasn't it?

"I have something for you, Wendi. Can you come outside for a minute?"

Wendi looked at Emma.

"I've got Emma and the pets." Shelly motioned for her to go.

"No, you need to see this, too, Shelly. Bring Emma."

"Ian, what's going on?"

He clasped her hand and gazed at her with complete focus. "Trust me." She followed him onto the porch, and immediately spotted three very large Christmas characters inflated on her grassy yard.

"Are you kidding me? You hate all this Christmas stuff!"

"I used to. Come here." He unfolded a blanket he carried over his arm and wrapped it around them. It felt as though they were alone under its warmth, even though Shelly and Emma stood on the porch behind them.

"Do you recognize them?"

She looked at the lit-up, bobbing nylon characters.

"Let's see. An elf, Mrs. Claus and Santa Claus?"

"Yes." Ian smiled. "I was going to get the Grinch instead of Santa Claus, but I remembered when you asked me if I wanted to be Angelville's Kris Kringle."

"And?" She was afraid to read the meaning she wanted to in the kitschy decorations.

"I'm thinking we can add a figure each year. I'm hoping we'll be adding more of the elves. It's you, Emma and me. A Christmas family. What do you think, Wendi?"

"Oh, Ian, I think it's wonderful! But what are you…"

Ian shrugged out of the blanket but kept it firmly around her as he sank to one knee.

"Will you marry me, Wendi?"

Wendi looked at the man who'd somehow, through some unexplained miracle, brought such intense joy into her life, giving her and Emma a sense of family she'd never believed possible.

"Yes, Ian, I will marry you. On one condition."

He got up, his expression serious. "Anything."

"You move into the house. Tonight."

"Yes, but I've got my own condition," he said

"What?"

"Integrity's bed goes in Emma's room."

Wendi kissed the man she loved. "That'll be the best Christmas gift for both of them."

* * * * *

ROMANTIC suspense

Heart-racing romance, high-stakes suspense!

BETH CORNELISON
brings you the next installment of
THE MANSFIELD BROTHERS miniseries
THE MANSFIELD RESCUE

Available December 2014

*A single father discovers the price of
revenge and the power of love...*

After his wife's murder, Grant Mansfield vowed to stay true to her
memory and to protect their children. But fate has other plans.
His temporary houseguest, injured smokejumper Amy Robinson,
has him burning with a white-hot attraction. And the single dad's
nightmare comes true when his older daughter is kidnapped.

Grant is just the man the adventurous Amy never knew she
needed, his children the family she never knew she wanted.
Before she can rescue his lonely heart, the handsome widower
must become a hero. Only Grant can rescue his little girl.
But time is running out...

Don't miss other exciting titles from BETH CORNELISON's
THE MANSFIELD BROTHERS:
PROTECTING HER ROYAL BABY
THE RETURN OF CONNOR MANSFIELD

Available wherever books and ebooks are sold.

HARLEQUIN®

INTRIGUE®

THE NEW SHERIFF IN TROUBLE, TEXAS, HAD A LOT TO PROVE. THE LAST THING HE NEEDED WAS A GORGEOUS CIA ANALYST GETTING IN HIS WAY—AT CHRISTMASTIME NO LESS!

Trouble's newly minted sheriff, Garrett Galloway, is determined to move on from his traumatic past. But when Laurel McCallister tracks him down and begs for help, he can't say no to the smart, beautiful CIA analyst. She's desperate to find the assailant who killed her niece's family—and now wants her dead.

On the run, Garrett, Laurel and her young niece escape to a Texas ranch, but danger follows. Garrett's courage lessens Laurel's initial distrust of the mysterious lawman, and sparks fly in the remote cabin. Now he must succeed for more reasons than avenging Laurel's family.

CHRISTMAS JUSTICE

BY ROBIN PERINI

Available December 2014,
wherever Harlequin® Intrigue® books and ebooks are sold.

New York Times Bestselling Author

LINDSAY McKENNA

She was caught in her past until he showed her a future...

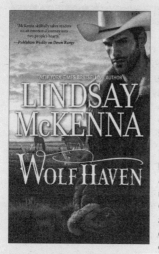

Some things can never be forgotten. A helicopter crash in Afghanistan. Capture. Torture. Now US Navy nurse Skylar Pascal is struggling to regain control of her life after a trauma that nearly destroyed her. After losing so much, an ideal job at the Elk Horn Ranch in Wyoming offers Sky something she thought she'd never find again...hope.

Former SEAL Grayson McCoy has his own demons. But something about Elk Horn's lovely-yet-damaged new nurse breaks something loose. Compassion—and *passion*. And even as Gray works with Sky to piece her confidence back together, something deeper and more tender begins to unfurl between them. Something that could bring her back to life.

But not even the haven of Elk Horn Ranch is safe from dangers. And all of Sky's healing could be undone by the acts of one malicious man...

Available now wherever books are sold!

Be sure to connect with us at:

Harlequin.com/Newsletters
Facebook.com/HarlequinBooks
Twitter.com/HarlequinBooks

HARLEQUIN® HQN™
www.Harlequin.com

PHLM903